The Book of Moon

George Crowder

Chelsea Press
Los Angeles, CA

Grateful acknowledgment is made to the following for his inspiration:
Remy Charlip: author of *Fortunately*, a perennial classroom favorite

First Printing, 2016

ISBN 978-0-9979358-0-6 (paperback)
ISBN 978-0-9979358-1-3 (e-book)

This novel is a work of fiction. Any references to real people, events, establishments, organizations, or locales are intended only to give the fiction a sense of reality and authenticity, and are used fictitiously. All other names, characters, and places, and all dialogue and incidents portrayed in this book are the product of the author's imagination.

Printed in the United States of America

Cover Design by Dane Low
Page Layout by Polgarus Studio
Chelsea Press logo by Luis Contreras

For my father,
with whom I took my first steps,
both as a writer and as a little boy...

Chapter One

The Book of Job

I WAS NOTHING.

People would inquire, "What are you? Lutheran? Baptist? Catholic? Jewish?"

I'd have to shrug and answer, "Uh, really, I'm nothing."

If they were stubborn, they'd offer me more choices, as if maybe one would be irresistible: "Episcopalian? Methodist? Buddhist? Islamic Fundamentalist?"

No, they're all delicious, I'm sure—but I couldn't. Really. *Nothing* for me.

I was supposed to become something, I guess. That seemed to be my mother's plan. One Sunday each month, she would pack my brother and me off to one of Los Angeles' numerous churches to try it on for size. We'd been doing it for years, but none of them fit any better than the cheap suits Moss and I kept growing out of.

My older brother and I would endure each and every service, wrestling tight, sweat-stained collars like a pair of horse thieves trying to slip the hangman's noose. We'd crick our strangled necks to peek at Mom, who was pursing her lips and shaking her head at whatever the minister had to say. The preacher's gospel was invariably her heresy, so we never went back to hear one a second time. I asked her about this once. She said, "Moon Landing, we are going to put a hell of a lot more thought into choosing your faith than we did into choosing your name."

If I hadn't been fighting for my last breath, I might have found the proceedings more interesting. The services were like a club, with passwords and secret handshakes. Everybody but us knew what they were doing. When they were sitting down, we were standing up; when we were patting our heads, they were crossing their stomachs. We had our signals completely crossed. God would never know what play *we* were calling.

Moss and I relaxed during the sermon. We could sit there and nothing was expected of us, except not to snore. Then I heard this story about Job that woke me up in a hurry.

Apparently he was an important character in the Bible—they even named a book after him. He was a devout man, and God had blessed him with a big family and lots of livestock. Since those were the low-tech days, I guess there was only so much the Lord could do for the guy. These numbers were remarkably specific and caught my attention: 7,000 sheep, 3,000 camels, 500 yoke of oxen, and 500 *female* donkeys. No lie, that's what the man said. *Donkettes.*

Everything was cool until God ran into Satan, and did a little bragging about what a God-fearing character Job was. Satan was not the devil for nothing. He had every one of God's buttons programmed on his remote, and he pushed them all. Sure, Job loves you now—and why shouldn't he? You buffed the man out but *good.* But what if his life went in the crapper—would he still sing hallelujah? Send up burnt offerings like he's Dickie's Barbecue Pit? I think not. He's just a fair-weather fanatic.

So God lost it big time. If they did a cartoon version of the Bible, at this point you'd see the sacred steam shooting out of His ears while His eyes would be rolling like pinballs. God told Satan to do whatever he wanted to Job—He was that convinced the man would still be faithful. They probably put money on it to make it interesting.

I can relate, 'cause I've known obnoxious characters like Satan. They make you say things you regret, like, "My old man can drink more beer than all your relatives put together." Glad Dad never actually heard about that little boast.

Still, this did not suggest a high level of emotional maturity on the part of God. I mean, would *you* allow the devil to torture your most loyal admirer just to satisfy your vanity? I certainly hope not.

Satan loves a challenge and he went right to work. While Job was on a coffee break, a servant ran in to tell him that his oxen and donkeys had been ripped off and many of his servants had been killed by the Sabeans. As soon as that guy got done talking, another messenger arrived with the news that a fire from heaven had fried Job's sheep and more servants. Then another guy burst in to exclaim that the camels had just been stolen and even more servants had been massacred. On *that* messenger's heels, somebody else showed up to say that the roof had fallen on top of Job's ten sons and daughters, and none had survived.

Tell me *that* won't make you give up coffee.

But Job still praised God—so the Almighty green-lighted waterboarding. Just don't kill the guy, He said. So the devil gave Job a disgusting plague that made him so nuts he tried to scrape his skin off with a broken plate. Job cursed the day he was born, but he still didn't curse God.

At this point Job's amigos came to cheer him up, but he was such a wreck that they just sat around for a week without saying a word. Finally they got helpful, annoying Job with various theories of what he might've done to wind up in the Lord's doghouse. They figured—

as most of us do—that when so many bad things happen to a good person, there's gotta be a reason.

Every time they floated a notion, Job shot it down. *No, that's not it. Nah, couldn't have been that.* Job couldn't think of a darned thing he'd done to get on God's bad side, which of course was right. These tortures were merely a little test of Job's loyalty, to see how much random crap and life-threatening abuse he'd take before he decided Our Heavenly Father wasn't Mr. Wonderful.

I guess Job got a passing score, because the Lord cured his skin disease and gave him double the animals he'd had in the first place. The kids were under warranty, so God replaced them, too. He and Job decided to let bygones be bygones, and they all lived happily ever after. Which was so many years that when he died, Job's age didn't even make sense in a base ten number system. The end.

Whoooooooa. Take a deep breath, dude.

I can't remember the point of the story, but I knew what I had heard. Give or take beaucoup asses and several centuries on Earth, it was the story of my life.

Chapter Two
So the Devil Walks into a Bar...

ALL RIGHT, I'M EXAGGERATING. How can any fifteen-year-old's tally of misfortunes rival the King of Woe's? Naturally I can't match the man donkey-for-donkey.

It's the general tone of Job's story that really gets to me—the way in which, just when you think things can't get any worse, they do. It reminds me of the TV pitches when they keep sweetening the deal— "For just three low payments of $19.99 we will steal your oxen and donkeys and two-thirds of your servants. But wait—that's not all! If you act fast we will throw in *the death of your ten children*. But wait—there's more! Do not delay! If you call in the next half hour we will include ULCERS, BOILS, AND LICE FOR *YOUR* ENTIRE BODY!"

The last year of my life has had that kind of downward spiral.

We're in the hot July sun, waiting out the line at CJ's coffee shop, across the street from Saint Mary Magdalena's Catholic Church. Mom's working the crowd, flirting with a lanky man who's half her age. He has a *New York Times* and the look of a surfer, a combination that's more than enough to catch her eye.

Moss and I exchange a look and a shrug. "Back in a few," he says,

5

jumps on his board and skates up the street. I take a seat in the shade and my eyes drift shut.

The story of Job rattled me. I don't believe in God, but if I *did*...

The lounge is a shadowy oasis, unremarkable save for the peculiar customers posed on barstools, immobile as marble statues displayed on pedestals. Hunched over cocktails, their backs to me, each bears a thick pair of wings.

The saloon door opens, allowing a momentary puddle of brilliance, and an enormous angel steps into it. He pauses as his eyes adjust to the gloom. There's no room at the bar, but the newcomer strides to the nearest seat and simply shoves its occupant to the floor, taking his place.

The deposed drinker looks up from where he's landed, still gripping empty stemware. "Satan!" he splutters. "I was just leaving."

The big angel smiles down thinly. "Take your veggies with ya," he says, daintily dropping a pick with three pimentoed olives onto the floored angel's chest.

Drifting to the new customer, the bartender plucks the soiled cocktail napkin, gives the counter a rub, and deposits a fresh serviette on the gleaming oak. His forearms are thickly muscled. I cannot see the bartender's face, but he seems somehow familiar.

"So the divil walks into a bar..." he says. His voice has an Irish lilt.

Satan grimaces in distaste. "If I gotta hear that one again, *you're* tippin' *me*."

"You laughed at it last time..."

"It's the way you tell it. Such a dark sense of humor, God. *Loved* your work in the Congo."

"Ah, that wasn't *me*. Boys'll be boys, and all that," God demurs, setting a tumbler filled with an icy dark liquid in front of Satan.

The devil sniffs the drink with satisfaction, and drains the glass in

6

a draught. He sets it down with a sigh. "You're too modest."

God refills the tumbler without comment, and the devil sips the new cocktail. "So…what's the line on your boy Moon?"

"*Moon?*" God's voice is incredulous. "Moon *Landing?*"

"Might like him with points…"

"Yer askin' for points…on an atheist?"

"*Agnostic.*"

"Ah, there's no sport in it, Satan. Take the Madre Garcia and six. Runs an orphanage in Juarez. Devout. She'll not forsake me."

Satan sips his drink, considers. "I like the kid."

"Then *you'll* give *me* six."

The devil snorts in disbelief. "Cut the crap. Little cancer, few deaths in the family. Nine outta ten unbelievers sing hosanna just the way you like it."

"No atheists in the trenches, eh?"

"My point. You oughta be fuckin' ashamed."

"It's not personal, just business. So you think this lad Moon is different?"

"Could be. You want the action or not?"

God polishes a glass, considering. "I'll give him to you straight up. My best offer."

"Done."

God's big hand enfolds Satan's hoof in a lingering handshake that suggests a certain affection. "You were my favorite angel," he sighs.

"Now don't go gettin' sentimental," says Satan, dropping a bill on the bar and heading for the door.

"Standard exclusions apply. Mortal diseases, fatal mishaps, natural disaster resulting in death, and I cover," God calls at the departing customer.

"You're gonna read the fine print to *me?*" says the devil, as Moss shakes me brusquely awake.

Chapter Three
Where's the Pony?

MY FATHER, DAVID LANDING, a Texan born and bred, was tall enough to stand out in most any crowd and so lithe he could have been a dancer. With his black eyes and chiseled features, Dad was the kind of man you assumed would take charge—though all he could really control was his sports bar, Fanatics. When he was off playing golf, Mom would sarcastically refer to him as "the lone Ranger." After things got bad, she called him "the *stoned* Ranger." But only under her breath.

Mom self-deprecatingly claimed to be a "Mediterranean mutt," with ancestors who principally hailed from Spain, France, and Italy. Like many mixed-breed animals, her looks were striking, highlighted by an olive complexion, flashing green eyes, and a strong jaw with the hint of a cleft chin. Throw in a vibrant shade of glossy red lipstick to frame her dazzling carnivore teeth, and it was no wonder that at Northwestern she had been the sweetheart of two different fraternities, at a time when such Greek accolades were going out of style. She still got looks from our friends that made Moss and me cringe.

A third-grade teacher who lived for culture, Mom liked life hot and spicy. Keeping the peace was not high on her list of priorities: femmes fatales and old movie bombshells had served as her role models. Mom's saving grace was her sense of the absurd. When that deserted her, we were all in trouble.

Probably my parents never should have married each other. Perhaps opposites attract, but in Mom and Dad's case, they *attacked*. Pretty much the only thing they had in common was their kids. It turned out we weren't enough.

Still, the news that their marriage was over came as a surprise to my brother and me. It happened last April, a little over a year ago. We were enjoying a rare mid-week pizza outing—which, in retrospect, should have been a tip-off—when my dad downed a brew, belched softly, and, ignoring my mother's scowl, declared, "Boys, your mom and I are throwing in the towel."

"Yo, hit me again, Daddy-o," my brother said, holding out his plate. He was listening to his iPod and rarely tuned in to the conversation.

Dad slid a piece onto Moss's plate, murmuring, "Eat up, son."

"You want to elaborate on that?" I said.

My mother had taken a back seat for as long as she could stand. She pursed her lips and shook her head. "David, you're not putting it well at all."

Dad shrugged. "Tomato, tomahto." He flagged a waiter and waved his empty beer bottle, calling for another.

"We—are—getting—a—divorce," my mother stated with clipped simplicity.

Moss ripped off his earbuds, a foolish grin plastered on his face. "A *horse*?!! Outrageous!"

"No, she didn't say that—"

"Rad!"

"Moss, we're not getting a horse."

"Well, why not? We could stash the nag in the garage and ride him around the bean field."

"Moss—"

"Hey, what're we gonna call him?"

I grabbed my brother by his shoulders. "They're getting *divorced.*"

Moss's jaw dropped open. He put down the pizza and looked from me to my mother, to my father, back to me, then around the horn again. The three of us watched him as he processed the momentous news, waiting to see what would finally emerge. At last, Moss looked at us and asked, "Does this have…*anything*…to do with the horse?"

Dad guffawed, spraying the table with a yeasty gout of beer. My mother dabbed herself with a napkin. "For heaven's sake, David."

But Dad was doubled over with laughter. "Just…just gimme a minute," he choked out. "This is not the way your mother planned this."

"What else is new?" Mom snapped.

"Why are you getting divorced?" I asked.

"You have to ask? Look at your father."

"Uh, Janice, that's not the way we planned it, either," my father said.

"Well, I'm not taking the blame for this."

"So Dad drinks," observed Moss, taking up for Dad. "Big deal."

"It's an occupational hazard," I added. "And it could be worse. Dad could be a dentist. They've got suicidal tendencies."

My father cleared his throat. "It's not just that, boys. You've probably noticed your mother and I haven't exactly been getting along too well…"

There was a quiet moment as we all digested Dad's statement. This might have been the first direct reference to the cold war that had existed in our house for at least the last year or two.

Tentatively, I broke the silence. "Everybody has their ups and downs…"

"True. But we've been more down than up for some time now."

"And we all deserve better," my mother summed up. "Our marriage is setting a bad example for you children."

"Yeah, for schizzle. Let's hope you two do a better job on the divorce, dog," said Moss.

"Please don't call me *dog*, Mr. Homie," said Mom.

Moss nodded. "Anyone want the last piece?"

We all shook our heads and my brother blithely took the pizza, then cut it in half. He tossed a portion on my plate. "Better munch, bro. Never know where our next meal's comin' from, right?"

Chapter Four

Moss

MOSS IS, AND ALWAYS WILL BE, two years older than me. He got his name from a small town in California where my father worked for a month—Moss Landing. Dad says that if he'd had another son after me, his name would have been "Crash Landing." Mom says over her dead body. Why she gave into him the first two times is a mystery to me, since relenting is not in her nature.

While we both got enough of Dad's height that we don't get teased about our names, Moss and I wound up with Mom's coloring: dark hair and eyes, and skin slow-roasted under the California sun where we spend as many hours as possible. Especially my brother.

My parents gave Moss a skateboard for his fifth birthday. It must've been like when Tiger Woods got a golf club, or when Kobe Bryant got a basketball. Something that was meant to be. My brother is blessed with the three most important qualities in a skateboarder: balance, agility, and a high tolerance for pain. To Moss, the world is just a bunch of rails there for the grinding.

Yeah, I know, the first-born is usually the anal worrier, but somehow my brother and I reversed roles on that. He's chill and I stress—about grades, parents, ruptured appendices, venomous snakes, leprosy, girls, global warming, the national debt, the meaning of life, the meaning of death…

Most of this is out of my control, though I still suffer some non-specific guilt. As evidence, I submit my recurring dream that I've done something to cause the destruction of the universe. It's called the "big antibang." The event has not yet occurred, but before it does, there's still time for everyone to find out it's *my* fault. Then I wake up. What an incredible relief that I haven't personally destroyed the universe!

As the little brother, I naturally tried to follow my sibling on the skateboard. My debut was not encouraging—I sprained a wrist. Then I got better—I broke an arm. Moss's crew was impressed, but I wasn't enjoying it. I switched to the unicycle instead. That *really* wowed them.

I spent one entire summer trying to ride that thing out of our driveway, every day for two, three, four hours. The sidewalk was sixty feet away. I never reached it. Moss and his friends would grind up and down the street, offering advice. They had never seen anyone with so much stubbornness and so little talent.

I have the ability to stick with something much longer than most people, which my parents say is a gift. They point out that every great success is bred of determination, persistence, and loads of failure. Of course, big losers share the same qualities, pouring resources down wishful ratholes until they exhaust both time and money. So we'll have to see how this all works out.

It's not that I have great self-confidence, because I don't. I do, however, have an overactive left hemisphere. It continually blessed—or cursed—me with inspiration for improvement. How could I enhance my performance to get another inch, another foot? The brainstorms would pelt my parched ego with hope. Reinvigorated,

I'd straddle the cycle, push off and pedal, expecting that would be the day Moss and his friends would watch me disappear over the horizon.

There's a Greek character named Sisyphus who is consigned to Tartarus, the depths of the Greek underworld. He has an eternity to complete a single task: rolling a boulder up a high hill. Each time he approaches the summit, after a long, agonizing climb, the boulder rolls back to the bottom, smashing him flat on its way down. Then he starts over.

That was me: Sisyphus of the unicycle. That's how I spent July…and August…and the beginning of September. Just trying to get to the end of the driveway.

On Labor Day morning, I came out and Moss was riding the unicycle. The other guys were eating donuts, watching him wheel up and down the street. He was riding forwards, backwards—he jumped the curb. He circled around and said, "Throw me a donut."

"What kind?"

"Any kind. Just throw it."

They tossed him a chocolate glazed. He caught it, circled around and said, "Throw me another."

This sinker was a powdered cake. He began to juggle the pastries while he pedaled in a circle. When he completed a circuit, they flipped him another. Then they did it one more time. After several revolutions, Moss was juggling four donuts and riding the unicycle.

After a few moments of this, he upped the ante, somehow taking bites out of the donuts as he juggled. The jelly donut leaked crimson goo as it flew through the air, but Moss didn't miss. He kept riding and juggling until he had consumed all four donuts. His friends were jubilant. "Drop out, homes! Join the circus and hook up with the bearded lady."

Then one of them saw me. "Hey, the grom's up, man."

Moss hopped off the unicycle and walked it over to me. "Sorry, Moon, mighta got it a little sticky."

I looked at him. "What am I doing wrong?"

"I dunno. I'd tell you if I could, but…it's just something I can do."

"And I can't."

"I'm not saying that."

"You don't have to. It's obvious."

That was it for the unicycle. I put it in the garage and never touched it again. Moss didn't either. I went back to sports with balls—baseball, basketball, football. I'm not particularly good at them either, but at least I can get out of the driveway.

Chapter Five

Mom and Dad

I CAN'T DENY that Dad was an alcoholic. It's not like he started the day with a beer, but he almost always ended it with a few of them. Or some Jack, or Johnny, or one of his other distilled pals. He wouldn't say no to a glass or four of vino. Dad wasn't the kind of drinker who played favorites: he simply didn't want *any* of his bottles to feel left out, so they all got their shot.

Abusing anything is unappealing, but Dad's drinking was nowhere near as offensive as Mom's smoking. For years we put up with the cigarette stench and her hacking cough. Moss and I constantly nagged her to stop, but Dad would tell us to give her a break. He didn't like her nasty habit, but he liked her.

Smoking is not the easiest thing for a teacher to do, since you can't indulge on a school campus. But where there's a will, there's a way. Mom hung with this old second grade teacher, Mable Walsh. Ms. Walsh was so hardcore that she actually moved to an apartment near the school so she'd have someplace to light up. The two butt buddies would shoot over to Mable's place every recess and lunch, have their smokes and grade papers, or whatever it is teachers do when there are no kids around.

Then Mable retired. Top of the to-do list was the trip to France she'd always dreamed of. This could've been a problem for Mom, if Mable hadn't given her a key to the apartment. The fish got fed while Mom got her nicotine fix.

Mom hung on Mable's every postcard, and I could see the tears in her eyes when she read them. France was all Mable had hoped it would be, and more. After thirty years of nagging seven-year-olds to take it easy on the tattling, she had been incredibly ready for something new, and the next chapter of her life offered big possibilities for exploring the world—and herself. She couldn't wait to start painting...to learn French...to cook coq au vin.

With all this good news, Mable's appearance when she returned was a shock. Instead of plump and sassy with crêpe suzettes, she looked gaunt and grey. Two months later, Mable Walsh was dead of cancer.

It hit Mom hard, but she didn't cry in front of us. Mable's sister came out from Buffalo, and Mom helped her clean out the apartment and pack up Mable's stuff. Moss and I felt bad and actually went over there to help. But when we got to the door, we could hear the two of them in there weeping and carrying-on. It spooked us and we couldn't go in. They were at it for three days. Then Mable's sister went back to Buffalo.

That's when Mom kicked the habit.

She didn't say anything about it, she just stopped. We didn't say anything about it, either. Not me. Not Moss. Not Dad. It should've made us happy, but it just made us nervous.

Turns out we had good reason. Six months later, when she felt she had it licked, she started in on Dad and his drinking. Said he was setting a bad example for us. Truth was, after watching Mom and Dad, there wasn't much danger of me or Moss wanting to smoke or drink. They'd done a fine job of making both those habits look revolting. But since Mom had given up *her* vice, she figured it was time for Dad to give up *his*. Except he wasn't ready to do that.

He tried to laugh it off. He liked to point out that all his best customers were alcoholics, so it would be hypocritical of him *not* to drink. When he'd say that, Mom would go into a blind rage. She'd take out her fury by cleaning the house in a way that made you feel sorry for the floor, the rugs, the toilet. When she did housework before, it was like she was restoring a cherished painting, removing a layer of grime and letting its radiance shine through; now it was as if she was punishing the place for getting dirty. Our normally spotless house became so dazzling that for a year we no longer really lived in it. We merely existed, like decorative props in a model home.

The writing was on the wall, even though Mom kept washing it off. I took a shot at it, too.

Chapter Six
The Scariest Person in My Life Is Me

"I THINK YOU'D really like this. Come on Friday." The girl who shoved a flier into Moss's hands was a couple years older than him, and hot. She graced him with a dazzling smile. My brother generally attracted attention from the babes, but this one was so smokin' she set off the fire alarm. Moss was momentarily tongue-tied and stared at the paper. I jumped in to help.

"Will *you* be there?"

"Do you *want* me to be?"

"Duh. And I think he does, too." I elbowed Moss.

"What, precisely, might you be selling, Miss?" Moss waved the flier. "Bottom line."

"The secret of happiness. Fulfillment of your dreams. The means to achieve your every goal."

Moss looked at me. "Oh, man, this is for that mop that cleans under beds."

I shrugged. "Or maybe the toenail clipper for dogs."

Moss looked back at the girl. "Are we warm?"

"Buddhism," she crooned. "Reveal your Buddha nature and

control the unlimited potential of your destiny."

"That's it? Nothing for the kitchen?"

The girl giggled and gave Moss a flirtatious shove.

"This would probably count as our monthly dose," I said.

"Ya think Mom'd go for it?"

"Don't know why not."

Moss looked at our comely salesperson. "But *you* better be there, Miss…"

"Gretchen. See you on Friday, boys." She turned and started to walk away, then called over her shoulder. "Don't forget your mom."

We took in the view as Gretchen exited. Moss looked at me.

"The momster could use some enlightenment, wouldn't you say?"

"Does a Buddha shit in the woods?"

The Buddhist center was not far away, on the corner of Fairfax and Venice, which helped us persuade Mom to give it a chance. The fact that we had instigated this affair lent suspicion, however, and as we walked in, Mom warily examined the small room.

I'd been expecting something kung fu-esque, with bearded Chinese monks in flowing robes dispensing wisdom to shaven-headed disciples seated on straw mats. Maybe some incense—karate or Zen archery if we were lucky.

Instead, it was a small conference room filled with rows of chairs facing an altar decorated with bits of greenery and a scroll inscribed with Chinese characters. The walls were bare, except for a tacky poster proclaiming the "Year of Youth!" Alliteration tends to rub me the wrong way. "Gargantuan Giveaway Galore!" No, *you* keep it.

About thirty people sat in the seats, chanting a mantra in a pleasant drone. Long accustomed to not understanding a word of religious proceedings, I felt right at home.

Gretchen saw us enter and crossed to greet us. Connecting the dots, Mom gave a slight nod of understanding.

"Janice Landing," said Mom, shaking Gretchen's hand. "Apparently sex sells, even in religion."

Gretchen shrugged. "If you meet Buddha on the road, ask her for a date." We all looked blankly at her. "Buddhist humor. In about a year, you'll get it."

Gretchen had enlisted a few of the regulars to fill us in on the protocols. She laid claim to Moss, and I was pleased to find myself with Claudia, a petite Hispanic girl about Moss's age. My mother was assigned a cheerful Japanese woman.

Claudia opened a thin prayer book and led me through the mantra with her finger. *Nam-myoho-renge-kyo.*

"What's it mean?"

"It doesn't matter." I looked at her blankly. "*Nam-myoho-renge-kyo* isn't a high-stakes contract you need to take to a lawyer. It's just a little chat between you and the universe."

"So…the universe will talk back?"

Claudia held up a cautionary finger. "If you're listening. Give it a try."

You wouldn't think it would be hard to repeat a few words over and over—but within a minute I was gasping. I made a conscious effort to breathe more frequently, noting the rhythms of the others around me as they inhaled. Many rubbed prayer beads and put surprising effort into their chanting, like they were really getting something done.

Claudia stopped me and directed my attention to the scroll on the altar. "That's the *gohonzon*. It helps you focus. Look at the top, the vertical line in the middle. See the white space?"

"Yeah…"

"That's the gateway to everything. Try to focus there."

"What am I focusing?"

"Your intentions. Your causes."

I looked at her blankly. She thought a moment, then said, "What you want."

"I should think about what I want?" I had just gotten here, and it seemed presumptuous to be starting off with a wish list.

"You're not going to get it if you don't think about it," Claudia said matter-of-factly. "And remember, you're never begging. You're just declaring your intentions."

We chanted like that for several minutes, though it felt much longer to me. Then the leader struck a metal bowl a couple of times and everyone turned their attention to a short man with a moustache who introduced himself as Gus. He explained that he'd be our moderator for the evening, and suggested that we all introduce ourselves and tell the group which superhero we'd choose to be. He also asked to know how long each of us had been "practicing," or, if we were a guest, who had brought us.

I hate this stuff. Schmoozing, ice breaking, fellowshipping. Mom doesn't mind attention of any sort, and Moss takes after her in that respect, but I wanted to crawl into a hole and hide. I listened distractedly, trying to come up with a superhero who wouldn't sound too lame. Everybody wanted to fly, which narrowed the choices if I wanted to be original.

It was Moss's turn. "Hey, I'm Moss, with the moms and the bro. We was fetched by Gretch. At the mall buying some kicks, and she was all, 'Hey little boy, how 'bout some enlightenment?'"

The group busted-up, laughing and hollering, the ice truly broken.

"Moss, you've been *shakubuku*ed by the best of them," laughed Gus.

Moss looked around theatrically. "Where's the camera, dude?"

22

"Don't worry, it's not a practical joke."

"To *shakubuku* someone is to introduce them to our Buddhism," said Gretchen. "Who's your superhero?"

"Gotta go with the Silver Surfer. He's the closest thing to a skateboarder, and you know, I gotta roll."

It was my turn. "I'm Moon." Everyone was staring at me. I tried to collect myself. "Uh, well, Moss just explained the Gretchen connetchen…" The play-on-words was accidental, but several people chuckled, and I relaxed. "You know, superheroes are some of my favorite people, so it's hard to single out just one of them…" There were nods of agreement. "Maybe I'll go with Daredevil. You have to admire him, 'cause he's blind and he still kicks ass."

"Get down with *nam-myoho-renge-kyo*, and you'll be kickin' ass, too," said a big guy near me.

"Karmically speaking," added Gus.

Mom said she'd like to be one of the *Desperate Housewives*. Moss and I cringed, but the crowd thought it was funny.

We watched a short video explaining the history of the religion, which was called Nichiren Buddhism. Mom had gotten to the lip-pursing point of the evening. "They're going to try to sell us a timeshare…" she muttered.

"*What?*" I whispered.

"This is a *pitch*. Nothing but a hard sell. Watch," she whispered. "They're going to have a come-on—something free to rope in the mooches. Then they'll make you a deal and try to close you."

"Sssshhh!" I said. Mom's whispering had gotten louder and she was starting to gesture. Several people were looking at her instead of at the video.

"*Try* it, just *try* it," Mom taunted.

"You're being rude," I said. She gave me a look, but she stopped talking.

After the video, people gave testimonials of how Buddhism had helped them in their lives. Mom was really getting restless now. "This is *so* AA," she said. "'I'm Harriet, and I'm a Buddhist,'" she mimicked. "'I've got six months of Buddhist sobriety.'"

The people seemed nice to me, but I could see Mom's point. Then a skinny Asian kid with baggy pants and a cocked baseball cap told his story.

"Yo, I'm Kim. I only been down with this a few months, you know... Couple years ago my folks split up and I took it hard. Let school slide, smoked dope, dropped Ecstasy, shrooms, whatever. Then dropped out. Spent days crashed, listening to music, Xboxing... It wasn't good. Then it got worse.

"My dad sent me to this summer camp in the old country. Blue Dragon Camp. Supposed to turn pussies like me into men. Dress up like G.I. Seoul in fatigues, run up hills, eat kimchi, and shout a buncha stupid shit. 'I will be strongest and coolest kid!' That really worked on me, right?"

Kim flexed his toothpick arm and the group cracked up. "Man, there was no way out of this bad trip. I *tried*. Me and a coupla other dudes went AWOL. We got to the highway and nobody'd stop for us. Dumb ass people saw our fatigues and musta thought we were North Korean spies. 'Oh, Daddy, don't pick up those guys! They will steal our bulgogi!'"

Pause for more laughter. "So, y'know, Blue Dragon really changed my attitude. I got home and I was done with marijuana. I started doing heroin. Why fuck around, right? Well, one thing led to another... I got convicted of a felony, one of my friends OD'd... I'm going through this shit and I run into my old pal Liz, who I hadn't seen since fifth grade. And she's like, 'Kim, I got the hook-up, and it's *nam-myo-ho-renge-kyo*. Check it out, man.'

"In a way, I can't believe I did. But somehow she got me here. And the *daimoku* and the *gongyo*, they got me high. Endolphins, whatever, I started feeling better. I mean, shit got *worse*…"

Several people laughed and nodded understandingly. "I'd made some bad causes. But I kept chanting, started making better causes. Man, facing *gohonzon* is some serious shit, 'cause it ain't nothin' but a mirror. *Gohonzon* introduced me to a sad and dangerous dude. No way around it, the scariest person in my life is me. *The scariest person in my life is…me*. Well…except for that old Marine asshole at Blue Dragon, who pepper sprayed us while we sang the South Korean national anthem. Can you imagine how long that took *me*? 'Oh say can you—whoops, wrong fuckin' country—Ack! Ack! Ack! *Donghae mulgwa* what the fuck!—Ack! Ack! Ack!'"

More laughs. Even Mom was loving Kim's story.

"Man, he kept yelling at me, 'Kim, your Korean is *nooooo* good!' Like twenty guys are looking at each other, wondering who he's screaming at, 'cause *everyone* is named Kim! 'No, *you*, you scrawny Americanized turd. *Your* Korean is *nooooo* good!' Well, no shit—I learned it off a menu!

"Hey… it's all good, right? You heard that one before? 'It's all good, man.' Dude, that is the *ultimate* Buddhist saying."

Shouts of agreement. This laidback crowd was getting worked-up. Kim had them eating out of his hand.

"It's all good *if* you can turn the poison into medicine. That shit…is deep. Workin' on it. *Workin'* on it."

Kim sat down. While the group caught its breath, I looked at Mom for her reaction. She gave a decisive nod of certainty.

"Timeshare," she said.

I stared at her.

Chapter Seven
A Small Box of *Nam-Myoho-Renge-Kyo*

ON THE WAY HOME, Mom was more animated than she'd been in ages. She was pissed-off as usual, but at least she was talking to us.

"Don't be so naïve, Moon, it was a pitch. Like I used to do on the phone. 'Hi, Moon, I tried to get ahold of you yesterday, must be your fishing day, huh? No? Maybe out taking your money to the bank? Listen, I'll tell you why I'm calling. One of our major suppliers kinda dropped a bombshell, gave us thirty-five free trips to enlightenment.'"

"They really bit on that enlightenment line?" asked Moss.

"Honey, it's an analogy. Really we were giving free vacations to Las Vegas."

"That sounds more appealing to middle America," observed Moss.

"They snapped it up. 'Now, I don't know what the connection is, Moon. Maybe we did some business in a past life, or we sent you one of our *gohonzons*, but my boss wanted me to give you a call on this. Have you ever had your worldly dreams fulfilled? Would you like to? Of course you would, who wouldn't? Well, Moon, this enlightenment comes with a small box of our imprinted *nam-myoho-renge-kyo*. Moon, what have you got there, a one-chair beauty salon? Mom-and-pop grocer? Little upholstery store? Dry cleaner?' Man, those were our bread and butter, we killed on those."

"How long did you have this job?" I asked.

"Three days. Changed my life. The scales fell from my eyes and I saw clearly. It's all sales."

"*What's* all sales?" I asked.

"Everything. Every darn thing you can think of is sales. Everyone's selling, twenty-four seven." She snapped back into the pitch, talking a mile a minute. "'Probably your customers walk away with your *nam-myoho-renge-kyo*. You'd like them to know where they got it, wouldn't you? Probably come back and give you some more business, right? Well, this is a real good *nam-myoho-renge-kyo,* the Graphomatic Three. It's a retractable, refillable—'"

"Ballpoint pen!" I said.

"'—got a guaranteed three year shelf life, comes with five lines of your ad copy on the barrel, and the enlightenment package on top of the box. You've seen these mantras selling at retail for a dollar twenty-nine. We normally sell them for ninety-nine cents, but right now we're blowing them out for just *seventy-nine cents apiece*!! Now, you know your business better than I do, what would be better for you, a box of five hundred or a box of three hundred?'"

"Hang up, bro!" laughed Moss.

"'You *do* want that enlightenment, don't you? Or at least the fulfillment of your worldly dreams? That's the main thing, Moon. Those benefits all come with the *nam-myoho-renge-kyo*. Listen, I'm a businessman myself, and I understand the importance of keeping your inventory low. Lemme tell you what I'm gonna do. I'm going to take a box of five hundred, break it down to a box of three hundred and a box of two hundred, and put your name on the two hundred *nam-myoho-renge-kyos*. That's going to come to—'"

"One hundred fifty-eight dollars," I snapped out.

"'—with five lines of ad copy and the enlightenment package on top of the box.'"

"No!" yelled Moss.

"'Don't you *want* to be enlightened, sir?'"

"I'd rather go to Vegas."

"'Well, sir, that *is* the opposite of enlightenment. Nevertheless, if you chant for a trip to Vegas with our *nam-myoho-renge-kyos*, not only will you *go* to Vegas, but when you get there, you'll *win*! Doesn't that sound great?!'"

"Uh...yeah," said Moss.

"'Of course it does,'" said Mom, coming out of character long enough to remark, "When you're pitching, every question is phrased so the customer must answer in the affirmative, or is forced to make a choice. You never ask, 'Do you want these shoes?' You ask, 'Would you prefer these shoes in black or in brown?'"

"Fiendishly clever, Moms. Like, 'Would you prefer to give me a Benjamin or a pair of U.S. Grants?'"

"Vaguely," said Mom. "Do you actually know anything about the presidents beyond their denominations?"

"I know they named the country after Mr. Grant," said Moss. Mom would've turned to see if he was serious if she hadn't been driving.

"What if you went through all that and they still wouldn't bite?" I asked.

"That's usually what happened, even though I knew the pitch cold and could counter every objection. But there's an art to closing, and not everyone can do it. Our closer was a special guy who could make them say yes. Frank DeMotta. He was a *dese*, *dem*, and *dose* kinda guy. But he could sell *anybody anything*. So about now, I'd start waving for Frank to get over there and take it home."

Mom started gesturing so wildly the car began to swerve and the lady in the luxury car next to us looked over in shock.

"Enough with the drama," said Moss. "That hag in the Lexus ain't Frank."

"What would Frank do?" I asked.

"Magic," said Mom. "It was like this." She flipped her cell phone out and started talking into it. "'Hey dere, Moon, you been talkin' to my gal Janice, huh? She tell ya 'bout the 'lightenment and the 'fillment of your worldly dreams? She did, huh? Dat sound awright?'" Mom extended the phone at arm's length. "Frank never listened to a thing they said."

Mom brought the phone back in and started talking again. "'So let's getcha down for some of dose *nam-myo-whatchamacallits*. Let's say a small box of five hundred to start ya off, see how it goes. You know, dis practice is based on evidence. It's gotta work for ya, or we don't stay in business.'" Mom held the phone out at arm's length. "Yada yada yada. Moon, I guarantee if you go back, they'll bring in a Frank DeMotta."

"Uh, Mom…" I said.

Mom brought the phone in tight and went into her closer routine. "'Whattsa matta, Moon, you got everything on dis deal but my shorts. You want I should throw dem in, too?'"

"*Mom*," I insisted.

"'Is dat a yes I hear?'"

At that moment the cop behind us lit his lights and hit his siren.

"Jesus H. Christ!" erupted Mom, coming out of character in a hurry.

"I wouldn't call that a yes," I said.

"I wasn't even really talking on the cell phone," whined Mom. "It was just a prop."

"Hopefully we'll get a cop who's a theater buff," said Moss.

"Yeah, Mom, ask him if he liked *Cats*," I said.

"Or *A Chorus Line*."

"Enough, boys! Start chanting *now*. Fast."

I thought Mom might be serious until I heard her snickering.

Moss and I did some quick *nam-myoho-renge-kyos* as Mom pulled over, rolled down her window, and got out her license. The officer exited his patrol car and sidled over to us. He was on the portly side, with a vein-riddled nose balanced atop a cookie-duster moustache.

"Evenin', ma'm, gentlemen…" His Western drawl seemed out-of-place on a portion of Pico Boulevard best known for wall-to-wall synagogues.

"Good evening, officer," said Mom, her voice suddenly unctuous.

"Wouldja mind showin' me your license and registration?"

"Certainly. I'll just reach in the glove compartment…"

"'Course you will."

Mom took her registration out of the glove compartment and handed it to the officer along with her license. We waited while he studied it carefully. He glanced up at Mom.

"I was several years younger then," she said coyly.

"Weren't we all? But you haven't aged a day, ma'am."

"Oh dear, I'm afraid this is going to be a *big* ticket."

The officer chuckled and said, "You know why I stopped you?"

"Because I was talking on the phone."

"*Were* ya?" The officer seemed genuinely surprised. "Nah, I know you were. That *is* why I stopped you."

"Officer, have you ever seen someone play air guitar?"

"Uh…yeah. I got a couple moron friends who purty much live for Guitar Hero."

"Would you call them guitarists?"

I looked at Moss, baffled at where Mom was going with this.

"Not hardly. But, ma'am, this is about talkin' on the phone, which I'm sure you know is illegal while you're drivin'. I'm not gonna write you for air guitar."

"My point is, your friends may look like they're playing guitar, but they aren't. I looked like I was on the phone, but I wasn't."

"Hmmm. You some kinda lawyer specializing in this here air guitar defense?"

"No. I teach third grade."

"I loved third grade. Miss Lemon let me be ball monitor all year." The officer put away his citation book. "So you weren't on the phone?"

"No, sir. You can check my call log."

"Then why were you talking on it and waving it around? I watched for half a block 'fore I lit you up."

"I was showing my sons how I used to sell ballpoint pens, key tags, and ice scrapers on the phone."

"You used to do phone sales?"

"Um-hm."

"Y'all were a telemarketer?"

"That's right."

The officer whipped the citation book back out and flipped it open. "I hate telemarketers. Gettin' so there's no point in answerin' the phone anymore."

"I only did it for three days!" Mom protested.

The officer grinned. "I'm just funnin' ya. I don't answer the phone at all. Have a nice night."

"Officer, can I ask you a question?" I blurted.

"Well, I reckon…"

"Where are you from?"

"The valley. Winnetka."

31

"Oh...I thought you were from somewhere else."

"Texas?"

"Well, yeah..."

The officer snorted appreciatively. "Taking an acting class and working on a character. So I hadja goin', huh?"

"Dude," said Moss, "You were the full redneck."

"Well, all right, then," grinned the officer. "Y'all drive safely."

Chapter Eight
Closed

"YOU WANT TO *WHAT*?!" You'd have thought I'd just told Mom I intended to join a voodoo cult that sacrificed barnyard animals.

"Go to another meeting," I repeated.

"Why?! What could you possibly have liked about the first one?"

"Uh…Gretchen?" suggested Moss. We were sharing a rare family dinner, and my stab at conversation was working perhaps better than I'd intended.

"Steak okay?" asked Dad.

"Perfect medium rare," Moss replied quickly. "Don't know how you do it, Dad. Lovely dinner, Mom. Could you pass the butter, please?"

Mom extended the butter, but stuck to the point. "If it's about the girls, I can understand."

"Great baked potato, honey," offered Dad.

"It's a really amazing recipe, David. You set the oven at three-fifty. Put the potatoes in. An hour later, they're baked. Imagine that."

"You make it sound easy…"

"I like that they never talked about God," I said, before Mom could snap Dad's olive branch in two.

"Yeah," agreed Moss, "That was, y'know, refreshing."

"No heaven, no hell, no sin, no guilt trip," I added, gathering steam.

"What good is a religion that doesn't make you feel bad about yourself?" demanded Mom.

We all looked at her dubiously.

Mom sighed with exasperation. "It's a cult."

"A cult? Like Jim Jones? Do these Buddhists have mass suicides?" asked Dad.

"Well, maybe not *that*," Mom conceded. "But...all right, *whatever*."

Dad put down his fork. "I don't get it. You've been dragging the boys to church for years. Now they actually *want* to go and you don't like it."

"We had an arrangement, David," Mom said. "It was your job to teach them different sports, and my job to expose them to different faiths."

Dad nodded thoughtfully. "To *expose* them...so they'd build up an immunity?"

Moss and I looked at each other as if we'd just found out Santa wasn't real. "You gotta be kidding," he said.

"I never thought my children would fall for any of this hokum," Mom sighed. "Did you ever notice the three-letter word hidden inside 'believe'?"

Moss, Dad, and I looked at each other, then I got it. "*Lie?*" I blurted. Mom threw up her hands, as if to say that I'd just made her point.

"Why don't we let them decide for themselves?" Dad suggested quietly.

Mom acquiesced with a nod and a final sigh. Moss gave me a shrug of commiseration when Mom wasn't looking, and the rest of the meal passed in silence.

So Moss and I went back, *sans* Mom. Then I went back, *sans* Moss. He was more interested in skating lines than chanting them, but I think I heard him muttering some *nam-myohos* under his breath from time to time.

I had mixed feelings, myself. On the one hand, I had Mom dying for me to throw in the towel and decide that the Nichiren Buddhists were a crock just like every other church we'd been to. That, of course, motivated me to prove her wrong and embrace the practice.

On the other hand, the Buddhists were so eager to see me commit that it made me skittish. I hated to admit it, but my mother was right. They introduced me to one closer after another. The third meeting, Yumi, the Japanese woman who had taken an interest in Mom, decided to fold me under her wing. She spent quite a while pontificating, but her accent was so impenetrable I had no idea what she was saying. I found myself nodding blankly, captivated by her assault on the English language.

These good people seemed just too interested in selling me their religion, and I decided this would be my last meeting. My conviction grew throughout the evening's testimonial from Robin, which featured a descent into his colorful alcoholic past, the act of siring multiple autistic children who were subsequently removed from his care, and ultimately, his incarceration. It somehow concluded on a hopeful note when he found Buddhism in the county lockup and returned to a wife who had slept with all his friends.

There was extended applause for Robin's speech. This portion of a meeting resembled the one-upmanship of a poker game, with each speaker attempting to top the previous story of recovery—*I will call your opiate addiction with my meth habit, and raise you a rear end collision that decapitated the other driver*—until all bets were in. There was a protracted silence, and it looked like Robin might just take the pot.

Then a black man in his forties named Phillip cleared his throat. I had spoken to him in passing, as all the Buddhists had made an effort to say hi. He looked over at me as he started his testimonial.

"Some of you guests may not be going through such rough times as Robin did. That's not how it is for all of us. My life was good when I came to the practice, about three years ago. Except my mother was sick with arthritis pain. We took her to different doctors and she was still suffering.

"That's when a friend brought me to one of these meetings. After listening, I thought I'd give it a try, for my mother's sake. My friend said, 'Okay, that's fine. But *you've got to follow the directions.*' 'What directions?' I asked. 'You told me I didn't even have to believe in it, and it'd work. Now you're telling me I've got to follow the directions.' 'Ain't nothing changed,' he said. 'This here Buddhism we practice is like a microwave oven. Whether you believe in it or not, it gonna heat things up in a hurry. But you gotta plug the machine in, you gotta set the dials right, you gotta *follow the directions.*'

"I guess that seemed reasonable, so I did it. Got the *gohonzon*, did my *gongyo* twice a day, lotta trouble with the words, but I got better, just like you will. Chanted *daimoku*. Said I'd give it a month to prove itself.

"Well, at the end of the month, Mama was so much better that she went back to doing her gardening. Doctors didn't know what to make of it. So I asked her, 'Hey, Momma. Anything else bothering you?' She said, 'Phillip, your daddy left me with a bad mortgage. If only interest rates'd go down, I'd refi into a long term fixed. That'd give me peace of mind.' 'Oh, that so, Momma?'"

Phillip slapped his hands into prayer position and chanted a couple of lines, while the crowd laughed appreciatively.

"Well, every day I'd check the newspaper, and I watched those rates drop a point and a quarter in a month. And Mama got her a new mortgage."

Phillip paused for a round of applause.

"Now, I'm relating these experiences for the benefit of our guests, since this sort of thing is pretty common to the rest of us, isn't it?"

There were nods and murmurs of agreement all around.

"Fact, we give it a name, call it the 'Hundred Day Test.' Here's how it works. You write down ten things you want to see happen, then you start chanting. Remember what I said. *Follow the directions.* Then like the commercial says—just do it. This Buddhism is no spectator sport. *Just do it.* At the end of a hundred days, *you'll* see some miracles, too."

Chapter Nine
Working for Cousin Rufus

SO I DID IT. I got a *gohonzon* and set up an altar in my room. Mom began to refer to me as "her son the Buddhist," and Dad called me "the Dalai Landing."

Like everything else, the Internet has revolutionized Buddhist practice. New folks like me can access online recitations of the Lotus Sutra done at a snail's pace by a digitized Japanese woman. Twice a day I'd poke along with her, surprised and pleased to find the foreign words becoming familiar. Even as I embraced the challenge, I found myself wondering if this had anything to do with Buddhism, or if I was just tackling this like any other project, such as memorizing an epic poem.

During the drone of *nam-myoho-renge-kyo*, there's a lot of time for your mind to wander, and that's the kind of doubt mine tended to return to. I was having a very hard time believing that I was tuning in to the mystic law of the universe. Chanting seemed a ridiculous waste of time, and I found myself thinking of the things I'd rather do instead. Perhaps this was the genius of the practice: it bored you into action.

Once a month I attended a special *Kosen-Rufu* meeting. *Kosen-Rufu* is loosely translated as "world peace." The Nichiren Buddhists believe that when enough people are practicing they will have such a beneficial effect on their environment that we will succeed in working out our problems and live together without killing each other. I explained this to Moss and he nodded wisely. Now when his skate crew asks what I'm doing, he says that I'm working for Cousin Rufus. That ends the conversation.

One day Mom asked me if I was experiencing any buyer's remorse. She told me that sometimes "Frank the closer" could talk people into buying the pens, but once the merchandise was shipped the customers refused to accept delivery. No longer under Frank's spell, they came to their senses and reneged on the purchase. Mom said that she kind of admired those people—they might have been suckers, but they weren't complete losers.

I guess I *was* a complete loser, because I was determined to stick with this for the hundred day limit I'd set for myself. The time went pretty fast. On the evening of the hundredth day my family unexpectedly went out to dinner. I hadn't told anybody about the hundred days, so I was surprised at the coincidence, but I thought this might be the universe's way of celebrating the completion of the trial period.

I was really savoring this karmic treat until I heard Dad say, "Boys, your mom and I are throwing in the towel."

Uh…the benefit the universe had prepared for me on completing my hundred days was my parents' divorce.

My wish list did not contain ten items, per Phillip's recommendation. It consisted of a single objective, on which I had staked everything. My only goal was for my mother to be happier.

Perhaps divorce was the only way the universe could accommodate me, but it sure seemed like a dirty trick.

Chapter Ten
Moss Rules

PRETTY MUCH EVERYTHING I know about family life comes from watching *The Simpsons*. Since Homer and Marge never divorced, I didn't know how to handle what was happening to my family. But I guess if you haven't watched it on TV, you just have to figure it out for yourself.

Mom and Dad sure must've had their ducks in a row, because within a week following the Pizza Night Bombshell, Dad moved out and got a small apartment near his bar. Mom said their agreement gave Dad "custody" every other weekend, which made it sound like Moss and I were going to be handcuffed and arrested. It was nowhere near that bad.

Like a lot of boys, our relationship with our father was mainly based on sports. When our parents separated, sticking with something that was familiar seemed like a safe way to ease into things. So on weekends with Dad, we'd spend a lot of time in the park.

Even Mom would give Dad credit for helping us become the best athletes we could be. Dad was never so drunk that he couldn't play catch with us. He taught me to throw a curveball, though he couldn't teach me to *hit* one. When the athletic genes were given out, my brother got the lion's share.

Moss is the most gifted natural athlete I've ever seen. He could throw a tight spiral forty-five yards, catch passes one-handed all day long, and beat high school basketball players at HORSE. But his capabilities were no big deal to him, and for that matter, neither were sports. He'd play a game just as long as he enjoyed it, and then walk away. Competition didn't interest him.

When he was eleven, some of Moss's friends nagged him into joining their little league team. He hit four home runs in the first two games, and his manager, Mr. Franken, was delirious. He imagined winning the league, coaching the all-stars, sweeping state championships, national championships, international championships. He came to see Dad, spewing these visions of glory and Dad tried to gently talk him down. When Mr. Franken left, Dad just shook his head and muttered, "That man does *not* understand your brother."

Of course, Dad was right. Moss decided there wasn't enough challenge playing by the standard rules, so he invented his own. He didn't disclose them, but Dad and I figured them out pretty fast.

Moss's first at-bat the next game, he took a pitch down the middle. *Strike one.* "C'mon, Moss, c'mon, babe," yelled Mr. Franken.

Moss took the next pitch as well. *Strike two.* "C'mon, Moss, shake the stick, c'mon, babe," yelled Mr. Franken, perturbed.

The pitcher delivered high and tight, maybe a strike, maybe a ball. Moss hit the pitch three hundred feet down the left field line, just barely foul. He missed a massive home run by a foot.

I looked at Dad, puzzled. "Did he do that on purpose?"

The next pitch was outside and low. Moss golfed a towering drive down the right field line, again foul by a foot. Dad and I grinned at each other.

Mr. Franken was a little slower to catch on. "C'mon, Moss,

c'mon, babe, just straighten it out, guy, you can do it."

Yes, he *could* do it—but I didn't think he would. The pitcher, who was pretty good, was also starting to wonder what was going on. He was way ahead on the count, but after the last two foul balls he wasn't feeling confident. His next pitch was so far outside the catcher couldn't snag it. Moss looked tempted, but laid off. Ball one.

The pitcher threw one a little closer, about a foot outside and just off the ground. Moss strode across the plate to get to it, and hit a line drive that hopped over the right field fence for a ground rule double.

By the end of the game, Dad and I had figured out Moss's rules:

1. He refused to swing at any pitch in the strike zone until he had two strikes.
2. With two strikes he would simply defend the plate, fouling off balls until he got a pitch he liked.
3. He liked pitches in the "Moss zone." The Moss zone surrounded the normal strike zone. These pitches would've been balls if Moss didn't swing at them.

Moss went four for four despite these self-imposed handicaps, but he didn't hit any home runs. His team won, so Mr. Franken wasn't too put out by his star's drop-off in production. He clapped Moss on the back and told him he had to work on his eye—lay off some of those bad pitches and swing at the strikes. Moss nodded respectfully.

In the short time that he played baseball, Moss's odd at-bats became legendary. After a couple of quick strikes, pitchers would test the limits of the Moss zone, sailing the ball high into the backstop or bouncing it in the dirt, scowling when Moss refused to swing at their most outrageous offerings. But if they got within a foot of the plate, Moss would shift his stance and attack with lethal results.

The team was winning, but the scores were closer. The Moss rules were taking a toll on Mr. Franken's nerves, and his chatter when Moss was at the plate suggested his deteriorating mental state. "C'mon, Moss, c'mon, babe, you're killin' me. Don't play with it, just *hit* it, for Chrissake!"

Mr. Franken offered to spot the opposition two strikes on Moss's at-bats so he wouldn't have to witness the best hitter in the league taking a pair down the middle like mighty Casey, but the umps wouldn't go for it. So Mr. Franken just looked down at the ground in disgust. When he'd hear the ump call, "Stee-rike two!" he'd reluctantly look up to watch how things would turn out.

One game Moss came to bat in the last inning with his team down four runs. There were two outs and the bases were loaded. Mr. Franken called Moss over before he went to the plate. We could see him pleading with his hitter to, just this once, abandon his rules for the good of the team. With one swing Moss could tie the game! Moss nodded and stepped to the plate.

No surprise to Dad and me, Moss did things his way. The result was a triple that scored three runs, an outcome that would have made most managers happy. But when the next batter popped up and his team lost by a run, Mr. Franken was apoplectic. He sat the team on the bench and railed at them all for letting him down, but especially at Moss.

When it was over, Dad took us out for burgers. Moss sucked hard on his milk shake and looked at us, tears in his eyes. "Mr. Franken takes baseball waaaaaay too seriously."

Dad looked at Moss gravely. "Son, this is a tough lesson, but it's time for you to learn it," he said quietly. "*What other people think of you is none of your business.*"

Moss and I looked at each other, completely confused. "I don't get it, Dad. What do you mean?" I asked.

"Moss made his rules and he stuck to 'em. That's what a man

does, how he lives his life. Sure, you'll take some heat for it—but you have to ignore that. *What other people think of you*—and this goes double for Mr. Franken—*is none of your business.*"

Chapter Eleven
Moss Cup

NIGHTS AT DAD'S PLACE were more awkward than the days. It was like camping out without the trees or animals or campfires—you know, the things that would make anyone *want* to go camping. There were no extra beds and not a lot else in Dad's apartment, so Moss and I bunked on the floor in sleeping bags. Dad never got cable and had only a tiny TV. We spent a few months of total boredom before he came to his senses and fetched us over to his bar. Turned out Fanatics Bar and Grill had something for all of us—sports, food, women, and liquor.

When we'd walk in, the waitresses would all rush over and try to seat us. Sometimes they'd have play fights and argue over who was going to get "the M&M's." When I said I loved M&M's and I'd take some too, they giggled. They said *we* were the M&M's. Moss and Moon.

Our popularity was due to Dad, and not because he was their boss, or because they liked him, though they did. It's because Dad was a big tipper.

As far back as I can remember, Dad put money in my hand and

taught me to leave the tip. Before I could even add, I could calculate twenty-five percent. Once, I pointed out that the waitress had forgotten to bring us water after we'd requested it. Dad said she looked stressed and told me to give her twenty-five. Another waiter sighed deeply when Moss ordered a hamburger without pickles. Dad suggested that twenty-five percent might help the man develop more patience. One of Dad's sayings was, "Twenty-five'll keep y'alive."

I wasn't getting a lot of practice with percent, since we always left twenty-five. I suggested maybe we should try twenty, even fifteen. Dad said maybe we ought to leave thirty. When I looked at him, I guess he figured it was time to explain more.

It was just Dad and me, sitting in a booth at a little coffee shop. Dad looked at me seriously. "Who's your favorite superhero?" he asked.

"Spider-Man, at the moment."

"I don't imagine he's a very good tipper."

"Probably not," I conceded. "He's usually broke."

Dad nodded. "He's got a lot of problems. Aunt Mae, a horrible boss, difficult girlfriends…"

"That's why I like him. He keeps it real."

"Yeah," Dad agreed. "Except for having spider strength, spider senses, being able to swing through the air, stuff like that…"

"Well, yeah, stuff like that."

"So Spidey's a bad tipper. But he makes up for it by fighting villains and saving people's lives, right?"

"Uh, I guess so…"

"Well, I can't fight villains or save anybody's life. So I try to make up for it by being a good tipper."

I guess I looked unconvinced, because he went on. "You must have noticed that life is not easy."

"Maybe even hard."

Dad nodded. "Maybe even. So everybody needs a break once in a while. I just figure that for anyone who deals with people for a living—which, believe me, is not a piece of cake—*we* can be that break. We can be the most polite, the most generous, the most understanding people we can possibly be."

"But what if they don't really deserve a break?" I said, probing for a flaw in his reasoning.

Dad shrugged. "Ask me, everyone deserves a break. Can't we afford to be wrong?"

This sounded kinda golden ruley—do unto others twenty-five percent, blah, blah, blah. But it was my dad's religion and I couldn't argue with it, any more than I could take exception to anyone else's religion. When we started hanging out at the bar, I came to appreciate it. For him to believe anything else would've been a lot more hypocritical than giving up the booze.

At first we'd just drop by Fanatics, have dinner, maybe watch a little TV, and then go home. Being a sports bar, Fanatics had TVs everywhere, and each of them could be tuned to whatever channel we wanted. And man, we *wanted*. We watched football, basketball, baseball, hockey, soccer, tennis, skiing, track and field, bowling, rugby, you name it. Then there were the skateboard competitions.

The Street League Skateboarding contest is the purest, most respected street skating event in the world. With nearly a quarter of a million dollars at stake, it also has the highest purse. Twenty-five of the world's best skateboarders ride a course laid out like an "idealized" city street—loaded with ledges, handrails, stairs, and ramps at varied heights, so skaters can launch their most outrageous tricks.

Dad and I were watching the competition with some interest, but

Moss was so bored he started yawning. Dad looked at him. "Not impressed?" he asked.

Moss shrugged. "Same old, same old."

"You can do that?"

"I could do that in pre-K while those little kiddies were taking their nappies." Moss always had his board. He grabbed it and headed for the exit.

"Where's he going?" Dad asked me.

"Moss Cup, Dad. You don't want to miss this."

The setting sun of September hit us smack in our eyes when we stepped through the door, and we squinted as our pupils adjusted to the surplus light. Meanwhile, Moss surveyed the landscape. To me, it didn't look like he had a lot to work with, but he could see a skatepark in a desert.

Moss launched. A group of regulars about to enter the bar stopped to watch along with us. He did three pop shuvits in succession—the board rotating 180 degrees, but his feet retaining the same forward orientation. The moves followed so quickly on each other that the silver board looked like a flashing knife. Then, without breaking rhythm, he executed a "front foot impossible," popping the tail and going airborne. He flicked the edge of the deck with his leading foot, sending the board rotating in a complete circle around that foot before he landed. Bada-bada-bada-BOOM.

He followed with a kick flip, a heel flip, and a varial flip, where the board both spins and flips—each trick building in difficulty from the previous one. What made Moss a great skater was not just the degree of difficulty of what he attempted, though that was very high. It was the style and ease with which he landed every trick, making the board dance while following a fluid line. This section was like a gunslinger twirling his pistols, showing off his dexterity before he blew everyone away.

All the while, Moss was skating slightly downhill and picking up speed, heading point blank at a brick wall. As he landed the varial he abruptly pivoted ninety degrees, dragging an index finger along the wall's face to show how close he had come to impact.

The four people witnessing this loosed four different expletives. One of them stuck his head into the bar, and a few seconds later a flood of customers poured out the door, some still holding their drinks, eager to see what the fuss was about.

They didn't have long to wait. Moss was just about done scaling a series of handicapped ramp switchbacks to a bank building next door. Other customers had to ascend—and descend—a flight of about twenty steps to reach the bank's entrance, which had a façade adorned with columns like a Greek temple. Moss slalomed through the pillars picking up speed, going faster and faster, the god of skateboarding rolling through the Parthenon. Then he slowed, veered toward the handrail, and went airborne.

The handrails in most competitions are maybe ten feet long, but this one was much, much longer, and it was do-or-die. Once he committed to the trick Moss either had to grind the entire distance or suffer a gory fall onto the cement steps of the staircase, since there was no bailout available.

My brother did not study academic science, but he was physics in action. He and his board were a diagonal vector—a force with direction—about to abruptly change course into a sheer vertical slide. To do this, he slightly pivoted body and board to execute a frontside smith grind. He took the rail between the wheels of the back trucks, the front of the board dangling precariously off the rail. His knees flexed and hands splayed to the sides, he shifted his weight back like a surfer plummeting down a wave face—as much a posture of artistic expression as one of perfect balance. His face showed dead calm with a trace of a smile. "Steez" the skaters called it. Style with ease.

Moss stuck the dismount and a cheer went up from the crowd, who had been holding its breath throughout the trick. A guy next to me murmured, "That's unreal."

"Not yet," I whispered.

Next to the bank was a post office parking lot, empty on a Saturday evening. Moss headed for the lot as the crowd ran to keep up with him. There were maybe forty bar patrons, some half in the bag, but no one wanted to miss this.

The US government had provided for his needs, installing a tasty array of raised concrete planters on the premises. Moss ground their ledges one after another, unleashing a display of the hottest street skating trickery. If he didn't kickflip into the trick, then he flipped out of it, his board rotating and spiraling, effortlessly mounting the ledges and grinding on every part of the deck, wheels, and trucks. I had seen my brother do this many times, and the ease with which he landed these tricks belied their true difficulty.

A decorative planter bed bordered the parking lot. Moss skated wide, picked up speed and sailed over the shrubbery with ease. He angled to the periphery of the sidewalk and jumped a trash can. Upon landing, he immediately veered left to avoid smashing into a lamppost, drawing a howl from the people who rushed to follow him.

He was headed back to the bank. I thought I knew what he'd do next. I waved the crowd away from the staircase, hoping I was wrong and he wouldn't try it. But I was right.

Moss gained the landing and skated away to start his run for the stairs. He approached at full velocity, and instead of mounting the handrail, this time he crouched, leaped, and went for the more spectacular jump.

He and his board shot into space, then separated for a time that seemed much longer than it actually was. Below him, the board arced through the air, spinning like a torpedo, as Moss hurtled the distance like a bionic long jumper. His leap had to cover a thirty-foot gap with about a fifteen-foot drop.

The board completed its revolution and Moss descended onto it, his feet finding the bolts on the deck as he and the board cleared the final steps together. On touchdown he sailed over the curb and into the street, which was, happily, empty at the moment.

Expletives from the crowd. Game, set, and match to Moss.

My dad's expression was wondrous, but his face was ashen. "We better head for the ER," he muttered.

"Why? Moss is fine."

"I'm not. I need an EKG."

Several folks near us laughed and clapped him on the back. Instead of the hospital, we went back to the bar and Dad bought a round on the house.

Chapter Twelve
Finding Goats

MOST PEOPLE HAD NEVER seen live skateboarding and were in awe of the performance Moss had put on. Several customers asked for his autograph, convinced that he'd wind up the next Tony Hawk and his signature would be a collector's item. Everyone was friendly and would greet us enthusiastically when we came in.

However, now that we were back in school, our nights at Fanatics took on an academic dimension. After dinner, we'd tune the TV facing our table to something neutral, then Moss and I would crack the books while Dad headed for his little office to work on his own books. The buzz of the bar made it feel like we were in a big, noisy house. It kind of replaced the home we'd had when our parents were together.

The only homework I don't mind is math, probably because it's so easy I could do it in my sleep. Mom has always seen to it that I was a couple years ahead of everyone. She tried to do the same for Moss, but somehow it didn't click for him.

Moss knows I like math so much that a while back he offered to let me do his homework if I paid him five bucks a week. I recognized this immediately as the scam from *Tom Sawyer*, where Tom makes his friends ante up for the privilege of doing his chores for him, so I didn't fall for it. I negotiated a much better deal. Moss agreed to let me do his homework *absolutely for free*!

One night I'd finished my math and was working on Moss's. Dad was in his office and Moss was out and about, so I had the table to myself. A waitress quietly refilled my water. Then I guess she must have stood there watching me for a minute; I wasn't aware of it, until she reached out and flipped over the textbook to see the cover.

"Aren't you a little young for this?"

I looked up, startled. "Are you going to card me for a textbook?"

"No," she laughed. "Geometry is non-alcoholic, although it would give me a headache."

"Well, you shouldn't do it on an empty stomach. But we had burgers and fries, so...*no problema*."

She laughed again. I noticed—and not for the first time, of course—that she was pretty. I mean, *very* pretty. She had long dark hair, eyes so big I could see myself in their reflection, and soft, full lips. She was very slim, but not in the important places.

"Seriously," she said, "I'm impressed. I couldn't even pass algebra."

This made no sense to me. "You have to pass algebra to graduate."

"Exactly. That's why I dropped out."

"You dropped out of high school?!" I must have sounded horrified, because she got kind of defensive.

"It's not such a big deal. A lot of kids drop out. And I'm going to get my GED."

"What's that?"

"You take a test to show you know the stuff you would've learned in high school. They give you a diploma and you can go to college, or whatever."

"Sounds better than actually going to the classes."

"It *is*," she agreed. "Except I can't pass the test, 'cause I *still* can't do the math."

"Well, *I* could do it for you," I said, joking.

"I wish. But maybe…you could teach me?"

"Me?" I choked out, my voice cracking. We both laughed. "You said I was too young for this."

She regarded me critically. "You actually don't look so young."

"Mom and Dad redshirted us, so Moss and I are older than most of the other kids in our grade."

"You're tall."

"Genetics," I said as I straightened up in the booth. "And good posture."

"At ease, soldier." I slouched and she smirked. "Are you getting them right?"

"Well, yeah…"

"Then you're *not* too young. You're hired."

Even though we were just talking about math, I blushed.

The waitress's name was Jasmine. We worked out a schedule where I'd ride my bike over to Fanatics after school. I'd teach Jasmine math for about an hour, then head home, and Jasmine would work her shift. Dad was around most days, so I'd get to see him. But above all, I'd get to see Jasmine.

Her problem in math was that she didn't know anything. That sounds harsh, but it's the truth. Okay, she knew her multiplication facts, and she could add and subtract, but decimals, fractions, geometry, algebra—*fahgeddaboudit*!

The first day she showed me some of her work and I studied it for so long that she finally asked, "Uh…are you okay?"

"Yeah. I'm finding your goats."

"My *goats?*"

"Um-hm."

She waited a few moments. "I don't know much math. I never heard about finding goats."

"It's just something one of my teachers used to say. It helped me a lot so I always do it."

"Well, maybe it'll help me, too."

It was worth a try, so I told her the story Mr. Riley told us in fifth grade.

Once upon a time there was a Bedouin sheik. He and his tribe lived in tents and traveled around the desert, herding their many goats and camels. One day his servants came running in, yelling, "Master, master—one of your goats is gone!"

"Find my goat!" the sheik thundered. The servants looked and looked all day, but they couldn't find the goat.

The next day a servant came running in, yelling, "Master, master—one of your camels is gone!"

"Find my goat!" the sheik yelled.

"Uh...you mean your *camel?*" the servant asked timidly.

"No, I mean my *goat,*" the sheik insisted. "Find it!" The servants looked and looked all day, but they couldn't find the goat.

The next day a servant came running in, yelling, "Master, master—one of your daughters is gone!"

"Find my goat!" the sheik bellowed. The servants looked and looked all day, but they couldn't find the goat.

The next day the servants came running in and said, "Master, master—"

"Don't tell me," the sheik interrupted. The servants looked at him expectantly.

The sheik sighed. "Okay, tell me. What happened now?"

"Your wife is gone!"

"Find my goat!" As the servants ran out, he added, "And if you find my wife, don't tell her I said that!"

The servants looked and looked all day, but they couldn't find the goat. So the sheik called all the servants to him and looked at them severely.

"Now we've got a heckuva mess, you guys. Someone is stealing goats and camels and daughters and wives—who knows where this is gonna end. If you woulda found my goat in the first place like I told you, the rest of this never would've happened!"

I wound up the story, thinking it was amazingly like the tale of Job, though not nearly so tragic. Maybe every story in the Middle East featured animals and servants running around like crazy.

Jasmine was staring at me, waiting expectantly.

"But what does that have to do with math?" she finally asked.

"The connection is not obvious," I admitted. "I think Mr. Riley just really liked telling this story, so he found a way to use it to make his point."

"Well, I'm waiting for it," she insisted.

"When you do math you make mistakes, which are the goats. If you don't figure out *why* you made a mistake and fix it, you'll make even more mistakes. We've got to find your goats and fix them—or things will just get worse."

"Can you really do that?" she asked.

I shrugged. "If you show your work…yeah, maybe. Like this problem…"

"I got it wrong, didn't I?"

"Uh, yeah…"

"What about the next one?"

"I haven't gotten that far. I'm still rounding up goats in the first problem. You multiplied instead of dividing, so I guess you're confused about that. You also made a mistake when you converted the mixed numbers to improper fractions, and you forgot to simplify your final answer."

"That's a lot of goats," she admitted.

"Yes, many goats."

"Ba-a-a-a," she bleated. I cracked up.

"I think that's a sheep. Fortunately, we don't have to find *them*."

Chapter Thirteen
Rigo's Ego

THERE'S NOTHING LIKE MATH for making you feel stupid when you don't get it. It's like a club that lets in anyone but you. Everyone's at the party and you're out on the sidewalk by your lonesome. That's no fun.

On the other hand, there's nothing like math for making you feel smart when you finally *do* get it. You think you're turning into Einstein, or at least one of those annoying kids who always have their hands up with the right answer.

Jasmine and I worked for a month. I could see her brain swelling, and along with it, her confidence. You wouldn't think a girl as pretty as her would have lacked anything in that department. Or at least *I* wouldn't have, with my limited knowledge of women. But now Jasmine was in the club and it put a little more strut in her step.

She did the learning, but she gave me the credit. She also gave me $10 a day for our sessions. I tried to refuse, but she insisted. She said I was a better teacher than any she'd ever had and worth five times as much.

This didn't hurt me in the confidence department, either. It's not too shabby hanging out with a gorgeous eighteen-year-old who laughs at your jokes and gives you money for being smart. But whenever I started to get carried away with my fantasies, I'd remember the tale of Rigoberto and that would hit me like a cold shower.

Rigoberto was a third-grade student my mother had a while back. Mom said Rigo was even more immature than the other childish children in her class. Either he wasn't housebroken or he was too shy to ask permission to use the bathroom. Whatever the cause, he had several accidents of the most embarrassing sort. These came to Mom's attention when kids held their noses and complained in pinched voices, "Rigo's stinky!" His shamed face provided tearful confirmation, and Rigo's mother was called to fetch a change of clothing.

In due time he outgrew this problem and his self-image took a leap forward. But it was the act of learning his nines that sent Rigo's ego into the stratosphere.

The major milestone of third grade is to learn the times tables. Of these, the nines are among the most daunting, an Achilles heel of students in even more advanced grades. My mother, however, knew all the tricks of the trade. She took advantage of a useful number pattern to help her students quickly memorize these facts. So while students in other third grade classes were still doddering over their twos and threes, the kids in Mom's class were bursting with pride that they knew their nines!

Rigo was the proudest of all. Despite topping out at three feet and lacking several front teeth, which made him look like a stubby vampire, he began to spend recess and lunch loitering at the fence that Mom's elementary school shared with an adjacent middle school. Gripping the chain links with bravado, Count Rigo would holler at passing seventh-and-eighth-grade girls, "Hey, I know my nines!"

The older girls thought it was cute and played along, calling to their friends.

Pretty soon Rigo had a crowd of girls towering over him and flirting so shamelessly that it put him at risk for a relapse of his embarrassing incidents.

To Rigo's credit he pushed his luck further, proposing to teach the girls the nines if they'd give him their phone numbers. Since most of them didn't actually know their multiplication facts, they took him up on the offer. At recess, separated by the chain-link fence, they'd sit on the asphalt and work problems in their notebooks, a diminutive Rigo standing eye-to-eye, teaching them the trick that Mom had taught him.

To their surprise, under Rigo's tutelage the middle school girls actually learned their multiplication facts, and true to their word, surrendered their digits. For a couple weeks Rigo tied up the phone lines with his middle school harem in a way that would have done Don Juan proud. Then the cell bill arrived and his mother hit the roof. She dragged the story out of him and went to see Mom. A new school rule was enacted, and third graders were no longer allowed to approach the fence and solicit the older women.

So when Jasmine gave me a dazzling smile…I'd think of Rigo. When I'd tease her and she'd elbow me and giggle…I'd think of Rigo. When she'd brush the hair off my forehead…I'd think of Rigo.

It was pretty much like Rigo.

Wasn't it?

Chapter Fourteen
Shoring Up the Ruin

WHEREAS DAD SEEMED to be handling his newfound freedom with restraint and dignity, the most generous adjective I can offer to describe my mother's approach to her single lifestyle would be "eager." Others might be more apt, but a son shouldn't have to say them about the woman who brought him into this world.

Mom's standard line became, "Forty is the new thirty." We pointed out that it was hard to find any thirty-year-olds who were acting like her, and she amended her defense: "Forty is the new *twenty*." That would actually make her our big sister, not our mother. But her antics were hard to take, even for an older sibling.

My mother is a goal-oriented person, the kind who makes a list every day. In fact, she includes items she's already completed, just so she can have the satisfaction of immediately crossing them off. Mom likes getting things done.

Number one on the agenda was to "shore up the ruin," as she put it. Apparently there's nothing like a divorce for motivating a mother to become a Victoria's Secret model. She set her mind to the task the minute Dad moved out.

For three weeks, she shot out of school every day and hit the fitness clubs for their free sessions. Curves, Sports Connection, LA Fitness, 24 Hour Fitness, Bodies in Motion, Gold's—Mom tried them all. The phone wouldn't stop ringing with reps from the gyms pestering Mom to cough up the membership fee and actually pay for her workouts. Fat chance. She always wound up talking them into one more free session.

Just when we thought Mom was never going to commit, she fell under the spell of a hunky trainer named Steve and joined LA Fitness. It was one of the cheaper places, and the trainer shrewdly convinced her she was better off paying less for a membership and spending the savings on his personal attention to her fitness needs. In that way he scored himself a daily four o'clock client.

I guess Steve was good at his job. Dripping with what she called "dew" and sporting a goofy grin from Steve's glorious TLC, Mom would fairly crawl through the door, much too wrung out to cook any dinner. She'd swallow several Advil, soak in the tub for an hour, and take to her bed while it was still daylight. Moss and I would shake our heads, get some fast food, and keep the noise level down. Being woken up would make Mom extremely cranky.

The combination of intense workouts and her fatigue-induced fast produced quick results, as the pounds poured off and the ones that remained turned to toned muscle. This only motivated Mom to redouble her efforts. She decided we were all going on the South Beach diet.

Purging the fridge of carbs was not hard: just don't go shopping. Mom wasn't doing much of that, anyway. However, she had lost all interest in cooking, and there was no way to follow a regimen of meat, fish, salads, and veggies without doing a little food prep. Who could she find to take over the chef chores?

After visiting a Sikh gurdwara one Sunday, Mom took me to a department store. This was not part of our routine, and I was quite sure this temple to consumption could not be considered another church. Without explanation, she led me to the housewares department and declared, "Moon, it's time you learned to cook."

"What about Moss?"

"He likes fire," my mother said simply. "He'll do the grilling. As I recall, you like knives."

She had me there. I *was* a big fan of cold steel. I'd been collecting pocket knives since I was seven years old, and had amassed about a dozen of them. I realized that at that moment I was looking at a display of expensive kitchen cutlery. Hmmm…this could be interesting.

Mom noticed a trim older salesman who was a little too involved in straightening up displays and called him over. His nametag said "Paul."

He listened to her explanation, nodded, and turned to me. "Wusthof Classic."

Mom balked. "Wusthof? Are you sure that's necessary?"

"Absolutely. When a young man cuts with Wusthof, he'll not soon forget it."

He unlocked the display cabinet, then took a large knife and a sharpening steel from a set embedded in a block of wood. They were on sale for the low, low price of $449.99!

"The steel should be used regularly to align the edge of the blade. Are you right handed?" he asked me.

"Yes."

"Good. Take the steel in your left hand and the knife in your right thus. Commence with the widest part of the blade near the handle. Draw the knife towards you." Paul demonstrated several strokes.

"The proper angle of the blade in relation to the steel is critical. It should be twenty-two and one half degrees." With a very careful inflection, he added, "Does that mean anything to you?"

"That would be half of a forty-five degree angle, or one fourth of a ninety degree angle," I said quickly.

He smiled. "Indeed it would. Your turn."

Paul coached me through a sharpening session of ten strokes for each edge, then produced a sheet of newsprint.

"A comparison is instructive." Paul took a cheaper knife and tried to cut the newsprint. It pushed the paper out of the way, but did not bite. Another knife tore the paper rather than severing it. Then he tried the Wusthof blade we had just sharpened. The knife sliced effortlessly through the thin paper.

I grinned. "Crude but persuasive," he remarked, pleased with my reaction. He handed me the knife and I slashed the sports section to ribbons. My mother sighed.

"We'll take them," she gave in.

"Obviously," said Paul. "I expect you'll be needing new pans, too."

"I think our old ones are okay," Mom objected weakly.

"New diet, new pans, I always say," said Paul, looking at me.

"Yeah, that's what I say, too," I jumped in.

"Yes, indeed. Young man, let me introduce you to Calphalon."

When we checked out, the total came to almost $800. I had a sudden attack of buyer's remorse.

"How are we going to pay for all of this?" I asked.

"Child support," said Mom.

Paul ran Mom's charge card through the machine and smirked.

Chapter Fifteen
It's Alive—Alive!!

"TRY NOT TO MAIM YOURSELF," was the extent of Mom's cooking advice. She didn't give Moss *any*, so I thought I'd assume the parental role. "Try not to torch yourself," I suggested. Moss usually has to learn things the hard way, though, and promptly singed his eyebrows while lighting the recalcitrant barbeque.

I avoided any bloodshed in the kitchen. Preparing the simple dishes for our new diet didn't really call for all the top-notch equipment we'd bought, but I did enjoy it. Between watching the cooks at Fanatics and on the food channel, I learned plenty of technique and could whack through veggies like a food processor. Slicing frozen meat for stir-fry was more of a challenge, but I learned to cut morsels you could almost see through.

After Moss's initial setback, he became a very proficient hand at the grill. Dad taught him to gauge a meat's doneness by touch, and after a couple weeks Moss could really nail "medium rare" versus "medium." Marinating the meat and fish was my end, then Moss brought them home to perfection.

This *was* an improvement over fast food, so I was starting to think maybe Mom's crazy self-improvement plan wasn't so crazy after all. Except it was only the beginning.

No question, Mom was looking better than I'd ever seen her—and that was pretty damn good. But she was still far from satisfied with what she saw in the mirror. So she went to Dr. Fisher to "have a little work done."

Dr. Fisher was a Beverly Hills plastic surgeon who must have apprenticed to a butcher. When Mom came home from her initial consultation, she had a diagram of a woman's body that looked like a schematic of how to cut up a steer: filet here, ground round there, prime rib, flank steak. He'd marked up the diagram to show what he could do for Mom's body. Dr. Fisher saw plenty of room for improvement.

When Mom explained the plan to me, I told her I was really impressed that our medical insurance would cover all that. She laughed so hard she choked. Then she told me the insurance wouldn't pay for *any* of it: she'd taken out a loan against the house.

This was just another of many things I didn't understand, but it gave me more to worry about. How was Mom's new body going to take care of us if we lost the house? And why did Mom think that was so funny? Had she lost her mind?

Maybe, but I don't think I could blame *that* on Dr. Fisher. Mom's brain was the one part of her body on which he did not perform surgery.

Dr. Fisher worked on her for most of the summer, one procedure at a time. Mom thought it best to withhold the details from me and Moss, but we couldn't avoid all of it. There was no one else, so we had to take care of her. She was swathed in bandages, moaning for painkillers, and sucking fruit or vegetable smoothies through a straw—the only thing she could eat for days.

In the end, Dr. Fisher's work was finished, and we beheld his greatest creation.

Frankenmom.

Chapter Sixteen
Target Practice

THE HUMAN BEING INHABITING Mom's room bore a faint physical resemblance to our mother. If she had been one of America's ten-most-wanted, and had gone to Argentina for a makeover to elude the authorities—well, it was like that. You could barely recognize some of her former features. Maybe her earlobes, or her incisors. She was a spectacular butterfly emerging from a chrysalis—a transformed creature. Yet, if anything, the psychological changes were even more dramatic than the physical ones. We were soon to learn that this new person had little to remind us of the woman who had seen us through the early years of our life.

In the months she spent recuperating from her operations, Mom had consumed tabloids and women's magazines as greedily as her pain medications. It was like standing for hours in supermarket lines, leafing through the crap rack literature about which star is diddling which star, how to have better bowel movements, and above all, intimate male/female stuff which mothers should not worry about. I believe it was responsible for reprogramming her mind in hideous ways.

Moss's theory is that Mom was always like this and kept it under control while she was married to Dad. He figured that was why she was so unhappy in the marriage, because she was hiding her true nature. That's a much simpler explanation, but I can't bear to think he's right.

At first Moss and I were mercifully uninvolved in the mechanics of my mother's new social life. She seemed to be busy almost every night, attending lectures, art exhibitions, chamber of commerce mixers, and other singles' events. She scaled back her gym workouts to a maintenance level so she'd have energy for her fresh exploits. But there were plenty of shopping expeditions to acquire a new wardrobe suited to her pursuits.

She also took on a partner-in-crime. Betty Bridges was a perky blond who'd been playing the scene for years. Moss and I called her "Betty Boobs" in honor of the dramatic work she'd had done in that area. Betty's breasts defied gravity like twin Hindenburgs, mammoth entitties that ascended to wondrous heights.

When we first met Betty, Moss elbowed me and muttered in awe, "Unchain those beauties." I was even more mesmerized, a fact that seemed to please Betty. On the rare occasions she could wrest my attention from her spectacular jugs and force eye contact, she would give me a complicit smile.

Betty claimed to be a secretary, but I think she was really a spy of some sort. She had compiled dossiers on the many single men who made the rounds. Had she wanted to, she probably could have extorted a lot of hush money; though she panned most of the men as "tight as a nun's you-know-what," so maybe they wouldn't have paid up. Instead, she blackened their names for free.

Mom and Betty took me to an art museum reception where I witnessed the two of them in action. Their behavior made me very nervous, but they seemed oblivious to my discomfort.

As we entered the museum's courtyard, their faces bore identical synthetic smiles, as if they were both in on a joke that I hadn't heard. Their heads swiveled quickly from side to side, and Betty remarked, "This is what you call a target rich environment, Janice."

I noticed an inviting hors d'oeuvres table. "Maybe we should have something to eat before you shoot anyone down."

Betty seductively clasped my arm and burst into gales of absurd laughter, her eyes dancing suggestively, as her other hand coyly covered her mouth. "Oh, Moon, you are *so* witty!"

Mom gave her a look usually reserved for disobedient students. "Betty, that's my son!"

Betty came out of it quickly. "Sorry, just a reflex," she apologized. She and Mom enjoyed a genuine laugh over this.

I tried again. "Food?"

"I could eat a bite," Betty agreed, taking a step towards the appetizers. But Mom grabbed her by the arm.

"Now, Miss Scarlett, I ain't aimin' for you to eat like a field hand and gobble like a hog!" she exclaimed theatrically.

"Fiddle-dee-dee! Ashley told me he likes to see a girl with a healthy appetite!" said Betty, with a campy southern accent.

"What gentlemen *says* and what they *thinks* is two different things!"

More riotous laughter. I noticed uncomfortably that people were starting to stare at us. Of course, that was likely the goal of the exercise all along.

"It's *Gone with the Wind*, dear," Mom explained. Her attention was suddenly riveted on a man standing in line at the bar.

"Betty, on your six, line at the bar, black blazer."

Betty surreptitiously looked over her shoulder. "That's Armani," she said with respect.

"He's much too young," Mom disagreed. "And better looking."

"Not the man, the jacket. I don't know *him*. He's fresh meat."

"Watch me beam him in," Mom declared, then remembered me. "Uh, Betty, would you mind escorting my son to the canapés?"

I kept my eye on Mom as Betty led me away. Mom cocked her head and leveled a gaze of laser intensity on the man in line, about fifteen feet away. He was restlessly surveying the crowd in the same way that Mom and Betty were.

I saw him make eye contact with Mom and raise his eyebrows in surprise. Mom gestured that she'd like a drink. He nodded and mouthed the question, "White wine?" She nodded and rewarded him with a smile of seductive gratitude.

Betty took me by the hand and gently led me toward the museum's interior. Before she could clear the crime scene, I witnessed my mother burst into gales of laughter and take the Armani man's arm. "Oh, Michel, you are *so* witty!" she exclaimed breathlessly, eerily echoing Betty's words to me a few minutes earlier.

Chapter Seventeen
Tahiti or Bust

THIS MUSEUM EXPERIENCE made me wary of women's wiles. I examined Jasmine carefully for indications that her words of praise were as hollow as my mother's and Betty's, but her enthusiasm during our tutoring sessions seemed genuine. This was on my mind as I sought my mother's counsel one evening.

Between ourselves, Moss and I referred to my mother as, "The person formerly known as Mom." Her attention was not easy to come by these days. However, I had noticed that when she was putting on her war paint before her nightly raids she was at least a shadow of her old self. I liked to lie in the empty bathtub and talk to her while she went through the familiar routine of anointing herself. Only half-listening, she was capable of the occasional motherly utterance.

I often guided our sessions to the same topic: my future. Like a loose tooth, I couldn't leave it alone. "What do you think I should be?" I asked.

"I think you could be anything, dear," she replied automatically.

"*Anything* is almost as bad as *nothing*. It doesn't help me narrow it down."

"No, I suppose not," she murmured, applying rouge to her cheeks.

"What about a teacher?"

"Why would you ask me a thing like that?" she snapped, suddenly peeved.

"I didn't mean anything by it, Mom. A lot of people are teachers. *You're* one. Do you think I'd be good at it?"

Moss and I had agreed that it was best to conceal all traces of our life with Dad from our mother. Fortunately, as she became more involved in her own activities, she inquired much less into ours. So I didn't mention I'd had a little on-the-job training that might be motivating my curiosity.

"Well, of course you would," she mouthed, putting on scarlet lipstick. She smushed her lips together, then blotted on a tissue. "You'd be good at anything, dear."

Mom had evaded the question, but I wasn't giving up. There were other teachers in my life besides her.

The next day at recess I asked my math teacher, Mrs. Johnson, what she thought of the idea. She took a sip of hot coffee, winced, then carefully stated, "Moon Landing, were you to become a teacher it would be the greatest disappointment of my thirty-six years in the classroom."

I thought I'd ask one more person. My English teacher, Mr. Desrosiers, might be approachable. Kids made fun of him because his French accent was thick and his hair was thin. He grew it long and combed it forward à la Napoleon Bonaparte to camouflage a large bald spot. However, he'd recently complimented my pronunciation of his name, so I thought he might have a better reaction than Mrs. Johnson.

When I ran the idea past him, Mr. Desrosiers made one of those inscrutable French noises to express disapproval. Then he gave a Gallic shrug that indicated—well, it can indicate a lot of things. I had to wait to see what came next. A long sigh, more little noises, drumming fingers on the desk. Then raised eyebrows, pursed lips, several head shakes. Clearly out of sorts, he ran his hands through his hair, exposing a hairless patch vast enough to resemble a medieval monk's tonsure. This was unprecedented: Mr. Desrosiers *never* touched his hair in public. I was growing concerned.

Finally he looked at me. "Monsieur *la lune*…"

Uh, yes, that *is* French for "Moon." Jeez.

"I am thinking about…eh…what *I* wanted to do when I was your age. I did not want to become a teacher."

"What did you want?"

He sighed deeply. "I wanted to go to Tahiti and live as Gauguin." It sounded as if he were confessing something dark and shameful.

"Gauguin?"

"*Oui*." He gestured at some colorful posters on the wall. "These are his work, of course. I wished to be a painter."

"Did you do it?"

"*Non*. Tahiti is not the same. And I…I am not Gauguin. So I became a teacher."

This did not sound like a ringing endorsement of the profession. "But what about me? What do you think?"

"What do I think?" Mr. Desrosiers stroked his chin. "I think you will sit at my desk in front of the class. For one hour *you* will see what *I* see for five hours, one hundred eighty days a year, thirty, *Mon Dieu*, *forty* years of my life. Then perhaps you will know."

This sounded ominous, but there seemed no graceful way to decline the proposal since it *was* my free period. I took a seat at Mr. Desrosiers's desk, feeling like an idiot. I might as well be wearing a dunce cap, or a sign that said "Kiss Ass."

Mr. Desrosiers was one of those touchy-feely teachers who liked to shake hands with the students as they walked into class. I recoiled as he clasped the booger-crusted mitt of Sammy Jenkins, a notorious nose miner. I figured I'd better make a learning experience of this, as Mom always says, and began to take notes.

1. Have a monster bottle of alcohol goo on your desk and apply it as if your life depends upon it. It actually does!

Mr. Desrosiers missed no opportunity to wallow in his Frenchness, so he naturally greeted every student with a cheery "*Bonjour.*" I noticed that several of my fellow students had trouble with the pronunciation, responding with, "Boner to you, too, Mr. D," amid rampant snickers.

2. Avoid language that can be easily corrupted into comical obscenities.

For a minute I was so busy dodging spit wads that it was impossible to make more notes. Then Mr. Desrosiers called the class to order.

There was silence. It was not, however, expectant, respectful silence. Instead, an assault of the most massive, concentrated boredom confronted Mr. Desrosiers, and his protégé, *moi.*

With growing panic I regarded thirty of the most vapid, empty, unpromising, lifeless, and hopelessly unteachable faces to ever grace a classroom. Moments ago, some of these had belonged to individuals who were, if not friends of mine, as least fellow members of the human race. But before the lesson had even begun, they had transformed into zombies.

3. Brandish a cross and hope it does some good.

Mr. Desrosiers, however, was unfazed, and plowed ahead.

"Today we will work on our conjugations."

Massive moan.

"Oh, I know you love it, don't try to hide it."

More groans, but a few reluctant giggles.

"Is that a verb thing, Mr. D?"

"Yes, indeed. When you conjugate the verb it changes according to tense, person, number, and mood. For example, Monsieur White, the verb, 'to do.' We might say, 'You do your homework.'"

"We *might* say that, but it'd be a lie," answered Bill White, not the most diligent of students.

"Yes, it would," sighed Mr. Desrosiers, as the class guffawed. "Let's try another example. 'On Thursdays I do the laundry.'"

A voice rose from a student slouched in the back. "What do you use to get out the skid marks, Mr. D?"

Mass derision.

4. Avoid all speech. Mutes are well-suited to this profession.

Mr. Desrosiers crossed to his desk, giving me a slight, "I told you so" look, as he pulled a form from a large stack. He quickly filled it out. As the laughter died, he replied, "I find office referrals are very effective for that. *Au revoir*, Morning Wood."

As the student took the referral, he stopped in surprise, blurting out, "Did you just call me 'Morning Wood'?"

Again, general hilarity. Mr. Desrosiers rolled his eyes theatrically. "*Mais non*, your first name is 'Morgan.' Perhaps it is my accent. Now, goodbye."

5. Amuse yourself (if you can get away with it).

Morgan Wood exited and Mr. Desrosiers returned his attention to the class.

"And now, I think, some work from the textbook…"

More groans. "No, Mr. D, we'll be good."

"We'll be *better*, anyway."

"But not the *best*."

"Very nice," admitted Mr. Desrosiers. "Comparative and superlative forms of the adjective. Perhaps for next week. For today, page two-forty-three."

"Can we just do the even ones?" asked a girl with long blond hair who was sitting with a football player.

"No, the *odd* ones," suggested an emo girl with streaked hair and so many piercings I cringed to look at her. I don't get the pincushion thing.

"Better yet," chipped in the football player, "how about we just do every other question?"

6. Before considering a particular school, check into the presence of nearby toxic waste sites or other factors that could drastically lower IQ.

Perhaps because he was not a math teacher, Mr. Desrosiers took their redundant suggestions with aplomb.

"I cannot choose between three equally commendable proposals. Therefore, I must request you answer *all* the questions. *Merci.*"

"*Merci,*" the class parroted back sarcastically.

As the students made a great show of opening books, shuffling papers, finding pens, and pretending to get to work, Mr. Desrosiers turned to me.

"So, Monsieur *la lune...*" He saw my notes. "Observations? May I?"

He picked up the paper and began to read silently. Chuckles became snorts, turned to knee-slapping laughter. The class ceased its simulated effort and stopped to watch with amazement. After a minute Mr. Desrosiers pulled himself together.

"Ah, Monsieur *la lune*. I see that today I *have* been a teacher. Perhaps you will be going to Tahiti?"

"Yeah, maybe I might try that. If I can figure out what my Tahiti is."

"Well, I can assure you, it's not *this. A bientôt,*" said Mr. Desrosiers, shaking my hand as I fled to enjoy what was left of my free period.

"Hey, Mr. D, why does he get to go to Tahiti?" complained the blond.

"Yeah, is that French for the bathroom?" asked the football player. "I want a Tahiti pass, too. I gotta use it."

Chapter Eighteen
Seymour Smith

AFTER A FEW MONTHS of reconnoitering the social scene, Mom began to accept offers from gentlemen callers. It seems Moss and I were to play a role in this too. Mom sat us down for an indoctrination session before her first date. She was dressed in a slip and chugging a glass of white wine, which she was now consuming in such quantity that she was in no position to point an accusatory finger at my father.

"When Seymour arrives—" she started.

"*Seymour*?!" interrupted Moss. "You're going out with a guy named *Seymour*? What's his last name, *Butts*?"

"Moss—" she tried again.

"Will you Seymour of *him*? Will he Seymour of *you*?" He turned to me. "What do you think?"

"I don't want to know."

"When *Mr. Smith* arrives," Mom insisted, "the two of you will attend to him until I am ready."

"We will, will we?" challenged Moss.

"Why won't you be ready?" I asked.

"Yeah, why not shag ass now instead of jawing with us?" suggested Moss.

"I will *intentionally* not be ready," said Mom crisply. As Moss began to complain, she added harshly, "Don't interrupt again if you value any aspect of your life on Earth."

Moss rolled his eyes, but closed his mouth. Mom continued, "A lady is never 'quite' ready. A gentleman must wait momentarily as she applies the finishing touches to her toilette before the curtain goes up. Obviously, this heightens anticipation. It has the further benefit of providing an opportunity for my callers to make the acquaintance of my charming sons, who will play the role of most gracious hosts."

Moss and I looked at each other. Throughout our childhood, Mom had at times adopted stilted speech, especially when she was ODing on plays, museums, concerts, and other mind-altering drugs. But this was something else. She was channeling Scarlett O'Hara meets Martha Stewart laced with a dose of fascism.

Moss required clarification. "You mean you want us to sit around with this guy?"

"There's considerably more to it than that, dear," said Mom.

"Such as?"

Mom thought for a moment. "Moon, you be Mr. Smith. Exit and ring the bell. I will model the role I expect you and your brother to play."

"Why do I gotta be Seymour?" I asked rhetorically, walking out the door. I pivoted and rang the bell.

A moment later Mom opened the door, beaming at me with a robotic smile. "Hello!" she said. "You must be Mr. Smith! Please come in! May I take your coat?!"

"He's gonna run for his life," predicted Moss.

"Hardly. Mr. Smith is a man of culture and refinement and will be perfectly at ease."

I saw a car pull up at the curb. "Mr. Smith is a man who's gonna see you in your underwear if you don't get out of here," I said.

Mom pulled me inside and shut the door. "Well, the show must go on. The two of you will just have to improvise. Offer him something to drink and make polite small talk. Perhaps he'll ask you something about yourselves, though that would be dreadful. Well, it can't be helped."

The doorbell rang. Moss and I looked at each other.

"After you," said Moss.

"No, after you," I said.

"Oh, I couldn't."

"But you must!"

"You first, I insist!"

"I insisted before you!"

The bell rang again. We looked at each other and walked to the door together. Moss opened it.

"Good evening, gents," said Mr. Smith with a crisp English accent. He was a tall man dressed in a conservative suit and tie. More importantly, he was at least twenty years older than Mom, which had the effect of rendering both Moss and me temporarily speechless.

This fact was not lost on Mr. Smith. "I take it you've never seen an octogenarian before?" he commented wryly.

Moss recovered faster than I did. "We've never had any pets, so we usually just go to the doctor. But Mom's spent a lot of time with the plastic surgeon lately."

"A matter which requires a tad more discretion, I might advise," said Mr. Smith conspiratorially.

"You mean I ought to kind of shut up about that, huh?" said Moss.

Mr. Smith nodded meaningfully.

To my surprise, Mr. Smith was actually getting through to my brother. "Would you mind not saying anything about that?" asked Moss.

"Mum's the word," he said with a wink. He turned to me and stuck out his hand. "Seymour Smith."

I shook. "Moon Landing. And I don't think you're eighty years old."

"Well, I would have said '*sex*agenarian,' but I thought it best not to bring up that word on the first date."

"Dude, did you say *sex*?" asked Moss.

"See what I mean?"

"Moss, 'sexagenarian' means sixty years old."

"Dude, did you say *sixty*?" he retorted, no less shocked.

Mr. Smith cleared his throat. "Um…were you going to invite me in?"

Moss came to his senses. "Oh, yeah, man…there's like a whole line we gotta grind. Rewind."

He shut the door in Mr. Smith's face, then abruptly opened it. "Hello, Mr. Smith! How *are* you! *So* good to meet you! We've heard *so* much about you! *Please* come in! *May* I take your coat?!"

Mr. Smith entered with a smile of amusement. "No, you seem a little too eager to get at my jacket, young man. I think I'll keep it," he said.

"Can I get you a drink?" I asked.

"Good man, Moon! Have you any single malt scotch?"

"Uh…I'm more of an expert on root beer than on whiskey."

"Well, lead me to the liquor cabinet and let's have a look."

Mr. Smith found a bottle that pleased him. "Ice?" I offered.

"Thank you, no. Scotch this fine should be taken neat. Will you gents be joining me in a libation?"

"Don't mind if we do," said Moss. He pulled out a couple of sodas and handed me one.

Mr. Smith took his drink and sat at the kitchen table. Moss and I joined him. Mr. Smith looked around appreciatively.

"Charming home you have."

"Thank you," I said.

"Dad did a lot of work on it," added Moss.

"I can see that he did," said Mr. Smith. An awkward silence ensued.

"It's not like it's your fault, or anything," said Moss.

"That's very good of you, Moss, thank you," said Mr. Smith. Another awkward silence.

"So, uh…do you know Mom from the museum?" I asked.

"Well, yes…are the two of you art lovers as well?"

Moss snorted derisively. "Oh yeah. A thing of beauty is a joy forever, you know."

"Well, that is a rather fruity line, but artists themselves are not necessarily fruity fellows."

"What about Gauguin?" I asked.

"A case in point. He had a lifestyle most men would relish. Do you like his work?"

"I've only seen a couple pictures—"

"So you're saying artists are not just a buncha fags?" Moss pushed on.

"There are artists of all proclivities," said Mr. Smith. "However, you must've noticed that women are rather drawn to art, aren't they?"

"Yeah, and they pose naked, too," said Moss.

"So there you have it," concluded Mr. Smith, raising his glass in a toast. "To art!"

The next time Mr. Smith came to call he brought us three art books. For me, he selected a book of Gauguin's work. For Moss, he chose a book about taggers and graffiti creators—"street artists," they were called. Then there was a book with pictures from his own favorite artist, Caravaggio.

It was the Caravaggio book we wound up looking at the most. Maybe it was the paintings, with their dramatic contrasts between light and shadow, their rich colors, their sensual textures. Maybe it was the subject matter of the paintings; depictions of desire, revenge, and raw emotions. Or perhaps it was the story Mr. Smith told us of Caravaggio himself, a rebellious, dangerous brawler, who could wield a sword almost as deftly as a paintbrush. By the time Mom was ready, Mr. Smith had sold us on the Italian artist.

Reluctantly, both Moss and I admitted to Mom that Mr. Smith was all right. In fact, we even liked him. To our surprise, Mom dismissed him as a "friend," not a "beau." She continued to see him from time to time, along with Harry, Walt, Dick, Mort, Bernie, Franklin, Felix, Stan, and a few others I forget.

Trust me, Moss and I got very adept at playing our part, and we couldn't help feeling a sympathy and kinship for these guys. We were all men snared in my mother's web. Moss and I decided we'd better take something away from this experience, and vowed that *we'd* never wind up getting involved with anyone like our mother.

Chapter Nineteen
Cereal Killer

"WHY THE C, MR. D?"

My English teacher turned from the whiteboard, nearly underlining Lori O'Neill's indignant nose, which was thrust deep into his personal space. She angrily waved a sheet of paper at him.

"You gave me a C on my story. I want to know why."

Mr. Desrosiers glanced at the rest of his fourth period English class. We watched with interest, guessing there might be more entertainment value in a student-teacher confrontation than in identifying objects of prepositions.

"Mademoiselle O'Neill, this is not an appropriate time for this discussion…" he protested weakly.

"It's cool, Mr. D, let her have it," called out Felix Hernandez.

"I didn't spell a single word wrong," said Lori, as much to the class at large as to the teacher.

"Girl down with the spell check deserve an A plus," said Lamont Bridges.

"Extra credit."

"Advanced placement."

There were several chortles. Lori looked chagrined, but she wasn't ready to back down.

"I'm just saying that he hardly marked anything wrong. There are almost no mistakes."

"Just sayin', Mr. D."

There was a general chorus of "just sayin'," the most courteous challenge to a teacher's judgment. Mr. Desrosiers considered a moment, capped the marker, and took a perch on his stool. He waved for Lori to take her seat while he gathered his thoughts.

"This will be a rather lengthy explanation…" The class nodded its indulgence. Mr. Desrosiers continued. "My family moved to California when I was seventeen. After two years of high school, I went away to college."

"What'd you study?" I asked. Unlike most teachers, Mr. Desrosiers tolerated *our* digressions within *his* digressions.

"French and Spanish literature."

"Spanish? *¿Habla español?*" asked Felix.

"*Por lo menos, me defiendo,*" Mr. Desrosiers answered.

"Sound pretty good, homes," approved Felix.

Mr. Desrosiers nodded, acknowledging the compliment. "I spent my junior year studying in Madrid, which helped. When I came back, I worked that summer at Hughes Aircraft Company, where my father was an engineer. What I can tell you about my job is that the best part was going out to lunch."

"What's that say about your work ethic, Mr. D?"

"I'm French, I can work up an appetite." Mr. Desrosiers gave a Gallic shrug, and the class laughed. "Once a week we'd hit a little Mexican place in Westchester. My dining companions were two engineers, Pat and Mark. They were learning Spanish, and I was trying to practice mine."

"Nerds eating nachos," observed Felix.

"Well, yes," agreed Mr. Desrosiers. "After a few weeks my new friends invited me to Tijuana for the weekend." Mr. Desrosiers fell silent.

"Well didja go?"

"I declined."

"Coulda gotcher party on, bro."

"That is what they alluded to," Mr. Desrosiers nodded. "However, one of them did not make particularly good eye contact. When the trip was suggested, Pat regarded the enchilada on his plate with surprising interest."

"Probably wishin' he'd ordered tacos," said Lamont.

"It was a small thing. I thought nothing of it at the time."

"What does this have to do with my grade?" demanded Lori, who'd been growing increasingly impatient.

"Who gives an excrement?" snapped Warren Grossman. "This is way better than infinitives or whatever."

"Thank you for your support, Monsieur Grossman. Mademoiselle O'Neill, the connection—which I admit may be tenuous—will be made shortly. In any case, I did not go to Mexico with Pat and Mark. No big deal. I worked the rest of the summer, then I went back to college for my senior year. Having no hot job prospects when I graduated, I returned to Hughes Aircraft."

Mr. Desrosiers paused a moment, then continued, "Walking down the hall my first day on the job, I saw my friend Mark, who greeted me with a handshake. I asked how he'd been, and how Pat was. He dropped my hand like it was a poisonous snake and looked at me. 'You haven't heard?' 'Heard what?' I asked."

Mr. Desrosiers blinked and stammered, "'Man...Pat was arrested.'"

"I *knew* this was goin' there! He was like, a perv, right?" said Felix.

Mr. Desrosiers ignored the comment and continued, "'Arrested?

For what?' He just stared at me. 'Turns out, Pat is a stone killer, man. Been wasting people for years. Then he chopped 'em up and put the pieces in trash bags. Dumped 'em in the desert. The last guy was still in the bag when the cops found the body at Pat's apartment. Know where he got the bags?' 'From right here—Hughes Aircraft Company,' I guessed. He nodded. 'Yeah. You know how we do things. Mil spec. Ours are the best. Thick. Sturdy. They don't leak.'"

"Dude, you're making this up!" said Felix, grinning nervously. "It's too *Chainsaw Massacre!*"

Mr. Desrosiers shook his head. "Sometimes I think so, too. But it happened. Monsters exist. This one's name was Patrick Wayne Kearney. There's plenty on the Internet."

"Like…what?" asked Lori, suddenly interested.

"When they caught him, he'd been at it for over ten years. His targets were young men, mostly hitchhikers. Since Patrick was not physically imposing, he developed a particular method of killing his victims. Driving down the highway, he would steer the car with his left hand, and use his right hand to shoot the passenger through the head."

Mr. Desrosiers demonstrated, cocking fingers on his extended right hand. Several classmates took the opportunity to chip in sound effects, including Tom Richardson's spirited rendition of a machine gun.

Mr. Desrosiers shook his head. "A .22-caliber pistol is not an Uzi. It makes a discrete 'pop!' And it creates no exit wound."

"Yo, slugs check in but they don't check out," said Lamont.

"Exactly. Less evidence to clean up," said Mr. Desrosiers. He continued, "Patrick said in interviews that he'd known since he was eight years old that he would be a killer. And in fact he became the most prolific serial killer in California history. He eventually confessed to thirty-five murders."

"Like, you coulda been number thirty-six, know what I'm sayin'?" said Lamont.

"But you read him, man, you knew!" said Felix.

Mr. Desrosiers shook his head. "I noticed…something. A very small vibration, just enough to disturb me. But I didn't *know*. No one did. Everyone described him the same way. A nice, quiet man. Calm. Reasonable. Perhaps a little dull. A *typical* engineer. All true, as far as it went. But superficial. Patrick Kearney was most adept at concealing his raging core. Mark had actually given his apartment key to the greatest serial killer in California history. The man had had it for three years."

Mr. Desrosiers looked at us with a tired smile. "So, who will google Patrick Kearney tonight?"

For once, every hand in the class shot up enthusiastically.

"Then you would say that my story was effective? It held your attention? It made you want to know more?"

"It made me want to know if you're lying," said Warren.

Mr. Desrosiers shrugged. "This was nonfiction. To compete with reality, fiction writers must have inventive minds. That is what I expect of you. Mademoiselle O'Neill, to be judged of truly high quality, your work must be more than error-free. It must be compelling. Write about something worthy of our interest and tell the story with conviction."

Lori O'Neill nodded in agreement. "That's cool. I can write some sick shit, excuse my French. Maybe even murder."

There were general calls of approval from the other students.

"Just one thing I wanta know, Mr. D. Why do they call them 'cereal killers'? What does murdering people have to do with corn flakes?"

"Yeah, that's a good question, Mr. D," agreed Warren and several other students.

Mr. Desrosiers regarded us with some amusement. "Ahhh. That would bring us to a discussion of the deadly homophone—which, by the way, can easily evade the pursuit of the computer spell check."

Before Mr. Desrosiers could start his explanation, I raised my hand.

"Monsieur *la lune*..." he acknowledged.

"Uh...I understand you told us this story to inspire us to become better writers..."

"*Oui*..."

"...but don't you think there are other lessons we should take away from it?"

Mr. Desrosiers nodded thoughtfully. "Perhaps...such as...?"

Martha Beasley's hand shot up. "Trust your instincts. You did, and it kept you alive." Mr. Desrosiers nodded in acknowledgment.

"Don't hitchhike," said Truman Hoyle.

"Like anyone *does*," said Warren derisively.

"Yeah, but they used to," said Truman. "My dad did—and he's always telling me I shouldn't do it. I guess maybe he's right."

"When you get in a car with a stranger, you are at a big disadvantage," said Mr. Desrosiers quietly.

Felix held up his hand. Mr. Desrosiers regarded the student's mischievous grin warily. "Señor Hernandez."

"Always use the best trash bags."

The class moaned.

Lamont Bridges called out, "Spend college years on a jerk-off major, probably wind up with a crappy job that might kill you."

The class laughed and Mr. Desrosiers nodded and said with distaste, "You might even end up teaching middle school English."

The class erupted into a chorus of vomiting, gagging, and farting sounds. Mr. Desrosiers held his nose dramatically. As the noise subsided I raised my hand tentatively. Mr. Desrosiers nodded.

"You can never really know another person," I said.

Mr. Desrosiers regarded me seriously. "Perhaps not, if, like Patrick Kearney, the individual conceals his essence."

"Even if they don't," I persisted, "you still can't really know them."

Mr. Desrosiers nodded. "'Know *thyself*,' advised Socrates."

"'Lay *low*,' advised Snoop Dog," yelled Lamont.

"That, too," agreed Mr. Desrosiers. Several students launched into a rap, with others bleeping out the frequent obscenities, signaling the end of any serious philosophizing for the day. Mr. Desrosiers gave me an understanding smile and a French shrug, as the bell rang for lunch.

Chapter Twenty
Magic Hands

MOSS AND I WERE gradually accepting that our parents' marriage was ended. This bitter pill slid down more easily with each virgin strawberry margarita we hoisted at Fanatics. The waitresses, bartenders, kitchen staff, and customers had become our extended family—a reassuring network of adults who helped us feel part of something larger and more nurturing than our disintegrated family. In a way, these people also helped us know and understand our father, who was half of the puzzle. For even as Moss and I became reconciled to our parents' divorce, we struggled to understand what could have ever drawn the two of them together in the first place.

Most of Moss's energy went into rolling, so I handled the investigating. Hidden like a private eye behind the cover of my textbook in our restaurant booth, I would stakeout my father for hours, studying him as he moved through his domain with the assurance of a giant cat on the veldt.

Dad's eyes never stopped moving, alert to customers to be greeted and seated, who might crave another drink, who'd dropped a fork, who wanted a check, who were waiting for their change. He saw plates to be cleared, repairs to be made, a waitress to soothe, a bartender in the weeds. He worked the room with a fluid rhythm, maintaining stability and control. He seemed happy and at peace.

My father didn't usually tend bar any more. But one busy Saturday, we were inhabiting our usual booth when the manager, Molly, came to tell him that they had an emergency. One of the bartenders had scarfed a piece of steak off a customer's plate before it went to the dishwasher.

"Tony?" asked my dad.

"Uh-huh."

"Figures. What a pig. So what's the problem?"

"He didn't chew it good. It won't go down."

"Serves him right. You give him the Heimlich?" asked Dad.

"No dice."

"Is he blue?"

"No, he's getting air, but not too good. He's scared."

"Yeah," said Dad. "It could get worse. He's gotta go to the ER."

"You want me to take him?"

"No...have Miguel take him."

"Miguel?" asked Molly, surprised. "Who's gonna pour?"

"I'll pour."

"Solo? We're swamped."

"It'll be okay," said Dad, getting up to go to work.

A minute later the two bartenders went out the front door, Miguel helpfully whacking Tony on the back so hard he almost knocked the smaller man down. Dad ducked under the bar and took over. I watched curiously from my booth, never having seen this side of my father.

The orders were already stacked up. I could see Dad visibly relax, yet grow more alert as he flipped quickly through them. Then he began to move.

There was no wasted motion as he glided gracefully around the bar, his large hands quickly icing glasses and, without a glance, finding liquor bottles where he expected them. He poured a line of drinks, topped them with the soda gun, started two blenders, pivoted and hit the coolers for a round of beer bottles, opened them and slid them to the waitresses. The blended drinks finished, he poured them off, filling glasses to the rim without overpour, rinsed the blender cups and readied them for another round.

Jasmine had told me that my father was a "mechanic," a bartender known for his ability to work with exceptional speed, precision, and style. I witnessed a man at home and at ease, performing with calm under pressure, confident in his ability. He didn't rush, but he never stopped or hesitated; he seemed to always be doing several things at once.

He wasn't making the winning shot in the last second of the NBA finals, nor was he finding a cure for cancer. But he was doing the job he chose as well as anyone possibly could. He ran the bar with grace and skill and pride, and I was happy for him. And I was relieved.

Maybe I've always worried about my parents; but when they divorced, I became keenly aware of my concerns. Not so much about my mother. But I fretted about my father. Who would take care of him if my mother didn't? He ignored the interested looks he got from women in the restaurant; polite to them, yet distant, withdrawn. He appeared to have other things on his mind.

But now, as he took care of business, he seemed to have nothing on his mind. He simply flowed through the night, wiping sweat from his forehead, pulling occasionally on a beer, relaxing into his labor.

I watched, and realized my attention had gradually focused on my father's hands. Large, deft, expressive, they roamed the bar, cleaning ashtrays, dealing cocktail napkins, mopping the counter, washing glasses, making and garnishing drinks, always where they were needed, never lingering, never faltering.

I looked around the bar and restaurant, suddenly struck by something so obvious I couldn't imagine how I'd forgotten it. This business was, literally, the creation of my father. The counters, cabinets, tables, moldings, doors—they were all crafted by his hands. With tools still in our garage, shrouded and long disused, he had hewn the lumber, formed it, stained and oiled it, and rubbed it to a silken sheen that thousands of customers had burnished over the years.

I might have been only three years old then, but now the experience returned to me in a rush. My father would start early in the morning and toil late into the night, the garage alive with the roar of his saws, his lathe, his router—off-limits to a little boy, and even to Moss. We were allowed entrance only with our mother, who would serve Dad his meals and bring us to visit. Dad would pause a few minutes to eat at his workbench and we'd linger, savoring the pungent smells of walnut, mahogany, maple, and pecan, the three of us marveling at the product of my father's hands. When he was done eating, my mother would take his place, resting on a stool at the bench as my father hunched over her, massaging her knotted shoulders, arms, and fingers, my mother sighing with pleasure.

At home that week I scoured old photos to confirm what I thought I remembered. Wedding pictures, baby pictures—my parents at the beach, at picnics, around the Christmas tree. The evidence revealed a man and woman who, through the camera's lens, appeared happy together.

It wasn't their faces that I studied for confirmation, but my father's hands, which seemed always entwined with my mother's, or caressing her shoulder, her hair, her arms. I thought one piece of the puzzle might be falling into place. But I wanted another opinion.

The next afternoon I taught Jasmine how to solve quadratic equations by factoring. She was delighted that it was so much easier than she had expected.

"You know what Einstein said," I teased.

"Uh, no…"

I put on a campy German accent. "Quadratics are easy, it's women I can't figure out."

Jasmine laughed, and cocked her head. "You know what Marilyn Monroe said. 'Just ask me, Mr. Einstein.'"

"Okay…it's about my dad…"

"Um-hmmm…"

"Uh…why would women like him?" I asked, suddenly wishing I hadn't brought it up.

Jasmine tried to put me at ease. "Your father is a very attractive man."

"Why?"

"The way that he carries himself…with confidence. Why are you asking me this?"

"I'm trying to understand something," I said.

"About your mother and father," she said. I nodded.

"Einstein couldn't figure us out because we're all different," she continued. "So this is just what I think. It may have nothing to do with your mother."

"Okay. What do you think?"

Jasmine jotted something on my notebook. "Download this and listen to it."

When I got home I went online and found the song. It was by an old band I'd never heard of. I burned it to a CD, and that night I played it for my mother as she was getting ready to go out.

She looked at me in the mirror as she worked on her eyes. "Where did you get that song?" she asked.

"A friend gave it to me," I answered. "Do you know it?"

"No," she murmured. She hummed, picking up the tune. On the final chorus she joined in, singing:

Your magic hands that cast a spell
The palms I've kissed,
Whose touch I'll miss,
Those fingertips that knew me well.

"You don't know this song?" I asked again.

"Maybe I've heard it," she admitted. She dabbed an eye with a washcloth. "Damn mascara."

Chapter Twenty-One
Cougarlicious

THE AMISH PRACTICE a conservative form of Christianity that might be labeled fundamentalist. Though my mother is not drawn to strict forms of worship, I imagine that if there had been an Amish church in Los Angeles, she'd have dragged me there one of these Sundays. She would not have appreciated their taste in hairstyles and clothing. However, Amish mistrust of nearly all forms of technology is a belief my mother deeply shares.

I don't think Mom would have enjoyed the Dark Ages either per se, but she certainly prefers to live in a world that is not well-lit. Dad had installed dimmers on all the switches, which was a start. But Mom's new lifestyle required considerably more drama.

A few months after Mr. Smith's first visit to our house, he returned to find Moss and me absorbed in our new chore of lighting the dozens of candles which provided the flickering illumination to our castle. These were to be fired-up before any gentlemen callers arrived. Moss and I were running a little late.

Mr. Smith paused in the doorway, exclaiming, "Egad, gents, has there been a blackout?!"

"Nope," said Moss.

"Hmmm. Forget to pay the electric bill, perhaps? I had a wife who did that once."

"Don't think so," I said.

"Just…something she likes, eh?"

"Now you're catching on," said Moss.

"Well…Caravaggio would have approved, you know. Lighting like this is dramatic."

"Mom calls it 'forgiving,'" I said.

Mr. Smith snorted. "That, too. Though one might wonder what the point of plastic surgery is if you still need to be forgiven."

"*You* said it, not us," said Moss.

"I didn't hear *anybody* say it," I said.

"Me neither," agreed Mr. Smith. "Now, have you equipped a seeing eye dog with one of those charming kegs around its neck? Here boy!" he whistled. "No? Well, then I'll be forced to seek the scotch by Braille." He began to carefully make his way through the living room and head for the kitchen. "If I can just avoid setting myself on fire, I'm sure we'll have a nice evening."

Mom didn't like phones much, either. It seemed like the only people calling us on the landline were her union or her school district, both of whom got on her nerves. We kept thinking about having the phone disconnected and just going with our cells, but there was the house alarm, a piece of technology that made Mom feel a little safer.

What Mom loathed above all else was the computer. As a teacher she couldn't avoid it completely. She had to check her email every couple of days, do an occasional Google search for something the kids were studying, and upload her grades. But that was about it. Mom believed that these "modern conveniences" ended up dominating your life and consuming more hours than they ever saved you. So she habitually spent as little time on the computer as possible.

Until now. The Amish Momish started out by hogging my computer. When I kicked her off, she took up residence on Moss's laptop. He booted her and she bought a mongo desktop, with a humongous monitor and enough memory and CPU to run the Pentagon. She upgraded our Internet connection to something that loaded pages so fast you got whiplash.

Mom had become obsessed with computer dating.

There must be a million single people in the greater Los Angeles area, and they're all online. Mom figured she needed a first class set-up to weed through the prospects and find the keepers.

With so much firepower brought to bear on the situation, Mom's choice of princes was baffling. Moss and I opened the door to Mom's first computer date and our jaws dropped. If Mr. Smith had been surprisingly old, Lance was horrifyingly young. He appeared to be in his late twenties.

Oblivious, he greeted us with fist bumps. "Yo, the offspring. What it be?"

"Uh, come on in," I managed. "Can I get you something to drink?"

"Like milk?" suggested Moss.

"Har, good one," said Lance. "Brew me, bro."

"Please," said Moss.

"Yeah, like Emily Post said—please," laughed Lance, splaying himself on the couch.

I got Lance a beer and the three of us looked at each other awkwardly. "So, you cats gonna make yourself scarce, or what?" he asked.

"We live here," observed Moss.

"Cool," said Lance. "We'll go to my crib." He looked around at the candles doubtfully. "This all a little gothic for me, anyway. I like to be able to see what I'm eating." He snickered and checked his watch. "What's takin' the Moms?"

"Are you on a schedule?" I asked.

"You'd be surprised. If this doesn't pan out, I got options."

Moss and I looked at each other.

"Options?" asked Moss.

"Man, a *night* is a *night*, know what I mean?"

"You don't exactly seem like my mother's type, Lance," I said mildly.

"Well, I'm not stepdaddy material—but didn't seem like her top priority was replacing the old man…" He quickly changed the subject, but not for the better. "So…is Moms as hot as her picture?"

"We haven't seen it," I said. "Is it good?"

"Good? It's *smokin'*! I'm just hopin' it wasn't airbrushed! I mean, she *looks* cougarlicious indeed! Rawrrrr!!" Lance pawed the air and snarled menacingly.

Thankfully, Mom now made her entrance. Lance took one look and leaped off the couch. "Good God, there *is* truth in advertising!!" he bellowed, delighted.

The next day Mom asked us what we thought of Lance. Moss got very chill, but I rolled my eyes and asked if Lance had been in the army.

"The army?" Mom asked. "I don't think so. Why?"

"'Cause that guy was a *major* tool." Mom snorted, so I added, "Or perhaps a *general* jackass."

She burst into laughter, but protested, "He liked you two."

Moss still wasn't saying anything and the scowl on his face had become darker.

"Please," I said. "He liked *you.*"

"Yes," agreed Mom. "He *did* like me. That's a point in Lance's favor."

"Mom, that's sick," I moaned. "You gotta change the way you keep score."

"Don't worry," said Mom, suddenly tired of the discussion. She got up and headed for the computer. "I'm not *marrying* him." She had a thought and turned to face us.

"And by the way, it's not all *him.* My screen name *is* Cougarlicious."

Moss and I looked at each other as Mom walked away. Moss stuck his finger down his throat like he was gagging.

We weren't worried.

We were *disgusted.*

Chapter Twenty-Two
Flow to Pro

THOUGH MOSS STAYS in the moment, even he recognized that adulthood would bring new responsibilities along with the allure of freedom. He still had a couple years before he reached the peak of the K-through-12 cliff. Plenty of time to line up a jump and stick the landing. But he had to be starting to wonder what tricks he could pull off for the next stage of his life.

Perhaps that's how his posse finally persuaded him to enter the Gatorade Free Flow competition. They'd been trying for years, and Moss was a conspicuous absentee at the local event. Most of the skaters were not even in his league, but given his disdain for competition, he had no compulsion to outshine them onstage.

When Moss casually let me know he was thinking about this, I initiated my usual keyboard recon. Along with the possibility of snagging a few shekels, some skateboard swag, and courtship by a host of sponsors, the top three placers in the open division would be invited to the finals in San Francisco, where the winner would receive invitations to compete professionally. Hence the competition's slogan: *From Flow to Pro.*

The local Free Flow qualifier was held at a place called "Woodward West" out in the Sierra foothills; not exactly bike riding distance, but it wouldn't take any travel money to get there, either. With just fifteen bucks and a board, a skater got to show his stuff, cop a prize bag, and guzzle as much Gatorade as his gut would hold. Or *her* gut, since there'd be some girl skaters, too.

That's how Moss sold it to Dad, who agreed to haul us out to Tehachapi, along with a couple of Moss's posse.

When we got there, Dad had no problem with the meager entrance fee, but the legal waivers gave him pause. No one wanted to get sued, so they ran skaters and their parents through a release that featured worst-case scenarios laid out in attention-grabbing capital letters that made it seem as if the lawyers were screaming at the top of their lungs.

I thought I saw the color drain from Dad's face as he skimmed the document. I looked over his shoulder and read, "THE ACTIVITIES OF THE EVENT(S) ARE VERY DANGEROUS...INJURIES RECEIVED MAY BE COMPOUNDED OR INCREASED BY NEGLIGENT RESCUE OPERATIONS." There was a lot more in the same vein.

Dad turned to us with a look of concern. "You boys sure this is safe?"

"Oh, absolutely," said Boosh, a near-sighted beanpole of a kid, named for his enormous curly Jewfro. "This is all legal beaglese. You know how they are."

Dad looked at another of Moss's friends, "Wee Wee," an homage to Wee-Man Jason Acuna, a four-foot-tall skateboarder of *Jackass* fame. Though Wee Wee was not nearly that short, he did look stumpy next to Boosh—and he certainly shared his namesake's go-for-broke approach to skating. "Did your parents sign this?"

"Yup. Since they couldn't be here, we had to get it notarized," he said. He waved his completed forms, and I saw Dad's eyes flick to the large black band-aid on Wee's elbow. It was completely covered with the message "FUCK! FUCK! FUCK!" in bold white text.

"Did they *look* at it?" asked Dad, still not convinced. "I mean, did they actually *read* it?"

"Well, I presume so," said Wee Wee, adopting his most formal persona. "It *is* a legal document and my parents take those most seriously."

Dad fretted over the release another moment. Boosh jumped in helpfully. "My dad said none of this really matters, anyway."

Dad gave him a look of mingled incomprehension and consternation. "Doesn't *matter*? What in the world did he mean by that?"

Boosh, who has a great deal more hair than common sense, ignored Moss's efforts to wave him off, and forged ahead. "He said it's not binding. If I break my neck, he's still gonna take 'em to court."

"Well that really puts my mind to rest, Boosh," said Dad, who couldn't help smiling.

"Yeah, he felt better, too," said Boosh. "Dad says it's un-American to give up your right to sue."

Dad snorted. Shaking his head, he muttered under his breath, "You've got good medical through your mother, I guess," and signed the documents.

Arriving well before the start of competition, we could have staked out good spots for spectating and defended them for the next few hours, as some were already doing. Instead we just wandered, taking in the scene. Moss and company slipped away before we'd even noticed, so Dad and I were left to enjoy the sights on our own.

Several padded-up riders stood ready on the halfpipe decks. One at a time, they'd take turns dropping in and flying through the air.

The skaters flipped and spun, accelerating throughout their runs to attain ever-greater speeds and loftier heights. It seemed they defied the laws of thermodynamics, like mechanical toys that wound *up* when they were activated, instead of winding down.

A shirtless skater showing several inches of boxers fluffed above the waist of his baggy pants rolled from the trough up to the top of the ramp. His front wheels cleared the coping and he quickly pivoted 180 degrees, then balanced for a moment, the midpoint of the deck resting on the edge, before he plunged back into the bowl.

"That's a disaster," I said.

Dad shrugged. "If you say so. It looked okay to me."

"No, I mean, that's a trick they call a *'disaster,'*" I said. "I don't really know why."

"Ah. So, do you speak 'skate,' Moon?" Dad asked.

"I'm moderately fluent."

A short skater in green shorts and an orange shirt was clearly superior to the others, catching big air at the end of his runs.

"Watch that guy," I suggested, pointing. The rider plunged down the half pipe and blasted up the opposite wall. He cleared the lip of the pipe and hung in the air, his board spinning cleanly off his feet, only to be caught by his trailing hand and thrown under the rider as he dropped sharply back down the steep face.

The crowd hooted in appreciation and Dad whistled.

"That's what they call 'diamondz,'" I said, imitating the vaguely disassociated tone of a skater. "Flawless."

Dad nodded. "So is hitting a golf ball 250 yards down the middle of the fairway—and a lot less dangerous."

As if on cue, the shirtless rider attempted a flip and went crashing to the bottom of the bowl. The crowd "oooed," but he popped up quickly.

"No harm!" he proclaimed, earning applause, then comically

crumpled to the ground, eliciting laughter. He got up, grinning, and exited the scene. Dad and I watched as several girls converged to make a fuss over him.

"See that?" said Dad. "Why do they go for the guy who crash-and-burned?"

"I think women appreciate a high tolerance for pain in a man. They know it will eventually come in handy."

Dad grinned and gave me his full attention. "So cynical so young?"

"I just call 'em the way I see 'em."

Dad put his arm around my shoulders. "You gotta keep the faith, man. They come to their senses when they get older," he said.

"Uh...like Mom?" I knew I shouldn't have said it, but it was too good a set-up.

Dad winced. "Well, let's not go there," he said. "Any place around here to get something to eat?"

"I think I saw a truck out front."

We ambled back to the parking lot, passing a proud mom cheering on a tiny boy with a huge mane of hair, who pushed off on a long, wide skateboard.

"How old is he?" asked Dad as we passed.

"Just turned *three*," the mother said. "He could ride before he could walk."

"Maybe the next Tom Schaar," I said, referring to the twelve-year-old prodigy who had just landed the first four-digit skateboard trick—the 1080, three complete revolutions in the air.

"That's what we hope," she said, then to her little boy, "If you get rich, will you buy Mommy a house?"

"*No*," he said curtly, skating away.

His mom rolled her eyes at us. "Yes, he *will*."

There was a short line at the truck, skaters whose diet was pretty much limited to chips, Skittles, Monsters, and Red Bulls. As if by magic, Moss, Boosh, and Wee Wee materialized next to us.

Dad noted their presence good-naturedly. "Get what you want, boys, I got it."

"Thanks, Mr. Landing," said Wee Wee, grabbing an energy drink.

"But not *that*," said Dad.

"Uh…I believe it contains the four food groups," said Wee Wee mildly. He idly picked at a band-aid on his other elbow that looked like a strip of bacon.

"You oughta eat some of that instead of wearing it on your arm. Have a breakfast burrito," said Dad, getting a bit irritated.

"Burritos bloat me, sir," said Wee Wee. The other skaters nearby hooted, and one farted loudly.

"Wee Wee," said Dad, trying to be reasonable. "Don't you have another name?"

"Well, yes, I do—but it's embarrassing," said Wee Wee.

"This is like *Alice in Wonderland*," murmured Dad. "I give up."

"Perhaps I'll try a Danish and some coffee," said Wee Wee.

"That's how mature people get their sugar and caffeine," said Boosh supportively.

Dad, Moss, and I got burritos, while Boosh and Wee Wee ordered their usual fare. We found a shady place and sat down, consuming our food in silence. Next to us, a group of skaters were chatting about their injuries with skaterish animation.

A guy with a DC hat worn backwards was on his feet, demonstrating a trick-gone-bad. "Yo, I tried to 360 flip off a funbox. Thought I had it, but in midair I lost it and the board went vertical—"

"Ouch!" said another guy.

"—I landed crotch first on the nose."

"We've all nutted, man," said a third guy with Nike Swoosh kicks, unimpressed.

"Not like this," said DC. "I put, like, a half-hitch in my left nut. The surgeon who got it untangled said it was a good thing he was an eagle scout since he knew how to handle knots and such."

"Save you the cost of a vasectomy later," said Nike dismissively.

"So you've bled, huh, dude?" DC challenged.

"Bro, I set off metal detectors at the airport. They think I'm a terrorist. I was bombing a sixty degree hill, hit about ten mph—"

"Got the speed wobbles and bailed," interrupted Boosh.

"I *didn't* bail, I got 'em under control, but while I *was*, a car backed out of a driveway."

"Oooooh," moaned Wee Wee.

"I hit it on the driver's side. It was this little old lady. She was staring at me with a look of horror that was actually hilarious. Fortunately, I missed her. I was, like, all Wile E. Coyote." He held his arms and legs out spread-eagled, putting on the pained expression of the Roadrunner's nemesis. "Concussed my ass and broke my clavicle. Also dented the shit out of the car and smashed its window."

"She have insurance?" asked Boosh.

"Fuck, yeah," said Nike. "It's the *law*." He looked over at us with more interest. "You guys got anything to offer?"

"Well, there was this time I was cavemanning out of a tree," said Wee Wee thoughtfully.

"Ha," said Boosh. "I skated off the *roof*." Nike shrugged dismissively. "It's a *two-story house*," Boosh added, upping the ante.

"Yeah?" said DC with interest. "How'd that go for you?"

"Very well, while I was in the air. After my head high-fived the driveway I needed eighty stitches," said Boosh.

"*Eighty stitches?*" said Dad, horrified.

"You can't even count that high," scoffed Moss.

"No, but the doctor could," said Boosh, pulling back his hair to reveal a scar. "He said seventy-nine wasn't enough."

"It doesn't look that long," said Nike, unconvinced. He pulled up his shirt, revealing a long, puffy scar. "Stab wound defending the turf. This bad boy only took about twenty, and it's longer than yours."

"Yeah, but look at the keloid," said Boosh. "Plastic surgeon did mine. They sew your shit up like Betsy fucking Ross."

"Fine work," observed DC.

"Plastic," said Wee Wee. "It's better than cash."

This lighthearted game of you-show-me-yours-I'll-show-you-mine wasn't exactly reassuring Dad about the safety record of skating. He ate the rest of his burrito, but that didn't prove anything, since Dad never loses his appetite no matter what happens. He gazed into the distance, chewing thoughtfully. I caught Moss's eye, and hitched my head in Dad's direction. Moss gave me a slight nod and a wink.

"You know, *I've* never gotten hurt," he said softly to Dad.

"You guys make Evel Knievel look like a pussy," said Dad.

"Thank you," said Wee Wee, pleased.

"I didn't mean it as a compliment."

"Nevertheless."

DC said, "Statistically you're more likely to be injured driving to the grocery store than skateboarding."

"That's ridiculous," said Dad. "Moon?"

"Uh...there probably *are* more auto injuries than skateboard injuries, since there are a lot more drivers than skateboarders."

"But that doesn't make it more dangerous," said Dad.

Wee Wee tried another tack. "Surely you must have engaged in risky behavior when you were young, sir."

"Not that I'd tell *you* about," said Dad. But a slow smile spread over his face.

"Oh, c'mon, Dad," said Moss.

"When I grew up, we didn't have *Jackass*, but we did have horses," said Dad. "And it was pretty easy to be a jackass on a horse. My personal specialty was the Cossack death drag. It was a trick-riding stunt where you'd keep one foot in the stirrup and hang head-down off the other side of the horse, dragging your hand in the dirt, like you'd been shot."

"And the horse was moving?" said DC.

"Duh," said Nike. "Like in the movies, when the Indians pretend the cowboys got 'em, and they hang off their ponies. Then they whip up in the saddle and shoot the fuck outta the cowboys."

"For reals?" said Moss. "You never told us this."

"Topic never came up," said Dad.

"How'd your horse like it?" I asked.

"Never complained to me," said Dad. "Until one day he got spooked and started bucking. It damn near *did* put the death in my drag. I was lucky to get outta that one with a broken ankle. Pretty much ended my trick-riding career."

There was a moment of silent appreciation for the story. Then Boosh commented, "I wonder if you could skate off a horse?"

"A *running* horse," added Wee Wee. "That'd be all *Cirque de Soleil.*"

Dad shook his head and focused on his breathing.

After eating, the skaters disappeared again, which was kind of a relief. Dad and I milled around, talking about this-and-that. We took in the vertical competition on the half pipe, which fortunately involved no casualties. The primo rider in the orange and green we'd noticed warming up won the whole thing, and I congratulated myself on my ability to recognize talent. Then it was time to go indoors for Moss's event, the Skateboard Park.

The competition featured a "jam" format, in which several skateboarders jointly skated the course for about five minutes, doing everything they could to impress the judges. Then the best rider from each of the eight jams would compete in a final jam, from which the top three finishers would be selected. All three would qualify for the finals in San Francisco.

Moss would skate in the fifth group. Dad and I watched impatiently as the other groups weaved through the course, an arrangement of ledges, pyramids, rails, and stairs which didn't present the degree of difficulty that Moss appreciated in natural landscapes. The stairs and rail were just an 8-sct, from which it was impossible to execute the most impressive tricks. But it was also a lot less dangerous, a fact not lost on Dad.

I thought the judges, professional skaters themselves, had a tough job. Though some competitors stood out as inferior, many of them seemed to be of similar skill level, and they mostly executed the same tricks. Without slow-mo, freeze-frame, and instant replay, it was hard for me to judge the relative quality between them. However, I found that keeping an eye on the videographers cued me to which skaters were the favorites. After a minute or so of action, the cameramen—who could discern subtleties that were lost on me—would jockey for coverage of the top one or two performers in each group, ignoring the others. They picked the winner every time.

Wee Wee skated in the third group. He did not embarrass himself, but his heat was won by an outstanding thirteen-year-old, who passed on the Junior Jam and was trying his luck in the main draw, which had the potential to get him to San Francisco.

Boosh was in the fourth jam. Coming off a jump on the 8-set, he missed his landing, snapped the tail off his deck and fell hard. The crowd applauded as he picked up the pieces and trudged off the track. Then it was time for the fifth heat.

Moss had been pretty quiet all day, and as he pushed out onto the course, I wondered if he was feeling any butterflies. If so, you couldn't tell it by looking at him. Whereas the other competitors seemed to be in a frenzy to do as many tricks as possible, Moss appeared calm, bordering on disinterested.

But his nonchalance suddenly transformed into action as Moss accelerated to the top of the 8-set and launched into a simple, unadorned jump. Lacking embellishment, he nevertheless got far more air than any other rider we'd seen, clearing the rail by several feet and landing the jump flawlessly. The videographers scurried to reposition, and I tapped my dad to look at the judges, who were actually sitting up and looking at each other. I saw one of them mouth a name.

"Landing," said Dad, reading their lips.

I watched the rest of the run in a daze. It was like spectating at the Olympics, where most of the athletes were amazing, but very evenly matched—and then someone put on a performance that was astoundingly superior to the others. And it seemed the judges might agree, since Moss predictably won his heat.

Dad and I watched the last two heats impatiently, nervously awaiting the finals jam. My throat was dry, and I wiped my clammy hands on my shorts. I could never be a professional athlete—I'd choke under pressure. Dad looked pretty cool, so that at least made one of us.

Boosh and Wee Wee joined us at the rail.

"The bro got the Flow," said Wee Wee.

"I hope so," I murmured.

"Oh, I *know*," said Boosh.

"Enough nursery rhymes," said Dad irritably. Maybe he *was* a little nervous. He looked at me. "Are there any 'Moss rules' to skating?"

"Not that I know of," I said. "But he's never actually been in a competition before."

Dad blew out a breath. Boosh and Wee Wee looked at each other quizzically.

"*Moss* rules?" asked Wee Wee.

"Moss *rules*," Boosh answered with an affirmative nod.

When the final jam started, the higher quality of the riders was obvious. There were fewer falls and less sketchiness in the tricks and landings. Still, within a few runs I thought I saw the main competition for Moss, a lanky skater in a black T-shirt. He looked a little older than Moss and wore a black helmet with a skull-and-crossbones drawn in white.

"Who's the guy with the Jolly Roger on his head?" I asked Boosh.

"Ron Nash," he said. "Won this thing last year but didn't do so good in the finals. He's got the full tricktionary."

"I can see that," I murmured. So could the videographers. By now they had focused on two riders, Moss and Ron Nash.

Moss just ran through his repertoire, mostly working the 8-rail, doing hardflips, kickflips, and tre flips. Ron Nash was doing very similar tricks, and it was honestly hard for me to tell the difference between the two skaters. I thought Moss had an edge, but knew I was far from an impartial judge.

"What do you think?" I asked Boosh quietly.

"Hard for Moss to get off-the-hook on the bunny slope," he said.

"There's a slight difference in difficulty, though," said Wee Wee softly. "Moss's combinations are technically harder."

"You think the judges will notice?" I asked.

"If *I* notice, they'll notice," said Wee Wee. "Could be some political shit, though."

Five minutes can take a long time if you're holding your breath. The heat ended and the judges conferred for a few minutes, with contestants and spectators milling around. The skaters pretended to be unconcerned, but they had to be nervous, too.

Then they announced the winners. Third place—Waylon Jacks from Ontario, California. Second place—Ron Nash, from Santa Monica, California. First place—*yeah*! Boosh and Wee Wee let out loud hoots at the announcement, and Dad clapped me on the back, grinning broadly. Moss made his way to the front with an "aw shucks" attitude. We watched as they bestowed more plunder than he could hold, then the three placers took positions on the podium for pictures, brandishing NK skateboards, backpacks, shirts, and hats.

But the day was far from over. There was still a video interview to shoot for the YouTube footage that would be posted of the event. While Moss waited to film his clip, we watched in fascination as he was besieged by a throng of little kids, cute girls, and representatives for board, shoe, shirt, hat, and helmet manufacturers.

And why not? SoCal was the hotbed of skating, and a lot of the guys who had won the Free Flow tour had gone on to pretty amazing careers. Like Timmy Knuth. Chaz Ortiz. The new guy, Brendan Villanueva. And—Moss Landing?

Moss flashed us a grin, fanning the phone numbers and reps' business cards out like a full hand in Vegas.

The lady we'd met earlier with the three-year-old skateboarder walked over dragging her kid. She reached out to shake Dad's hand. "Congratulations," she said. "He's gonna buy *you* a house." Dad laughed, and she flashed him a flirtatious smile. "Married?"

"Uh...no," said Dad, laughing.

"Me neither," she said, slipping him her number.

Chapter Twenty-Three
Cubs

I'M NOT ONE of those people who believes divorce has to be awful. Sure, a nuclear family with a mom and dad who still at least vaguely like, if not *love* each other—and put their kids' well-being before their own pursuit of whatever—sounds pretty good. I'd order it. *Give me Happy Family Special, please.* Also wonton soup, fried rice, and extra fortune cookies.

But back in kinder I learned that most of the time *you* don't get to order, it's done for you. "You get what you get, and you don't get upset," Mrs. McConnell would say. We'd snidely parrot it to Kimberly when she'd throw a fit about what color crayon she got, or to Franklin, when he'd fall apart because he wasn't chosen as office monitor.

Maybe it helps that divorce is so common. It's not like everyone you know won the happy family lottery but you. At least half the kids I know had divorced parents. The other half wished their parents would *get* divorced. I think it helped that our parents were so obviously miserable together, especially my mother. My dad probably could have hung in there, though it wouldn't have been satisfying for him.

Well…point is, you won't find me on some shrink's couch twenty years from now claiming their divorce ruined my life. I know that it's fashionable to scapegoat your parents, but if I'm a thirtysomething loser, it's gonna be on me, not on my folks. Turn the poison into medicine, right?

But if the shrink leads with the old cliché, "Tell me about your mother," well, I won't know where to start. *Which one?!*

Lance was but the first of Mom's boy toys, who, we were to learn, are referred to in singles' jargon as the cougar's "cubs." Ouch! Do *they* know that?

Playing our usual role as hosts for gentlemen like Seymour Smith was one thing. But accommodating Mom's new suitors was another matter entirely. One night I was doing homework in the living room when I thought I heard a faint knock on the door. I looked up at Moss.

"You hear that?" I asked.

He shrugged, shook his head.

I went to the door and opened it to find a tall young man with his hand poised to knock again.

"Bell works, dude," said Moss, joining me at the door.

"Oh, yeah, well sometimes it doesn't. Then I just stand there waiting…waiting…waiting…y'know. Uh…is Janice here?"

A sick feeling flooded my senses. "Are you…Greg?"

Greg nodded weakly. "I know this is a little awkward."

"Ya think?" said Moss, who was finally putting this all together. "The momster's dating a kid with peach fuzz and you think that's *awkward?!*"

"It's more of a five o'clock shadow," protested Greg.

"Get real! Italian women got more stubble than you do!" Moss was getting worked up. "And it's not 'Janice.' It's 'Mrs. Landing' to you, sonny boy."

"Mom!" I yelled, hoping my voice would carry upstairs. "Greg is here!"

"Invite him in and offer him a drink, of course." The note of annoyance in Mom's reply was loud and clear. It was the tone reserved for dealing with feeble-minded servants and sons.

"It's so hard to get good help these days," I mumbled, pulling the door all the way open. Greg gave me an apologetic look.

"Sorry about that, man," he said.

"Moms," said Moss. "You can't live with 'em, but you can fuck 'em."

"Get you a drink?" I offered.

"Beer, if you've got it," he said.

"Let's see some ID," Moss demanded, sticking out his hand. Greg rolled his eyes and grinned.

"C'mon, we're all adults here…"

"Or *not*," said Moss. He didn't withdraw his hand.

Greg considered a moment, then pulled out his wallet. He flipped it open to flash his license at Moss.

"Take it out," Moss demanded.

"What are you, the highway patrol?"

"Moon and I cannot be accused of accepting bribes. Please remove your license from your wallet, sir," said Moss. I snickered.

Greg snorted and took the license out. He handed it to Moss, who peered at it for a moment. His eyes tilted to the sky and his lips moved silently. Greg and I waited for the verdict.

"Fuck! I can't even fuckin' *subtract*! Here, you do it," said Moss, sticking the license out to me.

I glanced at it and broke into a grin. I looked at Greg who was smiling, too. "Made it by a week. Congratulations."

"Thanks," he said, replacing the license in his wallet. "I gotta update my profile. This puts me in a better demographic. Cougars actually prefer their cubs a little older…"

"Well, you've got that to look forward to," I said.

"Lower auto insurance rates, too," Greg added.

Moss led the way to the kitchen. He pulled a beer out of the fridge and offered it. "Bud okay?"

"Sure," said Greg, taking the bottle, "unless you've got something imported…"

"Think we have some Newcastle," I offered.

"That'd be great," said Greg, holding the Bud out for exchange.

Moss wagged a disapproving finger at him. "I'm afraid those beverages are reserved for the twenty-five-year-olds."

Greg laughed. His willingness to avoid confrontation was slowly defusing the situation. Moss took the beer, replaced it in the fridge, and pulled out a Newcastle. He popped the top and handed it to Greg.

"I ask you something?" said Moss.

"I guess."

"How do you feel about being called a 'cub'? Don't you find it—what's the word, Moon?"

"Demeaning?"

"Yeah," said Moss with satisfaction. "*Demeaning.*"

"It's not my favorite," Greg admitted. "But it's better than 'cougar bait.'"

"Or 'douchebag,'" said Moss.

"It's just a cute term cooked up on a website," said Greg, ignoring the insult.

"*Cute?*"

"Cute to mature women," Greg clarified. "They're a huge market. The online services cater to them."

"I'm not sure I'd call our mother mature," I said.

"It's kind of a euphemism."

"That's not what I mean," I said. "You'll see, she looks good. But going out with guys half her age is hardly mature."

Moss hurried to pile on. "So you like the old ladies, huh, Greg?"

Greg nodded. "If I'm bad, they spank me." Moss and I looked at him, aghast. "Just kidding. Relax."

"I'd relax if I was doin' *your* mom," said Moss.

Again, Greg ignored the challenge. "You know, younger women totally bust my chops. 'What do you do? Where are you taking me? Do you want to get married? Do you want to have a baby? Are my tits big enough? Is my butt little enough? Are you a bad boy? Are you a good boy?' You can't believe it."

Moss was unimpressed. "Mom'll say, 'Have you finished your homework?'"

"She's a teacher," I explained.

"*Really?*" said Greg with evident interest. Moss and I looked at each other. Greg threw up his hands in surrender. "Tell me you never fantasized about any of your teachers," he protested. "Or your friends' moms. Or your mom's *friends*."

"Betty," said Moss, conceding the point.

"She kind of hit on me," I offered. "Accidentally, I think."

"Well, now we have to wonder, Moon," said Moss, adopting an academic tone. "*Was* it an accident? Or are you in Betty's target demographic? Hmm? Wonder how Mom'd feel about you boinking Betty Boobs? Seems like, what do they call that?"

"Poetic justice?" I suggested.

"Yeah," said Moss. "*Poetic justice*. What do you think, Greg?"

"Go for it," he advised. "The thing about these, uh, cougars is, if they'll go out with you, well, it's, uh, pretty much a…" he trailed off.

"…*sure thing*," Moss finished with distaste.

But in this case, it *wasn't*. When Mom finally descended to meet her waiting suitor, she looked him up and down with a surprise that contrasted to his own appreciative reaction to 'Cougarlicious' in the flesh. Mom actually narrowed her eyes, squinting at him a little.

"Your profile said you were twenty-six," she accused.

"*Twenty*," he corrected.

"When zeroes start looking like sixes, it might be time for reading specs," suggested Moss innocently.

Mom scowled. "In your picture you look…older."

Greg shrugged. "The camera adds years."

"The difference in ages *is* the point, isn't it?" said Moss, increasing his smarminess.

"But *this* is…extreme," said Mom. "You're *twenty*."

"He just turned twenty-one," I said.

Greg took up the sales pitch. "It's not that bad," he said. "I've been out with older women. And you're no grougar."

"*Grougar?*" I asked.

"Uh…that's a grandma cougar," said Greg, wincing.

Moss and I were stunned. To our relief, Mom actually covered her face and doubled-up in shame. But when her hands came down, we saw she was actually convulsed with laughter, not humiliation.

"Greg," she choked out, "have you ever heard of 'Oedipus'?"

"You're asking *him*?" I burst out. "What about *you*?!"

"Not really," he said. "I pretty much stick to *Cougar Life*, but I'm open to new sites. How do you spell it?"

Mom burst into laughter again. "How do you spell it?!"

Greg looked at me uncertainly. Mom was laughing so hard she couldn't talk. "Did she say 'Oedipus' or 'Oedi*pussy*'?"

"She'll flip you the link," I advised.

Chapter Twenty-Four
Cougar Scat

THE EXPERIENCE WITH GREG served as a real world lesson on big cat dating mechanics: whenever possible, prospective cubs were to be isolated from a cougar's "litter," the offspring who might take offense at the particulars of their mother's mating ritual. For this reason, most rendezvous were scheduled in neutral territory such as bars, coffee shops, and gyms (if a cougar had assets she could truly flaunt). For cougars with kids, a premium was placed on cubs who had their own lairs, which were naturally modest in comparison to a cougar's cushy cave. However, assembling IKEA furniture, copulating on musty futons, and eating cheap takeout from the carton helped aging mama cats recapture their golden youth, an essential aspect of the relationship dynamic.

Thank you, Dr. Moon. In any case, though Mom was far from renouncing her perverse new lifestyle, for the most part Moss and I didn't have to have our noses rubbed in her cougar scat—with one notable exception…

It was Jasmine's night off, and she and I were at her place for an extended tutorial on algebraic word problems involving distance, speed, and time. These problems are notorious for trying the patience of even the most adept and persistent students, and Jasmine's emotional reserves were wearing thin.

"A passenger train leaves the depot an hour after a freight train left the same depot. The freight train is traveling ten miles slower than the passenger train. Find the rate of each train, if the passenger train catches the freight train in five hours," she read from her textbook, her tone growing more incredulous with each word. She threw down her pencil in frustration.

"Good first move."

Jasmine looked at me and raised her eyebrows. "No need to be sarcastic."

"I'm *not* being sarcastic. Are you familiar with the saying, 'First do no harm'?"

"Isn't that the motto of…plumbers?"

I couldn't help smiling. "Doctors, actually."

Jasmine laughed at herself, a good sign. "Blue collar girl. I knew I'd heard it somewhere."

"Good idea for plumbers, too. And mathematicians. Until you put pencil to paper, you haven't done any harm. Read it again," I said. "Slower, and read it silently. Focus on seeing the movie in your mind."

I waited a few moments while she followed my directions. Her breathing calmed and she looked at me.

"Tell me, in one word, what the story is about," I said.

"Trains."

"How many trains are there?"

"Two."

"What are they doing?"

"Moving."

"Are they traveling in the same direction, or in opposite directions?"

"The same direction, I guess. The second train leaves an hour after the first, but it catches up in five hours."

"Do they run into each other?"

"No, that's a different movie," she laughed.

"So, which train is going faster, the first train or the second train?"

"The second train," she said. "It leaves later and catches up."

"What do they ask you to figure out?"

"The rate of each train."

"*Rate*. What does that mean?"

"The speed. How fast they're going." I looked at her, and she made the connection. "Which is distance divided by time." I watched her eyes as the wheels began to turn and her face lit up. "Or *d* equals *rt*. The *d* is the same…"

"What about time?"

"One takes five hours, the other takes six…I think I can do this!"

She picked up the pencil as my phone rang. I pulled it out and checked the screen. "It's my mom."

"Oh," said Jasmine, putting a finger to her lips.

"Hi, Mom," I said into the phone. "Hello?"

I heard Mom's voice distinctly, but she wasn't talking to me. "I think this one would be better on you."

"Yeah, if I was a foot taller," said a voice which I recognized as Betty's.

Jasmine looked at me quizzically. "Musta butt dialed," I said. "Sounds like she's with her friend, Betty."

"Put it on speaker."

"They're just shopping…"

"Trust me."

I turned up the volume, hit speaker, and laid the phone down. Betty's voice exploded from the tiny speaker. "I'm working on a new screen name. What do you think of **I'll_ do_you_my_way?**"

"Too Frank Sinatra," laughed Mom.

"**I_deserve_a_dick_today?**" said Betty. Jasmine gasped and covered her mouth.

"Too McDonald's," said Mom.

"**Queen_of_cleavage?**"

"True, but... wasn't there a TV show?"

"**Booty_on_duty?**"

"Kinda ghetto."

"**TitsRUs?**"

"Perfect! You should be in advertising."

"Well, when you have a product you *love*," said Betty. "Mirror, mirror, on the wall—who's the cougariest of all?"

"*You* are," said Mom.

"No, *you* are," said Betty. The two burst into gales of girlish laughter. Jasmine gave me a look of amazed amusement. "Hey, are you still seeing Fred?"

"Nah," said Mom. "Been there, done him."

More giggles. "How'd you like his skinhead?"

"No big deal," said Mom. "I shave downtown, he shaves uptown."

"I went out with a guy who was *totally* shaved," said Betty. "Not a follicle on his body."

"How was that?"

"I thought something was wrong with him. I asked if he was getting chemo."

Mom burst into laughter. "What did he say?"

"We were looking at menus," said Betty. "He said he was getting *tacos*." The two women screamed with laughter. "He was more of a *schlub* than a *cub*," Betty choked out. "Or maybe even a *chub*! He looked like a big, giant tube of liverwurst!"

"Stop, Betty! I'm gonna have nightmares!"

I disconnected the call, shaking my head.

"When I say 'trust me,' you probably *shouldn't*," said Jasmine after a moment. I laughed, but I had to fight not to tear up. "Which one was your mom?"

"You know the one who was picking the new screen name?" I said.

"Yeah…" said Jasmine, her eyes getting big.

"That was Betty. The other one was my mom."

"I think Betty was worse," said Jasmine philosophically.

I shrugged helplessly. "Mom's already got a screen name that gets plenty of action. She calls herself 'Cougarlicious.'"

"You're kidding." I shook my head. Jasmine seemed to be having trouble incorporating such radical information into her world view. "And Cougarlicious was married to your *dad*?"

"She is Mom, hear her roar," I said tiredly.

"I don't think this is what the feminists had in mind," said Jasmine.

"I don't know," I said. "I just know she wasn't always like this."

"Maybe she's got a parasite in her brain. Would that make you feel better?"

"Maybe, somewhat. Meanwhile, what would definitely make me feel better is to see you solve this problem."

Jasmine gave me a long look and picked up the pencil. I watched silently while she worked the problem. She made an initial mistake, but I held my tongue, and after a moment's thought, she caught it. Setting up the equation is the hard part. After she got that right, she did the arithmetic and came up with the solution.

She looked at me proudly. "Fifty miles an hour for the freight train, sixty miles an hour for the passenger train."

"You got it."

"I almost messed it up. Why didn't you say something?"

I shrugged. "I thought you could do it. And you did."

"Do you feel better?"

"Yeah, a little."

Jasmine looked at me. "Maybe there's something else I could do…"

And just like that, Jasmine put her lips on mine. It felt surprisingly comfortable; my body parts seemed to have instincts I hadn't imagined, and I didn't feel as nervous as I always thought I would. I ran my hands through her thick hair and inhaled a scent incredibly fresh and exotic.

"I don't know if you should trust *me*, but I should trust *you*," she said. "Should we stop?"

"I think a little more would be okay…"

"Maybe just to second base," she said, wrapping her arms around me.

Wow. I'd never even gotten off the bench…

Chapter Twenty-Five
The Wheel of Time

I STOOD IN A cavernous room that reverberated with a low frequency guttural rumble that made my whole body vibrate. I *felt* this sound, more than *heard* it. It came from a dozen Buddhist monks, some of whom chanted, while others played horns so ridiculously long that the flared bells rested on the floor while the monks blew into mouthpieces, their cheeks puffed out like Tibetan Louis Armstrongs. All were draped in flowing robes of yellow and crimson, wearing foot-high headdresses that looked like giant lemony Mohawks.

The extravagant visual was like something out of a Dr. Seuss book. I closed my eyes and let the sound wash over me. My pulse and breathing slowed, and I swayed on my feet. Then a high-pitched chime rang out: finger cymbals, punctuating the droning dirge.

I opened my eyes and flinched away violently, reacting to the shocking sight of a multitude of wild animals poised to attack the performers—a grizzly bear, several wolves, a herd of buffalo! And then Seymour Smith's large hand was on my shoulder. "Steady now," he murmured, and with a rush I returned to my place in time and space.

Mr. Smith and I, along with hundreds of others, stood in the Hall of North American Mammals in the Los Angeles Museum of Natural History. We were there to witness the creation of a sacred sand mandala by the monks of the Drepung Loseling Monastery in India.

I had been confused when Mr. Smith had called to invite me the week before; it had taken me a minute to wrap my head around an outing with him that didn't include Mom. She'd made other plans, though, and Mr. Smith thought it was an event that would interest me, combining spiritual, philosophical, and artistic pursuits. It felt awkward to accept, but it seemed even clumsier to beg-off out of shyness. I hemmed-and-hawed, gripping the phone nervously, unsure of what to do.

"No pressure, old man," said Mr. Smith. "It *is* a bit of a once-in-a-lifetime opportunity, though. Kalachakra Wheel of Time, and all that. Monks have been making it since about 600 BC."

"And they haven't finished it?"

He laughed. "No, that would be quite an undertaking, wouldn't it? I mean to say they've been making *versions* of this particular mandala going back that far. They're going to complete the entire work of art over the course of several days at the museum. Naturally we won't stay for all of that, though. What do you think?"

"Let's go for it," I suddenly decided.

"Let's go for it, indeed."

So here we were. It felt weird to hang out with Mr. Smith without Mom, though it's not like I'd ever been out with the two of them together. And now that Mom's time was completely taken up with her juvenile admirers, Mr. Smith's visits were much less frequent, and I realized I missed him. There was something reassuring about the older man. When I was with him it felt like I was in a private club, and without ever explaining, he taught me what the club's rules were, and how to conduct myself.

When the performance concluded, the monks began to lay out the mandala on the marble floor of the hall. They used compasses, chalk, and string to carefully sketch the outline. I watched through Mr. Smith's video camera, zooming to observe the details as if I were looking over a monk's shoulder. But I wound up just staring at their faces, fascinated by their calm yet cheerful expressions as they collaborated wordlessly on the design. I've noticed most people don't look happy when they're working. They usually look bored or mildly annoyed, but not these guys.

After several minutes of watching, Mr. Smith cleared his throat. "Well, Moon, I'm getting a bit peckish. How about a bite?"

"Sounds great," I agreed.

"The monks'll be at this a good bit. Let's have lunch, then come back to see them start the sand painting."

A lot of people seemed to be having the same thought, because the crowd was quickly dissolving. Mr. Smith and I walked across the park and crossed the street to a Mexican restaurant.

He inhaled deeply as we entered, remarking, "Love that smell. Tortilla chips and a trace of mildew. Reminds me of Mexico."

"You've been there?"

"Oh, yes. Marvelous place. Delightful people, beaches, guacamole, margaritas—what's not to like?"

"Uh…poverty?"

"Well, yes," he agreed. "However, I grew up in India. If I hadn't learned to appreciate life's beauty amid squalor I would have been very depressed, indeed."

"I thought you were English."

He nodded. "But you know, the British played a large role in India, even after independence in '47. My father was a businessman, so we were primarily in India until I was eleven. Then we moved to the States. Oddly, I haven't really spent much time in England."

I felt like I was asking too many questions, but Mr. Smith didn't seem to mind. There was more I wanted to know, so I continued my interrogation. "Still, you have the accent," I said.

"Guilty as charged," he admitted. "Might've actually *emphasized* it. Seems to add about twenty points to my perceived IQ in the US. When I go abroad, people consider me a lot less intelligent."

We ordered and they brought our drinks. Mr. Smith raised his beer and toasted. "To art," he said. He clinked glasses with my Coke, and we each took a long drink.

I had a sudden thought. "You're not an artist, are you?" I asked.

"No," he said, chuckling. "I'm a realtor. At least I can appreciate beauty, even if I can't create it."

"Is that why you go out with my mom?" I asked. "Because she's pretty?"

"Well, it doesn't hurt," he said. "However, she has many other good qualities as well."

"Doesn't it bother you that she...uh...she—"

"Shh."

"—goes out with...uh—"

"*Shh,*" he said more sharply, gesturing with his beer. I stopped. "A gentleman is discrete, Moon." Then he thought, and added, "I have no romantic illusions regarding your mother. We really *are* 'just friends.'"

I felt suddenly glum. "I'm glad about that for *your* sake," I said, and shoved several tortilla chips in my mouth.

Mr. Smith looked at me thoughtfully. "You know, she's just going through a phase. In the long run, she'll snap out of it."

"In the long run we're all dead," I said.

"Touché!" he exclaimed, his eyes sparkling. "Do you know who said that?"

"A friend of mine."

"Not originally. The line belongs to John Maynard Keynes, a great economist. This *is* apropos," he said, grinning.

Mr. Smith was dressed in tie and jacket, as usual. I watched in fascination as he quickly shucked off his jacket and began to unknot his tie.

"Uh, Mr. Smith…"

"Don't worry, the trousers stay on."

Tie off, he unbuttoned his dress shirt half way, and pulled it apart to show me his chest. I could hardly believe what I saw. "You've got a tattoo!"

"Well, I thought I ought. Everyone seems to be doing it."

"Not like *that*," I said, looking more closely.

"It's from *The New Yorker*. Can you make it out?"

It was a cartoon that showed two old bald guys with glasses sitting in armchairs smoking cigars. One of them had his mouth open, talking, and the other guy listened with a frown. I read the caption aloud. "Between us, Flaster, there are two things I never did understand—arbitrage and dames."

"*Arbitrage?*" I asked.

"Economics term. Taking advantage of market inefficiencies to turn a profit." I looked at him blankly, and he gestured apologetically to his chest. "As it says, *I* don't understand it either. Nor the other topic under discussion—women in general, and your mother in particular."

"You're going to have to live with that tattoo for the rest of your life," I pointed out, realizing I sounded like an annoying parent.

"That's not quite as long in my case as it would be in yours," he laughed, buttoning up his shirt.

I was still having trouble wrapping my head around it. "You liked that so much you put it on your chest?"

"It was either that or my tombstone," he said with a wink.

When we returned to the museum after lunch, the monks had made a lot of progress. The outline was finished, and eight monks were seated cross-legged on cushions, bent low over their work.

I took a close-up look through the video camera and had a sudden irreverent thought. "It looks like a giant paint-by-number design!"

"Yes, it does a bit. But they're not painting," he said.

"What *are* they doing?" I focused on a particular monk. He was holding a long, tapering cone in one hand, and his other stroked it with a metal rod. I zoomed in tighter, and saw a fine stream of red particles exit the tip of the instrument, depositing in a series of tiny mounds as he expertly moved his hands. "What keeps the sand in place?" I asked.

"Gravity."

I looked at Mr. Smith. "That's it? No glue?" He shook his head. "That's not very permanent," I pointed out.

"Exactly. Two teams of monks will work sixteen hours a day for eight days to create a magnificent work of art. Then they will dismantle it."

I was appalled. "That doesn't make any sense. What if Leonardo da Vinci had destroyed the *Mona Lisa* as soon as he finished it?"

"Another way of thinking, isn't it? Puts the focus on the act of creation itself. And the transiency of this world. Like George Harrison said, 'All things must pass.' It's just that these boys really put their money where their mouth is," said Mr. Smith.

"Are you a Buddhist?" I asked.

"Can't say that I am. However, I hear *you've* done a stint with them."

I thought about my time at the Fellowship Center and shook my head. "The Buddhists I know didn't seem much like this. I have no idea if they share *any* of the same ideas."

"Some, no doubt," he said. "But you're aware there are as many different sects of Buddhism as there are of Christianity."

"And that's a shitload," I said, the profanity escaping before I could choose a more appropriate word.

"Precisely," he said. As usual, Mr. Smith took it all in stride.

We watched as the design slowly grew. Then Mr. Smith put his hand on my shoulder. "I'm afraid I've got to get to Beverly Hills for a showing. Have you any interest in seeing how this all comes out?"

"Well, yeah."

He nodded. "What if we come back next Sunday to see the finished product and the dismantling ceremony? It'll take a few hours."

"Can I bring someone?" I asked.

"Of course," he agreed. "Perhaps your mother will be available as well."

"Uh…"

Mr. Smith gave me a thoughtful look, then said, "On second thought, let's just make it the *three* of us, then. You, your friend, and me."

The finished mandala was an enormous, colorful, incredibly complex design. Mr. Smith, Jasmine, and I gazed at it, then Jasmine quietly said, "It's so colorful."

"Yeah," I said. "They used every crayon in the box."

"The one with forty-eight colors," she said.

"Or even ninety-two," said Mr. Smith.

"Uh, ninety-*six*," I corrected. "Crayons always come in multiples of eight or twelve. Ninety-six is actually a multiple of both." Jasmine gave me a look. "Sorry."

"Not at all," said Mr. Smith. "I stand corrected. Speaking of large numbers, if you look closely you should be able to make out 722 individual deities."

"I couldn't even do 'Where's Waldo,'" laughed Jasmine. "So I don't think I'll find them *all*."

"Maybe just the guy in the middle," I suggested. "He's supposed to be Buddha."

"Is he, like, their God or something? My mom always said you should rub his belly and make a wish," said Jasmine.

"My mom said that, too," I agreed.

"People have quite a proclivity for wishful thinking, don't they? Blow out the candle and make a wish. Throw in a penny and make a wish. Rub a statue's belly and make a wish," said Mr. Smith.

"Can you imagine someone rubbing Jesus' stomach?" asked Jasmine. "Instead of good luck, they'd probably get killed."

"It would be ill-advised," said Mr. Smith. "But Buddha is *not* the Buddhist God. The term means, 'One who is awake,' or, as we would say, 'enlightened.' In fact, there were many recognized Buddhas, some of whom did not take themselves too seriously."

There was music from the monks, more questions from Jasmine and me, and more answers from Mr. Smith. Then the monks got out their brooms. With their typical efficiency, they neatly swept up every grain of colored sand they'd spent the last eight days painstakingly arranging into an amazing design. In a few minutes it was gone, the remains packaged in Ziploc baggies that were distributed to the audience. I looked at the muddy swirl I held in my hand.

"I kind of feel like someone died," I murmured.

Mr. Smith nodded. "Ashes to ashes, and all that. I think you've got the point."

"What are they going to do with that?" asked Jasmine, pointing to a large urn one monk held while another poured the remaining sand into it.

"Ah! That's meant to be taken to the Santa Monica beach, where it will be thrown to the waves to bless the fish," said Mr. Smith. "We're invited, if you'd like to go."

I looked to Jasmine, who nodded. "We're in," I said. Jasmine excused herself to use the bathroom first. Mr. Smith and I waited awkwardly, then he cleared his throat and said, "She is quite lovely."

Jasmine and I hadn't been touching each other or anything, but I guess he could see there was something between us. "Mom would say she's way too old," I replied.

"What would *you* say?"

I wedged my hands in my pockets, thinking this was not my favorite subject. "I *am* a lot younger."

"Ah…you're an old soul, Moon. That's what counts. And she is certainly fond of you."

I shrugged, and Mr. Smith gestured at the monks. "Have you learned nothing from this? Live in the moment. Embrace the impermanence of life." He clapped me on the back and added, "And don't tell your mother. I certainly won't. None of her business, really."

When Jasmine returned we piled into Mr. Smith's car and followed about thirty other vehicles in a caravan to the Sand and Sea Club in Santa Monica. There, surrounded by bodybuilders, beach bunnies, roller skaters, bike riders, and homeless people who looked on with curiosity, the brightly robed monks flung the gritty remains of the Wheel of Time to mingle with less distinguished sand in the Santa Monica Bay. Then they seated themselves and began a prayer for the well-being of us all. As we lowered our heads, Jasmine discretely moved next to me and took my hand. After a moment, I reached for Mr. Smith's.

The sonorous drone of the monks' deep voices enveloped us with their benevolence. The best I could, I opened my senses to enjoy and record every detail of this fleeting, wonderful moment on the beach, knowing we'd never have another like it.

Chapter Twenty-Six
Fortunately/Unfortunately

MY FIRST GRADE TEACHER was named Miss Marsh. She was very tall and smiled a lot, but I knew that she was not happy about anything that would bring joy to her students.

I didn't trust Miss Marsh and I was afraid of her. Her eyes bored right through me with a knowing stare that penetrated to my evil first-grader core. Her gaze evoked shame and confusion. So I stopped looking up at her face, which was kind of like peering to the top of a towering redwood tree, anyway.

Instead I spent most of my time looking at her calves and feet. Miss Marsh always wore stockings and high heels. She mashed her feet into shoes that were far too small, and then compounded the self-inflicted torture by the ridiculous angle the heels forced on her feet and legs. Riding the prolonged acid trip of early childhood, I would meditate on Miss Marsh's legs, wondering why she was punishing herself, and if her pain was responsible for her perpetual ill-humor.

Since I avoided eye contact, I was often chastised for not listening to the teacher. But I *was* listening. At least once a week, Miss Marsh would read us her favorite book, which was called *Fortunately*. Then we'd play a game inspired by the pattern of the story, in which the class and Miss Marsh would compose a story together, alternating sentences. It would go something like this:

Chris: *Fortunately*, Jennifer got a new bike

Miss Marsh: *Unfortunately*, she didn't know how to ride it.

Barbara: *Fortunately*, the bike had training wheels.

Miss Marsh: *Unfortunately*, it *didn't* have brakes.

Greg: *Fortunately*, there was no one in Jennifer's way.

Miss Marsh: *Unfortunately*, there *was* a wall—and she smashed right into it.

And so it would go: for every *fortunate* turn of events, Miss Marsh would add an *unfortunate* complication to the story. As the narrative developed, the tension would steadily mount, with Miss Marsh inventing increasingly dire dilemmas that challenged the class's resourcefulness to conjure amazing ways to save the protagonist du jour.

Though the picture book happily concluded with a final *fortunate* occurrence, our games did *not*. Miss Marsh always wound up with the last word, ending things on a frustrating *unfortunate* note. She would smile with malevolent satisfaction as her students—initially seated in their best criss-cross-applesauce posture on the classroom rug—wound up writhing at her feet, deliciously frustrated that their best efforts were once more thwarted by their teacher's relentless ability to foretell disaster.

I now realize this routine served as a form of brainwashing, which, at least in my case, succeeded in its objective. I began to view life as a series of events in which nothing good occurred without subsequent catastrophe. In Miss Marsh's fairy tales, the heroes always wound up living "unhappily ever after."

Just as prison has its own currency, so, too, does first grade. Along with pencils, erasers form the backbone of the little kid economy. At the beginning of the year, every student was issued a ration of one gum eraser, which was intended to last all term. Like millions of children before and after us, our immediate action was to hold the erasers to our noses and inhale deeply. Ah, the smell of money!

Some kids developed such a reverence for their eraser that they refused to use their own, perpetually cadging one from their friends. I, however, did not use mine for a different reason: it was missing. This loss provoked guilt, insecurity, and a total dependence on Ellen Stacy, a blackmailing cutie pie who sat next to me. In return for the use of Ellen's eraser, I was forced to commit one of the seven deadly sins of elementary school: I had to let Ellen copy my paper.

The stress of the situation finally drove me to Miss Marsh for resolution. I explained the situation to her and she smiled knowingly.

"*Fortunately*, I gave you an eraser," she said. This was novel. Miss Marsh was reversing roles with me. But I was game.

"*Unfortunately*, I can't find it."

She nodded. "*Fortunately*, Ellen will let you use her eraser."

"*Unfortunately*, I have to let her copy my paper," I concluded, certain this could not be the end of the story.

But it was. Miss Marsh gestured expansively to indicate that the matter was resolved. It simply wasn't conceivable for her to say something like, "*Fortunately,* I can give you another eraser." All stories concluded with "*unfortunately*" and this tale could end no other way.

I marvel at people who adopt the opposite point of view, seeing good fortune in every crisis. Hit by a car? *I was lucky—it coulda been a bus.* A hurricane wipes out New Orleans. *Nature's form of economic stimulus—think of the jobs it'll take to rebuild.* Falsely convicted of manslaughter? *Take up bodybuilding and catch up on your reading.* Your five-year-old daughter dies of cancer. *God took her to a better place with Him.*

These relentlessly upbeat individuals genuinely seem to be comforted and reassured by their faith that the last line in the story will begin with the word "*fortunately.*"

Unfortunately, I don't believe that.

This was on my mind as our domestic situation began to contort under the weight of Mom's bizarre social life.

Fortunately, Mom did not go out with Lance again.

Unfortunately, she became a serial dater of a slew of equally abhorrent man-boys.

Fortunately, Moss and I saw less of this revolting spectacle since we now began to spend every weekend with Dad, giving Mom more "space."

Fortunately, Dad was careful never to inquire into Mom's affairs, so when we were with him we could make like ostriches and pretend none of this was going on.

Fortunately, I was still tutoring Jasmine, which obviously would tend to take my mind off anything less pressing than the detonation of a nuclear device in my immediate vicinity.

Fortunately, Moss was deep into his skating and preparing for the Free Flow finals, so he was in a good place, too.

One Saturday night Moss and I were at our usual table at Fanatics. I was working on an essay about *A Tale of Two Cities* and Moss was "reading" US history. Naturally, it was not holding his attention, and he spent most of his time gazing into space.

Suddenly he elbowed me, murmuring. "Bro, it's the Boobster."

"Betty Bridges, here?" I gulped out.

"Coming this way. Quick!" he said, sliding under the table. I followed suit and joined Moss on the floor.

We crouched and waited for Betty to pass, but instead of walking by us, she stopped.

"Hey, there's a table here, they just have to clean it," she called, oblivious to the textbooks still lying open.

"Look closer, you fool," breathed Moss. I stifled a giggle.

"Hey, can you clear this table? We'll sit here," suggested Betty. A waitress's shapely legs appeared beside Betty's. I recognized them as Jasmine's. Somehow I had regressed to first grade, once more obsessively focused on women below the waist.

"*Before* and *after*," observed Moss.

"I prefer *before*," I whispered.

"No doubt. But there's always the Boobster's better half," whispered Moss.

"More like three-quarters," I whispered. Moss snickered.

"This table's taken, miss," said Jasmine.

"I don't see anyone," said Betty.

"Maybe they're in the bathroom. It's the owner's sons. They always take this table," said Jasmine. I cringed, not exactly sure what we had to hide from Betty, but pretty sure it was something.

"Oh, I know them," Betty said brightly. "I'm a friend of their mother."

"Oh," said Jasmine. From her tone I could tell she realized it was time to stop being so helpful. "Uh, a customer needs me," she said and scurried away.

"Hm. I wonder where they are," said Betty, continuing to think—if you can call it that—out loud. To our relief, her legs took off back the way they had come.

Moss looked at me. "We're busted. Let's brazen it out."

"Yeah. It looks bad to be hiding under a table, don't you think?"

"Exactly. Like we've got something to hide."

"Right. What have we got to hide?" Neither of us made a move. Since Moss was the big brother I figured he had the honors. "See if it's clear."

Moss wriggled up the bench and stuck his head out. "Olly olly oxen free," he muttered.

I pulled myself up and promptly got back to work on my essay, just as Betty flounced over with a girlfriend.

"Moss and Moon, I've been looking everywhere for you two," she said, peeved but pleased.

"Why, as I live and breathe, it's Betty Bridges," said Moss. "Looking succulent as usual. Who's your little friend?"

Betty grinned. "This is Paulette. We came to watch the game."

"As did we."

"Are you Lakers fans?" I asked.

"No," said Betty.

"Warriors fans?" suggested Moss.

"No," said Paulette.

"You heard there were cute guys here," I said.

"You know me," said Betty.

"I'm not one to judge, girls, but I think you heard wrong," confided Moss.

"But the food and drinks are good," I said.

Betty noticed the blended beverages on our table. "What are you having?" she asked.

"Smoothies. Strawberry banana," I said.

"There's no liquor in them?" asked Betty.

"Betty, we're not of legal age," said Moss. She looked unconvinced and Moss held out a glass. "Please, have a taste."

Betty took the glass and sipped. "Well, I don't taste anything," she admitted. She held the glass out to Paulette. "You try."

Paulette made a face. "*I* don't want a smoothie."

Betty rolled her eyes and gave the glass back.

"We'll take a breathalyzer, but a blood test is out of the question," I taunted. But Betty wasn't letting it drop.

"I don't think you're even supposed to be in a bar," she accused.

"That could be true," said Moss, "but this is a *restaurant*."

"That serves alcohol," said Betty.

"Or you wouldn't be here," I pointed out.

"Got that right," said Paulette. "When are we gonna get some?"

"In a minute," said Betty, then turned back to us. "I don't think it's legal for you to be in here," she whispered.

"Betty, relax. Dad's got a pinkie," said Moss.

"A *what*?"

"A pink liquor license," I said. "It's what they call a 'type forty-seven,' for a restaurant. And under a type forty-seven, minors *are* allowed." Moss and I had been somewhat concerned about this ourselves, and had done our homework. If you sound like you know what you're talking about, it'll deter most harassment.

Moss opened his history book. "Well, we have some homework to finish, so why don't you two run along and have a good time?"

"Okay," said Betty dubiously.

"Nice to meet you," said Paulette.

"Absolutely," said Moss.

The two women headed for the bar. Moss and I looked at each other.

"That wasn't good," I said.

"No, not good," Moss agreed.

Unfortunately.

Chapter Twenty-Seven
Dakota

MOSS AND I had a rating scale for our parents' fights which we based on different types of severe weather. Conflict between our mother and father disturbed the atmosphere of our lives, so we thought of each fight as a storm. It could be a little scary, with thunder, lightning, high winds, driving rain—but it might blow over in a day, leaving rainbows, blue sky, and sunshine. A conflict of this variety we classified as a *squall*. Squalls featured a fair amount of emotional venting, but nothing that inflicted lasting damage to our world.

There was also an *ice storm*, when one or both of our parents became so upset that they would stop communicating at all for several days. They would go through the bare motions of domestic life, either with suppressed rage or obvious depression, and we would do our best to maintain a safe distance. When frost blanketed our land, we used care in motion to avoid painful slip-ups that could be hazardous to our health.

Then there were the *hurricanes*. These fights packed a wallop and produced serious devastation that could last for months. They were so significant that, like their meteorological cousins, Moss and I gave them human names. This made it easier for us to talk about them historically, since we could refer to "Hayden," the fight that happened after Thanksgiving three years ago; or "Skyler," which took place on Mom's fortieth birthday; or "Angel," which ruined last Christmas. It also gave us an illusion of control, since we were in charge of the rating and the naming, applying politically correct gender-neutral monikers. Unfortunately, that's pretty much all we could do—just like folks trapped by a major tempest couldn't flee for their lives and had to batten down the hatches to ride it out.

After Dad had moved out, we'd mothballed our scale, since our parents' infrequent encounters were marked by the same carefully regulated behavior as relay runners passing a baton—the baton being *us*. However, Betty's visit to the bar gave us a sense of impending doom, a severe barometer drop that presaged heavy weather. Moss and I decided it was best to fill Dad in on all the details so he wouldn't be blindsided. His somber expression as we explained the situation did nothing to reassure us. He listened without interrupting, nodding, asking no questions. When we finished he said simply, "Boys, you did nothing wrong. Not a thing."

"We don't think you did, either, Dad," I said.

"Yeah, right," Moss chimed in. "Strictly kosher."

Dad sighed deeply and nodded.

When Dad dropped us off the next night, Mom was waiting. She yanked the front door open when she heard Dad's car pull up, then loomed in the doorway, a glass of wine in her hand.

This was bad. Dad was pretty much the same, sober or drinking, but Mom became highly volatile after a couple of glasses of wine.

She ignored Moss and me when we walked up, looking daggers at Dad. "We need to talk," she said, holding the door open. Moss and I fled for cover, since the four words immediately identified the impending storm as a hurricane.

We headed for Moss's room, which was closer to the living room. We shut the door loudly for our parents' benefit, then silently cracked it open for ours. A hurricane was conducted at high volume, so we could usually hear every word. Sometimes we chose not to, but in this case, the hurricane would be about us, and we felt compelled to know the details.

"What in God's name do you mean by taking my children to a bar?" Mom demanded.

"Let's just slow down," Dad suggested.

"Are you determined to make them drunks like you? Is that what you're trying to do? Would that make you happy?!"

"I'm gonna get a glass of water," said Dad. "Is that okay?"

Silence where Mom must have nodded and Dad went to the kitchen.

Moss whispered, "What's the next hurricane?"

"Dakota."

"Hurricane Dakota," he mused. "Category?"

"To be determined. Currently a one, but quickly gathering strength."

"The liquor talk is bad."

"Yeah," I agreed. "But so far Dad is keeping his cool."

We heard Mom's voice and hushed. "What is that, vodka?" she accused.

"Only if you've got it coming out of the tap," said Dad.

"That's the way you would have liked it," said Mom.

Dad ignored the taunt. "Janice, the boys visit my restaurant. The food's good, they like to watch sports, they don't drink any alcohol."

147

"That's not the way I heard it."

"You heard wrong. No one who works for me would serve them liquor."

"Oh, you're so sure of that?!" said Mom sarcastically.

"Yeah, I am."

"There were drinks on the table when my friend Betty saw them."

"There were *beverages* on the table. Did Betty tell you she tried them herself and couldn't taste any alcohol?"

"Betty!" Mom scoffed. "She thinks a straight up martini's too weak. There could have been two shots in there and she wouldn't have known."

"She's *your* spy," said Dad. "Get one with a better palate."

The storm had reached a turning point. Dad had done a good job of sidestepping Mom's most personal attacks and de-escalating the conflict. They had reached a point at which Mom might potentially appreciate the absurdity of the situation, burst into laughter, and the hurricane might pass out to sea. Or it could head directly for the coast...

"What about that little waitress?" Mom demanded.

"Jasmine?"

"I don't know her name!"

"Probably Jasmine. What?"

"Are you seeing her?"

Uh-oh. Jealousy. This hurricane was now picking up moisture and wind speed, and heading towards land.

"That's none of your business," Dad said, getting annoyed.

"That means yes."

"That means I don't ask about your sex life and you don't ask about mine."

"Oh, you don't want to know about *my* sex life," said Mom.

"That's right, I don't—"

"—I *assure* you, you don't want to know—"

"—I *don't*, so shut up about it!" snarled Dad.

"Big man, going after a bar slut who could be your daughter," said Mom.

"Jasmine is *not* a slut," said Dad. I silently seconded him, disgusted with Mom for attacking someone she'd never even met.

"She dresses like a slut," persisted Mom.

"Everything about what you're saying is wrong! Jasmine's a nice girl who happens to be a waitress. Moon even tutors her."

"*What?!!!*"

Moss looked at me and shook his head.

"She's trying to get her GED. Moon is helping her with the math."

"Oh, great! What's she helping *him* with? Have you got no common sense? I can't even trust my kids to you for the weekend! Who knows what you'll do next?! Take them to Vegas, have some drinks, do a little gambling, hit the strip joints, get them prostitutes—"

"—That's ridiculous—"

"—I don't know—"

"—You *do* know I'd never do anything like that! Maybe I was not the perfect husband for you, but I've always been a good father."

"Amen," Moss whispered to me.

"Well, I'll agree that you were not a perfect husband," said Mom in a cutting voice.

"We're not going there!"

"You *aren't* a good father! You're a pitiful role model!"

"I can't stand this," I whispered to Moss.

"Enough! This is the whole point of being divorced, so I don't have to go through this anymore," said Dad.

"We still have children to raise," insisted Mom.

"Who do you think you are to lecture me, Mother Teresa? Is that why you had the makeover, so you can be the world's greatest parent?"

"Have the boys been telling you—"

"—I don't ask, and they don't tell! They've got way too much class for that."

"There happen to be a lot of men—"

"—I don't doubt it."

"—who are attracted to me—"

"—I don't doubt it."

"Men a lot better than *you!*"

"I *doubt* it."

"You *doubt* it?"

"Yes, I doubt it. But then, what you look for in a man is not the same as what I look for in a man."

"Oh?! And what is it I look for?" Mom demanded.

"Attention. You need a lot of attention. A good man is one who pays a lot of attention to you."

"Get out!" shouted Mom.

"I guess we've had our little talk," said Dad.

"This isn't over! You'll be hearing from my lawyer!" Mom raged.

"Oh, that's a great line, Janice, how original."

We heard the front door slam and just like that, Hurricane Dakota had dissipated.

Too soon, we would feel the effects of the devastation left in its path.

Chapter Twenty-Eight
Lawyers

IF YOU'RE STRANDED on a desert island with a Bengal tiger, a black mamba, a lawyer, and you have a gun with only two bullets, what should you do?

Shoot the lawyer twice.

What's the difference between a lawyer and a catfish?

One is a slimy, bottom-dwelling, scum sucker.

The other is a fish.

What's black and brown and looks good on an attorney?

A Doberman pinscher.

What's the problem with lawyer jokes?

Lawyers don't think they're funny.

No one else thinks they're jokes.

So Mom's lawyer *did* call Dad; and Dad called his lawyer; and Dad's lawyer called Mom's lawyer…

It went downhill from there.

At the end of the week, Mom and Dad summoned Moss and me

to a meeting in our living room. The two of us sat together on the couch. Mom and Dad sat in armchairs as far from each other as they could get. Dad had a somber expression I'd seen only a few times, when Moss or I had really screwed-up and Dad knew he had to do something drastic, but wasn't sure he was going to do the right thing.

Mom, on the other hand, adopted a bright, upbeat tone, as if she had come up with a delightful notion she knew we'd just love, and couldn't wait to share it.

"Well, the gang's all here," said Moss to get the ball rolling.

"Boys, your father and I have agreed that you need to spend more time with me," said Mom.

"That so?" Moss looked to Dad for confirmation. Dad threw up his hands and shrugged apologetically.

"How much more time?" I asked.

"You'll be staying home for the weekends," said Mom.

"*All* the weekends?"

"Yes," said Mom. "That way you can see more of your friends, which I'm sure you'll enjoy."

"And your little sleepover pals, too. It'll be great," snapped Moss.

"You are not to speak to me that way."

I glared at her. "So this is all being done to improve our social life."

"David, make them be civil."

Dad snorted. "I'm not going to defend your honor."

"You agreed to this, Dad?" I asked. Moss and I looked at him expectantly, but Mom interrupted before he could answer.

"Yes, we agreed it's for the best, given your father's drinking problem."

"He doesn't drink any more than you do," said Moss.

"Oh, I'm sure he does."

"Seems to me Dad's drinking less," I said.

"He's still an alcoholic."

"With all the Chardonnay in your veins, I wouldn't be calling anyone an alcoholic," said Moss.

Mom self-consciously put down the glass of wine that she was almost never without these days.

"It gets worse," said Dad.

"It has come to my attention that you have been spending considerable time at your father's bar. That is to stop," said Mom. "Entirely."

"We can't go to Fanatics?" I asked, incredulous.

"You mean, without Dad, right?"

"You are not allowed in that place at any time!" shouted Mom.

Dad held out a hand, as if to calm her. "Janice…"

"I do not trust the staff to refrain from serving you alcohol," said Mom.

"What about me and Moss, do you trust us?"

"You are minors. You are not expected to be particularly trustworthy," Mom retorted.

Moss and I looked at each other.

"Let me get this straight," I said. "We can't go in Dad's restaurant at all, because you're afraid we might get some liquor. Meanwhile, you have us playing bartender to your dates, pouring them drinks from our well-stocked, unlocked liquor cabinet."

"I think you're spelling it out," added Moss. "Then Mom will be out for the night, leaving us alone with all the booze."

"Perhaps your father will install a lock on the cabinet," said Mom.

"Perhaps *not*," said Dad.

"Well, the handyman, then."

"Are we going to see Dad at all?" I asked.

"Your visits with your father must be supervised," said Mom.

"*Supervised?*" said Moss. "Like we need a babysitter when we're with Dad?"

"Yes, Moss," I explained. "This is typical of situations in which a parent is abusive or a child molester."

"Oh, that's Dad, all right."

"Those are not the only situations," said Mom.

"I can't believe a court agreed to this," I said.

"They didn't," Dad admitted. "*I* did."

We looked at him, stunned.

"There, you see?" said Mom, as if this vindicated her. But Moss and I waited for Dad to explain.

"Why?" asked Moss.

"I can't say," said Dad. "That's part of the agreement."

"You agreed that you can't tell us the truth," I said.

"Yeah, pretty much."

"That's not quite so," objected Mom. We ignored her and focused on Dad.

"Did you do anything wrong?" asked Moss

"No."

"David," said Mom threateningly.

"I *haven't* done anything wrong. And I will sue you for slander if you say otherwise," said Dad, beginning to lose his temper. Then he calmed. "But if you go to court, who knows what happens," Dad shrugged. "What do lawyers do when they're dead?" he asked.

"They lie, still," said Moss.

Dad grinned and nodded. "That's all I can say."

"So Mom's threatening to take you to court," I said.

"Let's stop this right now," said Mom.

"What, she and her lawyer are gonna make up some lies?" asked Moss.

"Yeah, and maybe get the ABC to investigate Fanatics. Maybe close them down," I conjectured.

"You *swore* you would not tell them this!" Mom shrieked.

"Dad didn't tell us *anything*," I said.

"*You* just did," said Moss. He stared at her and let this sink in for a moment.

"So you're blackmailing Dad, threatening to make up lies in court, to keep him away from us," I said.

"Well, I certainly wouldn't put it that way," said Mom.

There was a long moment while we tried to come to terms with this.

"It's for your own good," Mom continued, trying to recover her dignity.

Moss moaned. I shook my head. "So who is going to supervise our visits with Dad?" I asked.

"Someone whom I trust," said Mom.

"Who's that?"

"We got a problem there, boys," said Dad. "There's no one who your mother trusts."

"You gotta be kidding," said Moss, looking at Mom. "You set up a plan that can't even work."

"What about Mr. Smith?" I asked.

"Seymour? Oh, he's much too busy—"

"—C'mon, you haven't even tried!" snapped Moss.

"Well, I'll ask him. He'd be acceptable to me, if he'd agree," said Mom. "There's one more thing," she said, looking at me. "You're not to see that young lady any more."

"What young lady?" I asked, trying to delay the inevitable.

"I believe her name is Jasmine."

"She's my student," I said defensively.

"It is an inappropriate relationship," insisted Mom.

"You're the expert on those, Cougarlicious," sneered Moss.

"She needs help with her math," I argued.

"There are many other tutors in the city," Mom insisted. "I'm sure she can find one her own age."

No one said anything for a moment. Mom clapped her hands and declared, "Well, I think that wraps it up."

"Isn't that what Hitler said after Australia?" said Moss.

"You mean Auschwitz," I said.

Chapter Twenty-Nine
Cold Turkey

SOME EXPERIENCES ARE NOT nearly as bad as you think they'll be. For example, the divorce, up to this point, hadn't been entirely miserable.

On the other hand, some things are every bit as gut-wrenchingly awful as you expect they will be, and then some. Anything involving a hypodermic needle falls into that category for me. I dread punctures like the Scarecrow fears fire. Also raw seafood items. Ewwww. Visits to my great-grandmother in a nursing home. Going to the vet to put our pet dog Otis to sleep. Bad trips, all of them.

And now, Mom's stupid new plan for our world. A dark cloud descended on us, and it just didn't let up. I'd wake up feeling okay, then remember what had happened and be plunged into gloom. As the specific constraints which Mom's straitjacket would place on our daily lives emerged, it only served to affirm my depression.

There were the obvious consequences—the loss of the people and places that had become important to me. I couldn't see Jasmine, though I continued to talk to her and tutor her on the phone. No more Fanatics. Above all, no time with Dad. Mr. Smith was out of town and no other suitable chaperone had been identified.

Moss and I tried to talk to Dad, but he wasn't good on the phone and sounded so depressed that it made us feel even worse. So we kinda stopped calling, and he didn't call much, either.

Even more upsetting was the transformation in our feelings towards our mother, the architect of this horrible scheme. When things were going all right, we could be somewhat tolerant of her self-indulgent behavior. But now that she had wrecked our lives for no good reason, we couldn't cut her any slack. The best we could do was to refrain from outright conflict, but we complied with every order and rule with resentment.

Oddly, Moss and I had grown closer to Dad after he and Mom had separated. We actually saw more of him than when they were married, and felt more attached to him than we had when they first divorced. So this separation felt a lot worse than the actual divorce.

Not seeing Dad made me worry about him even more. Jasmine became my best source of information, and the news coming from her didn't reassure me. She told me Mom had managed to squeeze more child support out of Dad, since we weren't spending the weekends with him. One of the bartenders quit and Dad picked up his shifts to help make the extra payments. Maybe staying busy made him feel a little better, I don't know.

She also told me that my father had become a clown.

No, a *real* one. Since he couldn't spend weekends with us, he took jobs appearing at children's parties. He wore the full clown outfit— white face, red nose, wig, giant shoes. I guess he knew a lot of clown shtick, like doing pratfalls, silly stunts, juggling, magic tricks, tying balloons. Jasmine helped him on one of his gigs and said he was really good. The kids loved him and the single mothers were all giving him the eye. She said he wasn't interested.

I remembered that Dad had spent time as a rodeo clown, but I hadn't thought it was a big part of his life. He had never talked about it. Moss and I weren't all that big on clowns, but we weren't scared by them, like some people were.

The only clown I could think of was the star in Mom's favorite opera, *Pagliacci*. She used to play that song over and over, singing in her bad Italian. I finally asked her what it was about and she told me the story, about a clown who has to make people laugh even though his life is ruined. After that, she started singing in English. I guess she thought I'd want to learn the song, too. I had no interest in that, but the words stuck, and they came to me now.

Laugh, clown, laugh, at your shattered love

Meanwhile, Mom bought a new red convertible. That *really* got her a lot of attention.

Laugh at the pain tearing your heart.

Chapter Thirty
Anti-theist

SO IS THIS APPROACHING the misery of Job? Nah, not even close. Okay how about this? Remember how Satan afflicted Job with a disgusting skin disease, and Job tried to scrape his hide off with a broken plate? Remarkably, that's starting to sound like a plan to me.

Last week I went to the doctor with a rash on my arms and legs. He diagnosed it as poison oak. I told him I couldn't imagine where I could possibly have run into poison oak, since I lead a concrete-and-asphalt-bound life. Yeah, right, he said. He looked at me like I was a pregnant lady claiming to be a virgin. Then he gave me some of that stupid pink lotion that turns to chalk and doesn't do anyone any good. He told me to wash all the sheets, towels, blankets, and clothes in the house and wipe down every possible surface I might have come into contact with to remove all traces of the poison oil. I guess he thought he was treating Cinderella.

Well, I did that. I've painted myself with so much calamine lotion that I look like the Pink Panther. The pink *itchy* panther. Mom says these things can take some time to clear up. It's been five ΩFΣ!ж days!

It's bad during the day, but it's unbelievable at night. After I put my cream on, there's a window of about five minutes where I feel some hope. Then my skin comes to life. It might start behind my knees, or between my fingers or toes. I try to lie still, hoping it will stop. I know that scratching just aggravates it.

But it *doesn't* stop. The itching builds until my leg or my arm spasms and twitches. So I give it a scratch. Just a little one. A drop in the bucket of my itch. Then I let the faucet drip—scratch…scratch…scratch. Open the tap wide to fill the bucket—*scratch, scratch, scratch.* Put a damn fire hose in the bucket and crank it wide open—SCRATCHSCRATCHSCRATCH!!!!!!! But there's no bottom to my itch bucket. My skin is bloody and raw and oozing like a festering carcass. The pain is better than the itch and I can drop off for a little while.

Last night I tried sleeping in the bathtub. With water, of course. I was somewhat concerned about the possibility of drowning, but sleep deprivation and itching have made death more appealing.

I got a couple hours sleep before Mom came in to pee and found me comatose and shivering in a cold bath. I was mumbling about Satan and God, which got her attention. She's taking me to a dermatologist tomorrow. Our next stop will be the exorcist.

According to the dermatologist, I've got scabies. He shook his head and gritted his teeth when he examined me and heard the doctor's diagnosis of poison oak. This new diagnosis makes me feel better since it somehow justifies the misery I've experienced, not because it's a less loathsome affliction than poison oak, which is, after all, just bad chemicals. Scabies are parasites, a whole new level of horrible.

They are microscopic mites that burrow into your skin like termites, creating tunnels, pooping, and laying eggs. When magnified, they're hideous creatures. The thought of these demons living inside me is even more repulsive than the itching they inflict, which is worse at night because that's when the pests feel like digging.

I asked the doctor if anyone had ever cured himself by excavating the bugs the way I was trying to. He laughed a little, but took me seriously. He said most people have the good sense to come to him long before that. He also said that if I'd kept going the way I was, I'd probably have contracted a serious skin infection before I killed all the mites. Instead he prescribed some cream that he thought would do a better job of exterminating them. And naturally, he told me to wash all the sheets, towels, blankets, and clothes in the house and wipe down every possible surface I might have come into contact with and left any stray scabies on. Or else torch the joint and relocate to the Antarctic, where they don't have a lot of these fiends.

Thank God for dermatologists and their chemicals. The bugs are dead and I can sleep again. I just hope this isn't like a horror movie, where the monster reappears to scare the bejesus out of you just as you're relaxing.

Uh...*thank God*? Did I say that?! Figure of speech, right? If He gets any credit for dermatologists and their chemicals, then He's got to take the blame for scabies, which are a really horrible creation.

Also, how about mosquitoes, bubonic plague, ticks, flesh eating bacteria, brown recluse spiders, leprosy, human wolf syndrome, vampire fish, alien hand syndrome, furious rabies, and snakefish, to name a few of His masterpieces I think we could do without. Were these hideous things absolutely necessary?

Or are they punishment for our evil thoughts and acts? That's what Job believed—that his misfortune was divinely inflicted for something he'd done to displease the Lord, though he couldn't imagine what it could have been.

It appears that I am no longer *nothing*. I am becoming…*something*. Not an atheist, because I take the topic a bit too personally. I'm becoming an *anti*-theist.

True believers are seriously getting on my nerves. In the last week, our door has been knocked on by Jehovah's Witnesses, Mormons, and some guy who wanted to sell me the Bhagavad Gita. Walking down Pico, I was accosted by a minivan full of Orthodox Jews who tried to convert me. Then there's the homeless Jesus freak on the corner in Westwood haranguing everyone to repent before it's too late. All are totally certain their unique explanation of the meaning of life is the only one that's valid. Why do so many religious people feel an overwhelming compulsion to talk you into enlisting with them? It feels like one giant pyramid scheme.

(It must be noted that an exception to this rule are the bow-tie-clad messengers of Nation of Islam I encountered selling their newspaper on the corner of La Brea and Slauson. They were not looking for any white converts, since their founder, Elijah Mohammed, considered Caucasians to be "blue-eyed devils." However, they were eager to sell me a bean pie, perhaps because my eyes are actually brown.)

Wondering just how many other faiths might be clamoring for my vote, I do a little research to determine the number of religions that exist in the world. It turns out to be a surprisingly tough question to answer, and I give up after identifying a few facts.

According to the Organization for Religious Tolerance, there are nineteen major world religions. That's not really so many, right?

Well…they subdivide into 270 different large religious groups. Okay. Still manageable.

Then it gets complicated. Take Christianity for example. Worldwide, over 34,000 different Christian groups have been identified! Most of these believe their particular interpretation of the Gospel is the only one that's valid, and that the other 33,999 are nothing but hooey.

How can people who accept the Bible as the word of God find so many different ways to disagree on what it means?

Wow—as Mr. Smith said, there are a lot of different Buddhist denominations, though I think the Christians have them beat. The funny names tire me out—Hinayana, Mahayana, Theravada, Nikayana, Sthaviravada, Mulasarvastivada—so I move on to another major faith. With only about 150 different sects, Islam is looking relatively homogeneous. Though it must be admitted, the Sunnis and the Shiites are frequently ready to kill each other. Do they each think the other guys are infidels, or what?

Well, religious people tend to blame this sort of bad behavior on man's imperfect nature, not the pernicious aspects of a belief in God. I think this is letting God off the hook on the question of faith and its merits. Does God really bear *no* responsibility for all the atrocities that are committed in His name? If so, just what is it that He supposedly is good for?!

I note that after his skin affliction, Job's next move was to confer with his amigos. What the hell. In for a penny, in for a pound. I'm going to call Macaroni.

Chapter Thirty-One

Aron

MY BEST FRIEND IN elementary school was a kid named Aron Patel. We went to an amazing magnet school, called, appropriately, Wonderland Elementary. It's located on Wonderland Avenue in the Hollywood Hills. If you get up there early you can sometimes see deer wandering in the hills next to the campus, and plenty of other wildlife. In Los Angeles, that's something to write home about.

There are other things that attract parents and kids to the school, however. Start with the insane test scores, just about the highest in the city. Lots of artsy-fartsy over-the-top parent involvement. A special event every day. Chinese New Year, Jewish New Year, Lunar New Year, Mardi Gras—though you can forget Lent, it's no fun.

Aron's dad was way cool. He worked for the department of agriculture. One day he brought a pair of German shepherds to class.

"They are vedy intelligent dogs, you will see. Here I have four suitcases. You there, young man. I will take the dogs into the hall. Hide the avocado in one of the suitcases. Don't worry, they will be finding it."

The dogs immediately identified the suspicious suitcase. They also ripped open a couple of lunches that had avocados. One dog peed on the floor. The other went for the teacher's desk and started barking like crazy. The kids loved the show.

Our teacher, Mr. Ruskin, turned red and murmured something about an avocado. Mr. Patel coughed and said, "They don't bark like that for avocados. They bark like that for a certain herb. Probably left by another teacher. You are a vedy good teacher."

Unfortunately, Aron's mom was *not* so cool. When he entered fifth grade, she decided he should skip a few grades and go to college. No kidding. She pulled him out of school for a couple of months to tutor him for the entrance exam. I mean, Aron is smart, but he's not Stephen Hawking, so this was a pretty crazy idea.

Anyway, he managed to pass the test, so he wound up getting into college. His dad put up a fight, though. So Aron went to fifth grade in the morning and Los Angeles City College in the afternoon. And guess what? He said fifth grade was harder.

Aron was never the calmest kid in the world, but this put a lot more pressure on him. He didn't react well and started quivering and shaking all the time. He also didn't have much time to hang out anymore, but before he went home he liked to go shopping.

"Shopping" meant "shoplifting." Yes, Aron became a kleptomaniac. I stopped admiring any objects, because if I did, Aron would go out and steal them. Books, CDs, electronic gear, whatever. Knowing my affinity for cutlery, Aron shoplifted a cleaver by stuffing it down the front of his pants. That's a good way to lose the family jewels.

A standard stop was a liquor store where a lot of the kids bought candy, sodas, and Hot Cheetos. I always paid for anything I wanted, but Aron naturally didn't subscribe to that credo.

It was not easy for Aron to be surreptitious because his body-in-motion attracted attention. People tended to stare at him, trying to figure out if he had Tourette's or MS or juvenile Parkinson's or whatever. Sometimes Aron would just confront the surveillant, demanding, "What are you looking at? Didn't your parents teach you it's not polite to stare? Everywhere I go, people are watching me!" Making a scene would invariably shame everyone into giving him enough privacy to steal something.

The owner of the liquor store was an Indian man named Gurmeet. He took a special interest in Aron, which made it more challenging for him to loot. But the proprietor was pinned down at the counter, which gave Aron the edge. Carefully playing the mirrors and the cameras, he wafted through the store and often bagged things that he didn't even want. Then we'd meet up at the counter to check out. Obviously, Aron never bought anything, which was pretty suspicious in itself.

One day, Gurmeet finally said, "You are never buying anything."

"You don't have anything I can eat," said Aron.

"Nothing?"

"It's my diet. I'm a vegan. And unfortunately I don't like most vegetables. Do you have any bean sprouts?"

"No. I do not have bean sprouts."

"Yeah, that's what I thought. I don't know why more places don't carry bean sprouts."

"That is all you eat, bean sprouts?" Gurmeet was actually getting interested now.

"Pretty much. I used to eat chicken and fish, but you know, it just wasn't right. I mean, how do you draw the line? Beef? No. Chicken? Yes. Pigs? No. Fish? Yes."

"Lamb?" asked Gurmeet.

"No."

"Shrimp and crab?"

"Yes and yes."

"Kitty cat? Puppy dog?"

"Ha ha. No kidding, does it make sense to elevate one creature with a central nervous system over another?"

"No, young man. That is why I say, 'kitty cat, puppy dog.' I am making a point. If you eat other animals, why not eat kitty cat, puppy dog?"

"Man, you're on your way to veganism."

"You misunderstand. I like meat. I will eat everything. Even, maybe, kitty cat, puppy dog. Maybe human being."

"I think that's illegal," I said.

"Okay, well, maybe not. But I do not have rules."

"You're what's called an omnivore with cannibalistic tendencies," said Aron. "There aren't many of you around."

Eventually Aron got careless. We were standing in line with several other people, and Aron decided to bag something right in front of Gurmeet. Without blinking, Gurmeet reached under the counter and pulled out a giant revolver. He leveled it at Aron and said calmly, "Stick 'em up, young man."

Aron twitchingly complied, clearly even more nervous than usual. His eyes bugged out as he stared at the gun. "Careful with that blunderbuss, man. It's like from the Civil War."

Gurmeet snorted. "This is Colt forty-four magnum, the most powerful handgun in the world. It can blow your head clean off. So you have to ask yourself, are you feeling lucky today?"

"*What?*"

"*Dirty Harry*," said Gurmeet. "Vedy good movie."

"I'll add it to my Netflix queue," said Aron. "Can I put my hands down?"

"Yes. Take candy bar out of pocket before it melts."

Aron pulled a candy bar out of his pocket and put it on the counter.

"*Ummmmm*," said a little girl in an accusatory voice. "That's *stealing*."

"Mommy," her little brother asked. "Is the man gonna shoot him?"

"I don't think so," said the mother. "But when you take what isn't yours, bad things can happen."

"*Lady*," pleaded Aron.

"Sorry," she said. "It's a teachable moment." She looked at Gurmeet. "Why don't you put down the gun and call the police?"

"Good idea," he said, putting the gun under the counter and picking up the phone. "I'll let *them* shoot him."

"What if you were to call my father, instead?"

"You would like that, would you?"

"It would be better than the police."

"Okay." Gurmeet handed him the phone. "Call."

Aron dialed, waited, then shook his head. "Voice mail."

"What about Mommy?"

"Uh…I think I'd rather deal with the cops."

"*They* will call Mommy."

Aron put his head on the counter. "But you talk to her, okay?"

"Okay. Dial the number and I will talk."

Aron dialed without raising his head, then passed the phone to Gurmeet. The shopkeeper switched to another language, rattled off several sentences, then waited. He raised his eyebrows, then replied angrily. He nodded several times, said a last word, and hung up.

"She is vedy bad," he said somberly. "And her Hindi is not good at all."

"That's what Dad says," Aron agreed.

"Too bad we are not getting him," said Gurmeet. He looked

down at the candy bar on the counter. "Why do you take Snickers bar if you eat only bean sprouts?"

"I'm pushing myself to try new things."

We didn't have long to wait for Aron's mother. She screeched into the parking lot and gunned her SUV into a space labeled for a compact car. She slammed her door open, smashing it into the car parked next to her, then contorted her bulk to wriggle out of her vehicle. As she launched herself towards the liquor store, the owner got his first good look at her.

"Oh, my God," he murmured. Mrs. Patel was a very large woman. Dressed in a brightly colored sari, she wore a multitude of necklaces and bracelets that jingled like a Hare Krishna festival. Her hair streamed out behind in a flowing mass, and dark eyes blazed from beneath a protruding, sweat-beaded brow.

"I told you," murmured Aron, as his mother burst into the store. It was the last thing he would say for some time.

"What is the matter with you?" demanded his mother. "Who told you to come here? Who gave you permission? Why are you not at home studying, as your brother and sister? Stand still! What is the matter with you? Do you need an operation? Shall I take you to the hospital? They will cut off your feet. Stop moving around. What is the matter with you? This man says you are stealing. Are you stealing, or is he a liar?"

"I am not a liar," objected Gurmeet.

"I cannot take your word for this. A liar would say he is not a liar."

"Everyone saw."

Mrs. Patel turned to me. "What about you, Jupiter, did you see?"

"Uh, yeah…he took it." I gave an apologetic shrug to Aron, who nodded understandingly.

"Hmph. Some friend you are, Mercury. He is probably taking it for you."

"Yes, that is a possibility," commented Gurmeet helpfully. "It was a Snickers bar, which he does not eat."

"He does not eat a Snickers bar?"

"I am aware of his dietary restrictions. He is a vegetarian who does not like vegetables."

"What does he eat, then?"

"Well, you should know. Bean sprouts."

"*Bean sprouts*? You think my son eats nothing but *bean sprouts*?!"

"That is what he told me."

"You are a gullible man," said Mrs. Patel. "You remind me of my husband, who is a fool. He is always being taken advantage of. We go to buy a car. 'What is the price?' says my husband. 'Here is the price on the sticker,' says the salesman. 'Can you do better?' says my husband. 'No, I cannot. This is the most popular color. You are picking the color all people are wanting. For this color I must charge you the price on the sticker.' 'Vedy good,' says my gullible husband, who I should not have married. My mother told me that, but I did not listen, just as my children are not listening to me. My son has probably stolen half your store. *Bean sprouts*! Do you think a boy could get so fat on bean sprouts?"

"He is only plump…"

"He is a pig. But you give me an idea. For two weeks he will live on bean sprouts and water."

"*Two weeks*?" exclaimed Aron.

"Yes. Then you will not be a pig. And, perhaps, you will not be a thief. Also, you must not associate with Uranus. He is a bad influence."

"This wasn't Moon's idea."

"Pluto is beneath you, my child. You need to meet some nice college boys."

"They're ten years older than me…"

"Your son goes to college?" asked Gurmeet incredulously.

"Oh, yes. He is vedy intelligent. Of course, he does not get that from his father. Stand still! What is the matter with you! Stop moving around! We will go to Home Depot and get a chain saw. Don't worry, we will take care of this problem."

Chapter Thirty-Two
Mac

WHEN WE LEFT WONDERLAND I didn't see Aron as much. He skipped middle school and stuck with college, while I followed a more conventional academic path.

Which turned out to be pretty boring after Wonderland. I was on an honors track, so there were many bright kids in my classes, but the teachers often left something to be desired. I started to think maybe Aron's mom wasn't totally nuts to put him in college.

American history was particularly dreary—so boring that, in comparison, TV static was high-octane entertainment. The drone of Mr. Grogan's monotone was punctuated by students' occasional snores, real or simulated, which he ignored. However, his dullness was redeemed by his negligence, since he tacitly allowed all forms of cheating, which resulted in stellar GPAs for all but the most honest or oblivious students. The facts of life in Mr. Grogan's class were well known to us by the second week of class, and upon entering his room each day we all settled down to quietly endure fifty-four minutes of torpor.

I sat next to a skinny short kid named Solomon MacAndrew, who dressed in a uniform of flood pants and yellowed T-shirt. He had black wire rim glasses that ran in a cockeyed diagonal across his face, with masking tape connecting one of the temples to the frame front.

I had noticed that when Mr. Grogan started lecturing, this kid would begin rocking back and forth, mumbling under his breath. I thought he might be Asperger's and left him alone. But my curiosity got the better of me and I asked him what he was doing.

"Davening," he said. "Praying."

"You're praying?"

"That's what I said. You got a problem with it?"

"No. Just wondered."

"Well, now you know." His words were aggressive, but I didn't take it personally.

"I'm sorry to bother you."

"Apology accepted."

He kept davening and I tried to listen to Mr. Grogan's drone for a few minutes. But Mac's praying was much more interesting.

"If you're praying," I whispered, "does it mean that you believe in God?"

"Interesting question. Not particularly."

"What are you praying about?"

"For this consummate cretin to say one thing that's true."

I was quiet for a moment, shocked that he could be so disrespectful to authority. I hadn't really considered whether the history Mr. Grogan was teaching was accurate or not. My only goal was to learn the answers that he expected so that I could regurgitate them on the test.

"Lies," said Mac. Then, louder, "*More* lies." Other kids were starting to raise their heads off their desk and look at him, but Mr. Grogan was oblivious. It seemed that I had upset Mac's equilibrium. He got louder. "*Damn* lies!"

Now even Mr. Grogan heard. He blinked in confusion. "Excuse me?"

"Are you aware that virtually every word you have uttered for the last week has been either totally false, slightly inaccurate, or an error of omission?"

"Uh…no. That comes as something of a surprise to me."

"More's the pity," said Mac. Kids were rubbing sleep out of their eyes and waking up in a hurry.

Even Mr. Grogan seemed a bit refreshed by the turn of events. "Would you care to support your allegation?"

"Delighted. First let's examine the reasons you've stated for European exploration. Why did they feel the urgent need to go looking for Asia? Anybody?"

A kiss ass girl in the front row raised her hand.

"Yes, Jennifer, one reason," said Mac, playing the role of teacher to the hilt.

"Europe was becoming richer and the people had money to spend on luxuries."

"An accurate recitation of what Mr. Grogan has imparted. Patently false, however. Having endured waves of bubonic plague which killed at least a third of the population, Europe was suffering a severe labor shortage and was *not* prosperous."

"But that's what the book says," Mr. Grogan objected.

"You're familiar with the expression, 'Don't believe everything you read'?" asked Mac. "That should be our mantra for the textbook."

Another hand went up. "After the fall of Constantinople, the Turks closed the trade route to Asia."

"Another correctly incorrect statement," said Mac. "This was debunked almost a hundred years ago. In fact, the Turks had every reason to keep the trade route open, since they made money from it."

"But wasn't there a war between Spain and Turkey?" asked Mr. Grogan timidly.

"*That* is true. The Turks also fought with Portugal. So they may indeed have shut out those two European countries for a time," Mac admitted. Mr. Grogan smiled with the quiet self-satisfaction of an inferior student who has said something smart for a change.

"But the Turks were Islamic," pointed out another student. "Didn't they have a problem with all infidels?"

"Depends what you mean by a problem," said Mac. He got up and walked toward the front of the class. Mr. Grogan discretely retreated to his desk as Mac took center stage. "Perhaps you're thinking of the Crusades, which might have—*might have*—had some legitimate motivation at first. Once the Muslims took over the Holy Land, they came down on the Christian pilgrims and there *were* atrocities. But the Muslims realized which side their bread was buttered on and they stopped stirring things up. After all, Christian pilgrims were the tourist trade. Cha-ching."

"So why did we have the Crusades?" asked a big guy.

"I note your use of the word *we*," said Mac. "Apparently you identify with the Christians."

"I guess I do."

"It's good to be aware of your biases. Especially after you've watched lots of Hollywood flicks that demonize the towelheads as a bunch of terrorists, right?"

Jennifer sucked in her breath in shock and Mac looked at her pityingly. "That's a politically incorrect word," she said.

"Yes, it is, Jennifer. It's very derogatory. I use it for dramatic effect only. Please don't report me or I'll lose my teaching credential," Mac said. Several kids laughed. It was the most enthusiasm I'd seen in middle school apart from recess and lunch.

Mac continued his explanation. "Ironically, one of the main

causes of the Crusades—which were, remember, Christian missions to ostensibly free the Holy Lands—*was* terrorism. But the terrorists were the Christians. There were a lot of trained warriors in Europe with time on their hands, who spent it beating up and killing civilians. Remind you of anything?"

"Police brutality," I said.

"Bingo. Goons with guns equals violence. Of course, the Crusaders didn't have firearms. They used swords, battle axes, maces, ball-and-chains, that sort of thing. Crush 'em, stab 'em, kill 'em. So it seemed like a pretty good idea to have the military go terrorize the Middle East instead of Europe. Give the thugs an indulgence and let 'em go beat on someone else for a change."

"What's an indulgence?" I asked.

"It's a Catholic get-out-of-jail-free card. If you slid the church some money, or did them a favor, they'd give you a pass for whatever sins you had committed."

"That doesn't sound right," said Jennifer. "It's like you could buy your way into heaven."

"You and Martin Luther would have agreed on that, Jennifer. It was one of the main causes of the Protestant Reformation."

"So—and don't make fun of me, okay?" said Lori Boggs, a pretty girl with long blond hair.

"Then don't say anything stupid," snapped Mac.

"I don't *try* to say stupid things, they just come naturally," said Lori. Everyone laughed and she blushed.

"Fair enough. What's your point?"

"So you're saying the Muslims weren't, like, 'the bad guys'?"

"That *is* what I'm saying," said Mac. "You should be aware that in Spain the Moors allowed freedom of worship at the same time that the Catholics persecuted the Jews and Muslims. After all, it was the 'good guys' who brought us the Spanish Inquisition, an enlightened process to torture and, frequently, execute anyone whose Catholic faith was suspect. History is a great story, but it's not just about good guys and bad guys. People are more complex than that. So it's not all that easy to just take a side and root for them, like a football game."

It turned out that Mr. Grogan actually knew more than he'd been teaching. However, over the years, he'd developed a conviction that kids had no interest in historical accuracy—all they cared about was their grade. He'd given in to the same apathy that he'd assumed on the part of the students and taken the path of least resistance—the textbook.

Now, with Mac's cantankerous leadership, our class embarked on a journey down the road less traveled, which we hoped might lead to something like the truth. We determined to sift the evidence, reading first sources and alternative analyses of important events, to draw our own conclusions about what most likely had happened in the past.

Mac and I became friends. The rest of the class respected, admired, and even feared him, but they were not drawn to associate with him. Mac's every instinct led him to adopt idiosyncrasies that made him a social pariah. But none of his peculiarities were repellant to me.

Like Aron, Mac was very entertaining. He had a strong belief in genetics and traced his character and temperament to his ethnic roots. He preferred to be called "Mac," from his last name, MacAndrew. His mother was Jewish, and his father was Irish. Given this mix, he wound up in a lot of fights and invariably got his butt kicked.

"I figure I deserved it, anyway," he said. I was helping him pull himself together after he'd been knocked down by a couple of future members of the Aryan Nations.

"Why?" I asked, surprised that anyone would imagine they merited misfortune.

"Jewish guilt. I musta done something, right?"

"Yeah. Your face got in the way of Butthead's fist."

"Exactly."

I handed him back his glasses. When he put them on they were oddly straight across the bridge of his nose. I was about to say something, when he twisted them into their usual skewed position.

"There. Good as old," he said.

The broken glasses were not the only defective hardware in Mac's life. Even more egregious was his bike. In an age of designer mounts, he rode a creaking, rusting wreck. Then it got two flat tires that Mac "repaired" by filling them with sand.

I had the honor of assisting him in this unique procedure. "Let's see *that* leak out of there," he muttered, admiring his handiwork.

I contemplated the pathetic conveyance, its tires sagging like lumpy diapers carrying a full load. "Really great, Mac. You'll be a regular Lance Armstrong."

"Just watch. I'm gonna have legs like the Incredible Hulk from riding this thing," he said.

Witnessing Mac ride his tenth-of-a-speed bike was a study in determination, for both rider and spectator. This was one bike that didn't need any brakes: if Mac coasted, he'd wind up at a dead stop in a few feet—if he was going down a steep hill. It didn't need a saddle, either, since Mac had to stand on the pedals constantly just to keep the thing moving.

His body was under severe strain, and the stress found its most graphic expression north of his shoulders. Sweat streamed from his scalp and curly hair, cascaded in a torrent alongside his dripping nose, poured over angry pimpled cheeks. His neck contorted like a chicken with its head stretched for the death blow, fighting to evade the axe.

This enormous effort was in pathetic contrast to the results, since Mac's bike moved, on level ground, at about the pace of a brisk walk. There was simply no way to propel it up even a modest incline, let alone a genuine hill. Thankfully, these were abundant, and it was a relief to see Mac dismount and catch his breath as he pushed his bike up a slope.

After a couple of weeks of this, I dug through our garage for an old ten speed I didn't ride any more. I cleaned it up a little and gave it to Mac, along with a lock.

He greeted this gift with mixed emotions. Clearly touched, he also appeared somewhat insulted.

"What'll I do with *my* bike?"

"Perhaps it's time to retire it."

"Why?"

"Other conveyances make better use of the wheel."

"But it's unique. It stands apart from the common herd."

"Apart, and far *behind*."

Mac shrugged sadly. "Everyone needs a backup," I suggested.

Unfortunately, my words were far too prophetic. A week later we came out of school to find Mac's new bike rendered a crumpled wreck. Without even undoing the lock, one of his numerous tormenters had managed to lay the bike down and run it over several times.

Mac heaved a sigh, then looked at me. "You were right. It's good to have a backup."

He seemed oddly relieved to return to his old bike.

I figured that if anyone could help me make sense of Job's story of suffering at the hands of God it was my two friends, Mac and Aron. Macaroni.

Chapter Thirty-Three
Macaroni

"DOES THE NAME 'MRS. ROBINSON' mean anything to you?" asked Mac.

My horndog friends were plastered to Aron's iPhone, studying Mom's online profile, which I had stupidly mentioned to them.

"I hope you got the model equipped with a drool-guard," I said.

"This? Don't worry, I dropped it in a toilet and it's still working fine," said Aron, never looking up.

"Really?" Mac was impressed.

"No," said Aron. "You're awfully gullible for a Jew."

"That's the Irish. On the other hand, I'll beat the crap out of you if you try to take advantage of me, so it evens out."

Aron grunted. "You think Cougarlicious would go out with a college man?"

"Maybe," I said. "You know any?"

"Seriously. Your mom getting action off this ad?"

"Major. Take one out for yours. It makes a great Mother's Day present."

"You could call her *Curry*-licious," said Mac.

"Oh, man, if *my* parents ever got divorced…" Aron moaned softly. "*Now* I'm feeling your pain."

"It's about time," I said.

"As a Jew, I always feel pain, some of which may, or may not, be *yours*," said Mac.

"Dude, I may, or may not, appreciate that," I said. "Let's get some pizza."

"Absolutely," said Mac. He looked at Aron. "Will pepperoni offend your cow-loving sensibilities?"

"Despite rumors to the contrary, I have *never* loved a cow. How about a little *pork* sausage on there? That okay?"

"The more pig the better. Fat back, chitterlings, go whole hog, won't bother me."

All triangles have a dynamic. Ours was marked by considerable competitive bickering between Aron and Mac.

The waitress approached and I ordered. "One extra large with everything. No anchovies. Three Cokes."

"You're paying, right?" asked Mac, who never had any money.

"Moon's rich from his little tutoring job," said Aron. "Or, *was* rich, but I guess Cougarlicious threw a wrench into the gravy train…"

"Jasmine's not online, is she?" asked Mac. "I'd love to see her. Purely vicarious, you know."

"Not online, but I do have pictures." I pulled out my phone, set up the gallery, then tossed it to Mac. He and Aron bent over the tiny screen hungrily.

"Sweet Jesus, who I don't believe in," Mac groaned appreciatively. "Slow down, man, this is something to savior—I mean, *savor*."

"You don't get out much, do you?" said Aron. "But this *is* impressive. Sorry, Mrs. Robinson, youth trumps plastic surgery." He looked up, suddenly serious. "You had something going with this girl?"

"Not really. I was just teaching her math."

"Please. You were her algebra gigolo," Mac frothed. "She paid you to stroke her equations."

"Ummm," said Aron. "I'd say her breasts have a very positive slope."

"Nothing negative about the rest of her, either," said Mac, grabbing the phone. "Enquiring minds want to know, Moon, did you get into her variables?"

"That will remain an unknown," I said.

Mac tossed my phone back. "No wonder you've got a bone to pick with God, but I think you're barking up the wrong burning bush. It's no deity's fault that your mom's a piece of work—no offense."

"None taken."

"Have you considered the possibility that this is your karma?" asked Aron. "Some Hindus believe that children actually *pick* their parents—and vice versa."

I made a sick face. "Do you believe that stuff?"

"No. But *you* can, if you want. Another spin is that you're paying for the sins of a past life."

"I don't remember committing them. Doing time for unknown crimes doesn't make sense to me. I'm not buying it."

"So thumbs down for the principle of reincarnation?" asked Mac, gesturing.

"I'm out," agreed Aron, thumb down. "It's too 'blame-the-victim' for me."

"Me, too," I gestured. "No metaphysics that offend my sense of justice."

"Hear, hear," said Mac. "If I were to believe in God—which is very doubtful—I would create him in *my* image, not vice versa."

"A scary thought," said Aron. "But I agree in principle."

"This puts us totally out of step with the religious left, right, and center. They relish the opportunity to worship at the altar of unreason," said Mac.

"Faith *is* belief without reason," I said.

Mac looked at me more seriously. "You said you wanted to talk about Job."

"I do."

"Old Testament. Right up my alley," said Mac.

The pizza arrived and we momentarily busied ourselves with serving out slices.

"There's something about that I'd like to know," said Aron. "Is there any connection between the words 'Job' and 'job,' or is that just a linguistic coincidence?"

I spit up my Coke, but Mac didn't miss a beat. "Biblical scholars have argued about that for years, and ultimately they've agreed that it's a really stupid question, Aron."

"It's a relief to know they figured it out. My dad explained it to me different. One day he looked kinda depressed as he headed out to work and I asked him about it. He shrugged and he told me, 'That's why they call it a *job*, not a *blow*job.'"

This time Mac spit up *his* Coke.

"So about that Job..." I persisted.

"Oh, yeah," said Mac, mopping Coke off his face, "God 1.0. Lotta bugs in that version. Major hard-ass. Tended to overreact, like a giant killer bee. Got slightly miffed at Moses and let him wander in the desert for forty years."

"Yeah, but that's on Moses. He coulda asked for directions," said Aron. "Moon, aren't you taking this too seriously? It's just a story."

"That hundreds of millions of people consider to be God's word, upon which they base their life, their laws, and their politics," I retorted.

"No," said Aron.

"No?"

"People *say* they do, but the vast majority *don't*. They treat the whole religious deal like going out to dinner. They, or more likely their parents, pick the particular buffet at which to worship. Once inside, they walk around with their plate. I'll take a little of this, a little of that, go very light on commandments, thanks; load up on consolation, God's love, hope for a good afterlife, reinforce my prejudices…"

Mac regarded Aron thoughtfully. "I only have one problem with your analogy. My family takes buffets very seriously, and we would *never* compare them to something as mundane as religion."

"You know, that Old Testament God is not what most people would consider a model authority figure," said Aron.

Mac added, "He says so Himself. He's a *jealous* god, He's an *angry* god."

"He's got issues," I said.

"Big time," said Aron. "He's working his shit out. Sorta like, if I may, your mom."

"Another authority figure," said Mac, "who you can submit to out of fear or respect, but you can't exactly trust."

"So…you think my problem with God is mostly a problem with my mom?" I asked.

My friends regarded me with wordless pity. I looked back at them, stunned by the obvious truth of what they were saying.

Chapter Thirty-Four
Hot Links

IN THE LAST BLISTERING DAYS of August, Moss, Dad, Mr. Smith, and I were getting set to tee off at a public course out in Camarillo Springs. After my pizza therapy session with Macaroni, I had decided to see what I could do to end Mom's reign of terror.

All summer she had been telling us Mr. Smith was out of town, and thus unavailable to monitor our visits with Dad. I had found it odd, since the summer is usually a busy time for realtors. Finally, realizing I had Mr. Smith's phone number on my cell, I just called him myself.

There was dead silence on the phone when I explained this to Mr. Smith. He cleared his throat and said quietly, "Moon, I have been here all summer. What's more, I'm sorry to say that I've run into your mother at two events, and she's not mentioned a word of this to me."

Now it was my turn to search for words. I decided to avoid the subject of my mother's bald-faced lies and work towards my actual goal of seeing my father. "So you don't know the situation with my parents?"

"Apparently not. You say your mother is preventing you from spending time with your father?"

I briefly explained. "Well," said Mr. Smith, "I'm terribly sorry that you and your brother are the victims of forces beyond your control. Though I have always appreciated the wisdom of Falstaff's admonition that discretion is the better part of valor, I personally find it hard to live up to."

"Uh, Mr. Smith, you lost me there."

He chuckled. "What I mean to say is, I'd be glad to help. Did you have a particular get together in mind?"

"Kind of. Do you play golf?"

"Love the game! Though my affection is not always requited."

"Whose *is*?"

"Just so! It's an inspired idea, Moon. A foursome might be the least unnatural way to do this peculiar thing."

As we took practice swings, I became wrapped in a daydream about what would have happened if Job had been a golfer and the devil had gone after his game. Naturally, with all his good fortune, Job would have been a scratch player; that would give him a long way to fall.

Probably the first thing the devil would do is give him a wicked slice. I've got one myself, so I could imagine Job's sick feeling as he watched a promising tee shot execute a large, inexorable turn to the right and sail out of bounds. That'd have Job playing his second shot—if he could find his ball—from behind trees on another fairway. Limbs and leaves have a way of finding your ball no matter what you do. More wasted strokes, more frustration.

Then Job'd top his fairway wood, shank his long irons, and finally catch a wedge and send the ball over the green, maybe into a bunker. Once in the sand, I could imagine him hacking away in a perpetual cloud of dust, with the promised land of the green just a few impossible yards away.

Job might not curse God, but he'd curse his clubs. I've seen plenty of guys throw their sticks, and a few break them. One guy actually tried to strangle his driver. Apparently it was fighting for its life, since he tussled with it on the ground, panting and gasping—*him*, not the driver—as the rest of us looked on in amazement, trying not to laugh. Finally the guy declared, "There!" with some satisfaction, and stuffed the club's corpse back in his bag.

On another round I saw a guy come unhinged much more quietly. His putting had been rotten all day, but he'd suffered in silence, never letting on how much it was torturing him. Out in the parking lot, though, he pulled the putter out of his bag, threw the rest of the clubs in the trunk, then methodically tied the bad club to a length of rope he attached to his bumper. Then he tossed the tethered putter on the ground. He saw me watching and stated matter-of-factly, "No way that son-of-a-bitch is riding in the car."

He jumped into the driver's seat, ran over the club as he backed out, then gunned the car forward. The putter followed with an abrupt jerk, hopping over the parking lot pavement. The man took the exit to the street very fast, the putter swinging wide on its rope, like a wild water skier whipped hard by a turning speedboat. It smashed into the stop sign the golfer had just ignored; but the rope was stout, the knot held, and the club went airborne. The golfer pulled up short in traffic. Flying high, the club descended blade-first in an elegant parabola and smashed through his rear windshield. Evidently that putter had more than one way of inflicting pain on its owner.

I was thinking about what the devil might do to the rest of Job's psyche, when I realized I was up. Since the others had all hit good drives, the pressure was on me to hold my own. After waggling my way through what felt like several self-conscious minutes, I finally gave up any hope of feeling comfortable, and just swung the club. My initial relief that I had outwitted my habitual slice and hit the ball straight was replaced by chagrin that I was at least thirty yards shy of the shortest ball, which was Mr. Smith's. There were murmurs of "That'll play," and we were off to the carts.

We'd decided that Moss would ride with Dad on the front nine, and I'd ride with him on the back nine, so I jumped in with Mr. Smith. He quickly drove to my ball, which was the farthest from the green. I got off the cart and considered my choice for a moment. The distance from the green warranted a fairway wood, but I grabbed my hybrid four. A hybrid has a shorter shaft than a wood, which makes it easier to swing; but it has a fatter head than an iron, which makes it easier to get solid contact. All things considered, it's my favorite club, and I reach for it most of the time.

The hybrid didn't let me down. I hit it good, about forty yards short of the green.

Mr. Smith grinned at me when I jumped back in the cart. "Like that hybrid, do you?"

"It likes *me*."

He nodded understandingly. "*I'm* terribly fond of my seven iron. Nevertheless, I seldom use it more than twice a hole." I laughed, since hitting a seven iron twice on a hole would mean you pretty much screwed everything up.

We pulled up at Mr. Smith's ball. "Unfortunately, this calls for a bit more clout than the seven. You're good with maths…what's seven minus two?"

"Five?"

"Sounds about right," said Mr. Smith, smiling, as he pulled out his five iron. A quick practice swing, and he put his shot on the green about thirty yards from the pin. He gave the head of his club a quick kiss. "Keep that up, and we'll make the old seven jealous, won't we?"

Mr. Smith kept things light like this for several holes, and I began to relax and enjoy myself. Truth is, I hadn't known exactly how this plan was going to work, and I felt responsible for facilitating everything, since it was my idea. But Mr. Smith was a lot better at social lubrication, and I was glad to let him take over.

Dad rolled in a long, breaking putt on the fourth. Moss and I cheered and Mr. Smith whistled. "Nice read, I'd say!"

Dad shrugged, smiling. "Better with greens than books."

"Wish I could say the same," said Mr. Smith.

Dad hit a monster drive off the next tee. Moss and I grinned at each other. "He's warming up," said Moss.

"Little bit."

Dad and Moss pulled out first in their cart. Mr. Smith started up, then abruptly stopped and stared at me. "Your father is quite a golfer."

"Wait'll the back nine," I said. "He always plays the second half four or five strokes better."

Mr. Smith lifted his eyebrows. "Does he have a handicap?"

"I guess that'd be drinking."

"I mean—"

"Just kidding," I said. "I don't really know. I don't think he takes it that seriously, though."

"Amazing," murmured Mr. Smith, stepping on the gas. "If I could hit a ball like that, you'd have to pry me off the course."

"Yeah, me too. Moss is like Dad. They take their athletic ability for granted."

"Must be nice."

As we played the hole I filled Mr. Smith in on Moss's skateboarding triumph and his upcoming competition. "You mean to say that if your brother wins this tournament he will become a professional skateboarder? At his age?"

"Well, he wouldn't *have* to, but that's usually how it goes."

"What do you think his chances are?"

"Pretty fair," I said, and explained my thinking. There were nine regional qualifying events, which meant a total of twenty-seven contestants in the finals. The results of each qualifying tournament had been posted at the Free Flow website, so it wasn't hard for me to get the names of the other finals competitors and actually do a little online research. There was YouTube footage of most of them, in addition to the video coverage of the qualifying competition, so I was able to watch almost all of them skate.

They were certainly a lot better than Boosh and Wee Wee, and Moss's other skating companions. But I didn't see them do anything Moss couldn't do. Of course, anything could happen in a competition, but I figured there were only a few skaters who were really going to be in the same league as my brother.

"What does *he* think about it?" asked Mr. Smith.

"We don't talk about it."

"Superstitious or nervous?"

"He's neither, but I'm *both*."

"What's your mother think?"

"Uh…"

Mr. Smith looked at me. "She doesn't know." I shook my head. "How can that be?"

"She's been preoccupied."

"Nevertheless, this is her son. Don't you think you should tell her?"

I shrugged. "Hard to say how she'll react. I don't want to screw up anything for Moss."

After the ninth hole, Moss and I switched our bags and I rode with Dad. At first I felt a little awkward; I hadn't seen him for a couple of months, and I was worried about him. I kind of didn't know what to say. But then my dreaded slice reappeared, and that gave us something to talk about.

I was pretty dejected after playing through a couple of miserable holes. Fortunately, my awful play didn't seem to be dragging Dad down: he birdied one hole, and parred the other.

Golfers are circumspect about offering advice, even to their own sons. Dad volunteered nothing, so it was up to me to make the first move. As we rode to the next hole, I asked, "What do you think, Dad?"

He shrugged. "Figure it out."

"I can't."

"Everybody's game goes south. Good golfer's gotta be his own swing doctor."

"How, Dad?"

"Same way you figure out a math problem. If you can teach Jasmine algebra, you can fix your slice."

"Did you read that in *Golf Digest*?"

Dad ignored my sarcasm and laughed. "I'll get you started. What causes a slice?"

"Club face not square at impact," I said mechanically. "Or cutting across the ball from right to left."

"Good. What can cause that?"

"About a million things."

"Too many to consider. Simplify."

"Setup. Backswing. Downswing."

"Okay. What do you think?"

"I *think*—" I started, ready to express my frustration. But somehow Dad's coaching *had* started me thinking. "I think my setup is okay," I said more calmly. "But I think I'm stiffening-up and not releasing my wrists through the shot. I'm blocking through the ball, instead of swinging, and the face isn't closing."

Dad nodded thoughtfully. "Could be. Make an adjustment."

I set up carefully on the next tee, taking pains to square my feet and shoulders to the target. I started the club back, turning my hips and shoulders and allowing them to pull my arms and hands through the backswing. At the top, I felt my wrists cock in response to the weight of the dangling club head—my favorite part of the backswing, since it feels powerful and fully charged. As I began my downswing I concentrated on keeping my head still and my left shoulder and chest square to the ball, and my hands somewhat relaxed. And as the club passed my right leg, I felt my wrists begin to snap just before the club face contacted the ball.

I raised my head hopefully. Even the worst slice starts out looking good, so the verdict wasn't in for a few seconds. But the shot stayed dead straight, and I couldn't help grinning. I looked at Dad, who gave me a wink and tapped his head, as if to say, "File for future reference."

As we rode to the next shot, I said, "Thanks, Dad."

"You figured it out yourself."

"That's what I'm thanking you for."

Dad laughed, and threw his free arm around my shoulders. "I've missed you boys."

"We've missed you, too."

I guess we both choked-up, since neither of us said anything for a while. Then Dad turned the conversation to other things and we just enjoyed the morning, hitting balls, riding around, and being together.

It should have been no big deal, but thanks to Mom's meddling, it was. Then again, I realized I had taken something for granted that really *was* pretty special. If we could ever get this mess straightened-out, I'd have to try not to do that.

We finished our round and Dad shook hands with Mr. Smith. "Seymour, you've done us a big favor, and I'm grateful," he said.

"Not at all," said Mr. Smith. "Lunch?"

"Well," said Dad thoughtfully, "would you consider doing us *another* favor?"

Dad explained and Mr. Smith smiled. "If only all wishes were so easily granted, I'd be a magic genie."

When the four of us walked into Fanatics the servers on duty shrieked with delight. I was disappointed that Jasmine wasn't there, but the waitresses who were gave us plenty of love. After hugs all around, Beth grabbed my right arm and Helen grabbed my left, and they both tried to drag me to their section. It looked like a tug of war over a stuffed animal, and I have to say I enjoyed being the teddy bear.

"Better flip for it before you tear him in half," said Dad. Beth lost, and Dad slipped her a twenty as we headed for Helen's section.

At Dad's urging, Mr. Smith ordered a ribeye, medium rare, with a beer. To our surprise, Dad got iced tea.

"No brew, Dad?" said Moss.

"Been on the wagon for a couple months," said Dad.

"You're not drinking?" I was having trouble processing this news.

Dad shook his head. "Seemed like it had something to do with…the situation. So…" He shrugged. "To be honest, it hasn't been a big deal."

Moss and I looked at each other. *We* thought it was a big deal. "Even after a round of golf on a hot day?" I asked. We knew that had always been prime time for a cold one.

Dad winced comically, and we laughed.

"Do you feel like a new man, or anything?" asked Moss.

"I can't say I do," Dad laughed, a little embarrassed. "But I have lost a few pounds, and that feels better. Easier on the knees."

Mr. Smith's eyes widened after the first bite of his steak, and he declared, "I know where *I'm* going to be watching the playoffs."

"Glad you like it," said Dad, pleased.

"Have you been here long?"

"Eleven years."

"Really? Good lease?"

"The best," said Dad. "I own it."

Mr. Smith carefully put down his fork. "You own this building?"

Moss and I watched with interest, not entirely understanding what was going on, but knowing from Mr. Smith's reaction that it was important.

Dad nodded. "Bought it early on, before real estate shot up. Janice got the house, I got this."

"Mortgage?"

Dad held his thumb and forefinger close together.

"Wise decision, David," said Mr. Smith. Then realizing that Moss and I were paying a bit too much attention, he abruptly changed the subject.

Chapter Thirty-Five
Joseph Kony 2012

OUR FIRST MONITORED VISIT with Dad was more successful than I'd ever thought it would be. Both Moss and I really liked Mr. Smith, and we were glad that Dad did, too. It probably helped that when Dad hesitantly inquired about Mr. Smith's relationship with Mom we could honestly answer that they really were "just friends."

Employing the services of Mr. Smith as an escort was not a long-term solution, but it was a first step in breaking Mom's embargo on Dad. Moss and I felt as triumphant as if we'd just dressed up as Indians and pulled off the Boston Tea Party. We could only hope that King Mom would not overreact and send in the redcoats.

When she found out about our golf game she wasn't happy, but she had agreed to the plan in the first place, so she could hardly go ballistic. For our part, Moss and I decided it was probably better, both for Mr. Smith and for us, not to tell her we knew he'd been in town all summer. Admitting she was wrong was not among my mother's virtues. Even so, it was entirely possible she might find some new way to rein in the rebels.

Before I could stew on this, my life took another turn for the weird as I embarked on the adolescent rite of passage known as "public high school." Going to middle school had been a bit of a shock; ascending the next link on the food chain was bizarre.

The first thing that struck me was the incredibly organized and premeditated cliquishness of the campus. We'd had a bunch of little groups in middle school and a few clubs, too. But the choices in high school were mind-boggling. In just one summer, three basic flavors had evolved into the panoply of frozen offerings from Ben & Jerry's.

Apparently the administrators were afraid that any kid who didn't have a little group of pals might either kill himself or everyone else. Hence, we were all required to officially join one of more than eighty sects. There were clubs that catered to academics, such as the Math Club, Chess Club, Robotics, French Club, Spanish Club, Mandarin Chinese Club. Do-gooders had lots to choose from, including American Red Cross, Because I Care, Breast Cancer Awareness, Children's Cancer Society, Feeding America, and a bunch of others that were even more depressing. On the lighter side, there were plenty of choices for active people—Cycling Club, Equestrian Club, Tennis Club, Golf Club, Guitar Club, Passion for Dance. There was even a Sandwich Club, where I suspect they ate club sandwiches. Naturally the Christians had 34,000 groups, but I didn't see a single club that catered to atheists, let alone, anti-theists. Outta luck there.

I've always had trouble making up my mind when there are too many choices, especially when none of them sound particularly appetizing. I'm not much of a joiner. On a whim, I opted to tail a pretty girl to see where she'd end up for the designated "Club Meeting" period. "Hey—I'm in Detective Club," I thought to myself.

Trying to be sleuthy, I walked behind at what I hoped was a discrete distance, appreciating the swing of her hips and her short brown hair. She entered a bungalow and I snuck in like a shadow.

Uh-oh—lost her. I peeked in the first open door and I made her.

She made me, too. "Come in!" she exclaimed. "Greetings! Welcome!" She had a slight overbite that looked really cute, along with her bangs and librarian glasses, so I took a few steps inside.

"Thanks," I said. "Uh…welcome to *what?*"

"You've come to the first meeting of the Invisible Children of Uganda Club. I'm the president. Sarah Nellis." She stuck out her hand and we shook, smiling at each other. She had a sudden thought and her hand went limp. "You *did* mean to come here, didn't you?"

"Uh, yeah," I improvised, "if you're the president."

Rather than being flattered, she was annoyed. "This is a serious club. What's your name?"

"Moon Landing." She frowned at me, so I added, "*Seriously.*"

She thought for a moment, and said, "Are you Moss Landing's brother?" I nodded, and she shook her head, as if to say it wouldn't do.

"He got the athletic genes, and I got the serious genes," I explained. "And I'm wearin' 'em." I tugged on my pants for emphasis.

She snorted. "See, you're joking. Do you know the first thing about the Invisible Children of Uganda?"

I shook my head apologetically. "I'm an empty vessel for you to fill, Sarah."

She frowned at me again. "Are you a freshman? 'Cause you don't talk like a freshman."

"I'm as surprised about that as you are." Which was true. I guess the tutoring sessions with Jasmine had made me feel comfortable to actually do a little flirting. And it wasn't so hard. "Uganda's in Africa, right? Idi Amin country?"

"He's been dead since 2003."

"I think I did hear something about that. You want to tell me about the Invisible Children and I'll be quiet?"

"First of all, they're not literally invisible. If you're looking for something like that, you'd better head for the Comic Book Club," she said with a sniff, daring me to leave.

"Nothing against the X-men, but I'm staying here." I made a show of getting as comfortable as a human could in a school chair. "In what way *are* they invisible?"

"They are invisible because the world is not aware of their suffering," she continued, sounding like a professor. "Since 1987 a despicable military leader named Joseph Kony has kidnapped more than 30,000 children, given them training and weapons, and used them as an army to terrorize small communities throughout central Africa. Usually the first thing he has them do is kill their parents. He prefers that they chop their mother and father to death with a machete since it seems more 'personal' than just shooting them."

"That's twenty-five years," I said. Sarah nodded. "And nobody's stopped him?"

She shook her head. "But *we* will." I raised my eyebrows, and she continued. "Not *just* you and me. I want you to watch this."

I noticed she had an open laptop hooked to some external speakers. She clicked on an icon and a video called *Kony 2012* began to play.

It was a very slick, highly-produced piece of work. It told the story of a young man named Jason Russell and his friendship with a Ugandan boy named Jacob, who was one of the children abducted by Joseph Kony. I guess Jason Russell had the habit of capturing his life on video, because the film dramatically included footage of a promise Jason made to young Jacob that he would do everything in his power to stop the atrocities.

Unlike most of us, Jason took his promises seriously. "Everything possible" became his life's work for the next nine years, as he tried and failed to enlist the support of American politicians to intervene in the conflict. Republicans and Democrats alike explained the cynical truth: that if the United States' economic interests weren't directly involved, military forces weren't going to be committed to save the lives of strangers in a foreign country.

That's where Jason got creative. The rise of social media made it possible to build enormous human coalitions across states, nations, and continents, and he resolved to make Joseph Kony famous—or rather, *infamous*. He believed that if the public mobilized and made repeated demonstrations of outrage, governments would have no choice but to act. The movie claimed the strategy was starting to work—the Obama administration had finally committed a hundred military advisors to assist the Ugandan military in pursuit of Kony. However, he still had not been caught, and Kony's troops continued to rape, kidnap, loot, terrorize, and murder.

"Why are Kony's kids called the 'Lord's Resistance Army'?" I asked suspiciously. "Is this some kind of religious movement?"

"Kony claims to be a prophet, and says his goal is to create a society based on the Ten Commandments," said Sarah. "However, he seems to break most of them every day, especially 'Thou shalt not kill.'"

I shook my head disgustedly. "You'd think legitimate Christian groups would be offended by someone who commits such horrific acts under the pretense of religion."

"No comment."

"From *you*, or from *them*?"

"From me. I don't know about them."

"Well, count me in. What do we do now?"

"For a start, we get T-shirts. I hope you like red."

"Oh, I do," I said. "Especially on *you*."

She snorted and blushed. "Big talker. You have a credit card?"

"No...."

"Neither do I," she admitted. "But my mom gave me her number. You have twenty-five bucks?"

"Stiff for a T-shirt. Are you getting a cut?"

"*No*. It all goes to the cause. Can you afford it?"

"Sure. I'll give it to you tomorrow."

She looked up from the computer. "You better. What size?"

"Have they got an extra extra large?"

She looked up again and measured me with her eyes. "Large'll do."

"If you already knew, why'd you ask?"

"Bad habit."

A bell rang announcing the end of "Club Time." I hefted my backpack. "So I'll meet you for lunch tomorrow," I said. Sarah looked up, surprised. "You know, to give you the money."

She nodded dully. "Are you *sure* you're a freshman?"

"Cafeteria. Twelve thirty." She nodded again and I headed for the door. "I don't know, Sarah. Maybe I'm a senior."

"No, you're not."

"I might be," I yelled. "I forget."

"You're *not*."

I smiled to myself as I walked to geometry, thinking about Sarah; about Joseph Kony; and about a man who made a promise to a boy, then spent his life living up to it.

Chapter Thirty-Six
Esutbo

IN MIDDLE SCHOOL, no matter how dumb, lazy, or absent you are, you move forward. No one fails, no one repeats. It's like prison: you do your time and you get released. It's absurd to have a culmination from middle school. If you've got a pulse, you get a diploma. If you don't have a pulse, you get a death certificate.

High school is another matter, which comes as a shock to many students. You actually have to pass classes and accumulate units to progress through the system. At the end of their first year in high school, many students are surprised to find out they're still freshmen, since they failed so many classes they didn't achieve sophomore status. High school teachers don't go out of their way to let students in on the change in the academic game rules. They mention it in passing, sort of under their breath. I guess they love the look of amazement in the eyes of kids who never turned in a homework assignment and figured they'd get away with it. Mom says that's what they refer to as "non-monetary compensation." Teacher humor. It's not for everyone.

I worked my way through middle school and took the academic

demands of high school in stride. However, many others were not so fortunate, particularly when it came to math classes.

There were quite a few upperclassmen in my geometry class. Boosh and Wee Wee were among them. They had failed algebra, passed it in summer school (a joke), then failed geometry. Due to the latest budget crisis, there was no summer school make-up option, and they were back for a second dose. Thanks to Moss, they became new clients for my tutoring service.

Though not nearly as cute as Jasmine, they actually had plenty of mathematical ability, which school had never managed to tap. Skateboarders have a working knowledge of geometry, and they just need a little help to translate it into formal mathematical terms. Mainly I scraped away academic jargon so they could apply what they already knew.

Our first session started with a review of angles.

"Why's it called a three-sixty?" I asked.

Boosh shrugged. "It's two one-eighties."

"Yeah, that adds up," agreed Wee Wee.

I tried another tack. "Then why's it called a one-eighty?"

Boosh grinned. "'Cause it's half a three-sixty."

I raised my eyes in defeat. Wee Wee came to my rescue. "I have a feeling you want to tell us something."

I nodded. "It goes back to the Babylonians."

"The Baby-*who*?" said Boosh.

"Ancient civilization—very advanced in astronomy. They were the first to peg the measure of a circle at three hundred sixty degrees."

"You're saying it's called a three-sixty because the board makes a full circle," concluded Wee Wee. I nodded. "Why'd they pick that number? It's kinda off-the-wall."

"They were primarily farmers. So the most important circle in their life was the one the earth makes around the sun, which determines the seasons. And that circle takes approximately—"

Boosh jumped in, pressing an imaginary buzzer. "Bzzzzzt! Three hundred sixty-five days. So why doesn't a circle have three hundred sixty-five degrees?"

I began to think there was hope for both of them. "Their number system was different from ours. It was based on sixty, and three hundred sixty is six times sixty. It's also a great number to work with—you can divide it by two, three, four, five, six, eight, nine, ten, twelve—a lot of numbers."

The two skateboarders were looking at me with surprised interest. Boosh was particularly delighted. "That's a rad once-upon-a-time, bro. Is that shit for reals?"

"I think so."

"Screw the fact check," said Wee Wee. "It's a good story."

"Affirmative. Dr. Boosh prescribes one of those to start each tutoring session, and the patients," —he indicated Wee Wee and himself—"will recover."

"I'll see what I can do…"

"Try those medical marijuana places," said Wee Wee. "I believe they have them in stock."

I thought for a moment, then picked up two pens. I held them up to form a small angle. "Once upon a time a baby angle was born. Babies are cute, so it was called an…"

"Acute angle," they both answered.

I continued to rotate a pen to make the angle larger. "But it kept growing to become a…"

"Right angle!"

"Which measures…"

"Ninety degrees!"

"So an acute angle is what, greater or less than ninety?"

"Less!"

"But it keeps growing to become an…

"Obtuse angle!"

"Which is what, greater or less than ninety?"

"Greater!

"But less than a straight angle, which measures…

"One-eighty! There it is! Half a three-sixty! Boo-yah!" yelled Boosh.

It's tough to find a student who doesn't like school when he knows the right answers, and Boosh and Wee Wee were no exceptions. Pushing my luck, I picked up a protractor. Boosh cringed and comically hid behind Wee Wee.

"Little problem with the protractor?"

"Hate 'em. Like bloodsuckers hate the cross, Superman hates kryptonite, pappy hates taxes."

"Well, you've lumped this guy in with some bad company, and he doesn't deserve it. This here's a simple tool for measuring angles," I said mildly. "Just put the little X-marks-the-spot on the vertex of the angle."

"*Vertex*? There you go again."

"It's just the 'point,' dude. Chill," said Wee Wee.

"Then line up the zero on one of the rays, and see what number the other one goes through."

"That's where I bing-bizzle," sighed Boosh. "Is that sucker thirty degrees or a hundred fifty degrees? It says both."

"Is it an acute angle or an obtuse angle?"

"A cute little angle," said Boosh.

"Which is what, greater or less than ninety degrees?"

"Less," said Wee Wee. "So you're saying it has to be the thirty?"

I nodded. Boosh was grinning broadly. "I *get* it. Four down, on the bolts. But what's the one-fifty there for, just to mess with you?

"It's actually pretty useful. Sometimes you run across an angle that's looking backwards…" I drew a large obtuse angle with a vertex on the right and a horizontal ray that extended to the left. "Then you use the other zero mark."

"Get down, it's riding fakie," said Wee Wee.

"That's an *esutbo* angle," said Boosh.

"*Esutbo?*" I asked. "I don't know that term."

"That's 'obtuse,' spelled backwards," said Boosh. He and Wee Wee grinned at each other delightedly.

"Even *you* learned something today, Moon," said Wee Wee.

Boosh nodded seriously. "Perhaps *you* should be paying *us*. Ever think of that?"

Chapter Thirty-Seven
Trashed

SARAH AND I WERE wrapping up the fourth meeting of the Invisible Children of Uganda Club. We continued to be the sole members of the group; neither of us had made any effort to recruit reinforcements, instead enjoying the chance to get to know each other on the school's dime. I was beginning to think Club Time was a pretty great idea.

Sarah was a sophomore, only a year older than me, so I seemed to be ratcheting-down my attraction to older women. It turned out she was pretty good at math, so I couldn't play the tutoring card. Seems I didn't have to. Being myself was good enough.

That, and my appreciation for Sarah's quirky, intense intelligence. Her father was a corporate lawyer and her mother did legal work for the unions—or, as Sarah put it, "Dad works for the Man and Mom works for the People." This led to many heated discussions at their house, so Sarah was prone to be argumentative herself. Sometimes I'd play devil's advocate just to keep her on her toes.

At the moment, however, I was debating the finer points of the Invisible Children of Uganda by sticking my tongue into Sarah's mouth. She didn't seem at all offended, however, since she responded in kind. She pulled back abruptly, gasping for air, her glasses fogged with my breath.

"Some people breathe through their nose when they're kissing," I pointed out.

"I keep forgetting," she said. Oddly, I had more experience at this sort of thing than Sarah did.

"If you lose consciousness, I'll start CPR."

Sarah had a lot of different laughs, but my favorite was her nerdy snort, which she often employed as a form of punctuation, followed by a rejoinder. "No need—my autonomic nervous system will kick in and I'll breathe on my own."

"Rats. I thought it would be another excuse to kiss you."

"You don't need an excuse, Moon." Sarah looked at me very directly. "Do you have a girlfriend?"

"Uh…" I should have just said "no," but I hesitated, thinking of Jasmine, who I hadn't seen for months. "Not exactly." Sarah raised her eyebrows inquisitively. "It's complicated, I guess."

"Really. Unfinished business at fifteen?"

I grinned and shrugged awkwardly, wondering how to explain the situation. Even with my newfound confidence, dealing with girls seemed to require a far better sense of balance than I possessed. I hoped my learning curve with women would be less steep than it had been with unicycling, but I kind of doubted it.

I caught a break when the bell rang and we both had to hustle to our next class. I headed for geometry, cutting through a seldom-used passage that took me past the parking lot. Moss and his buddies were there meeting with the rest of the Skateboard Club, ollieing up and down the staircases. I hollered at Boosh and Wee Wee to get their butts to geometry class, then cut past the gym.

There was a knot of big guys wearing letter jackets clustered in front, probably the remnants of the Football Club. I hate to stereotype, but their smirking, hulking, self-satisfied essence gave off noxious fumes of dangerous stupidity that I imagined I could actually smell. *Eau de idiot.* I gave them a wide berth.

As I did, something caught my eye. It was a pair of skinny legs, sticking up out of the trash can. The scene began to make more sense, as I realized the reek was actually coming from overripe garbage rather than the jerks clustered around the can to block their actions from the view of anyone who happened to be walking by.

I stopped, figuring out what to do. The biggest guy, who I recognized as our star linebacker, Brian Doyle, had a small victim by the shins, and was shoving the kid's head and shoulders deep into the stinking can. One of the other guys noticed me and yelled at me to keep walking. So I did. Right at them.

Maybe it was the Invisible Children thing that made it impossible to ignore cruelty and walk away. After all, I was wearing my red Joseph Kony T-shirt. How could I protest injustice committed on another continent while allowing a bunch of Neanderthals to terrorize the locals at my own high school?

Besides which, I was pretty sure I recognized the legs in that trash can. They were sticking out of flood pants usually worn by my friend Solomon MacAndrew.

The football players regarded me with amused aggression as I approached them. "Let him out of there," I said, trying to keep my voice level.

"Moon?" Mac's muffled yell could be heard from inside the trashcan.

"Yeah, Mac, it's me." I raised my voice so he could hear me through the garbage.

"Moon, go away. I got this under control."

The football players laughed, and even I had to smile and roll my eyes. This was not a random encounter between Mac and the jocks. For reasons that would probably have deeply interested a Freudian analyst, Mac had become a manager to the football team. "Manager" is a euphemism for gofer, lacky, lickspittle, slave, toady, serf, and other similarly demeaning terms that were hardly likely to recruit candidates to the position. But we all knew that the main duties of the manager were to allocate jockstraps and pads before practice, fetch water bottles during practice, and shag wet towels after practice. And, of course, to be the object of pranks and derision from muscle-bound bullies at all times. I could only be in awe of the creative ways in which my friend's masochistic streak manifested itself.

"He's got you where he wants you," sneered the smallest guy, who I recognized as our quarterback. He had a face that reminded me of a big, clean-cut rat.

"Yeah, he's pullin' my arms down," said Doyle, shoving Mac deeper into the can. The other players hooted and guffawed, like a bunch of sidekicks.

The ratback looked at me. "You heard him. Leave."

"I don't think so. Get him out of that can. Now."

"I *can't*," said Doyle, mugging. "*He's* in control. I can't do a thing about it."

"You know what?" said the ratback, looking me up and down. "It's a big can. I think *you'd* fit in there, too."

"Yeah, he could keep his friend company," said another guy who had a Mohawk. "C'mon," he said to the others, moving towards me.

This didn't seem to be the way to save Africa, or Mac. I reached into my pocket and pulled out my cell phone.

"Calling for help?" jeered Doyle.

I shook my head, backing up. "Ever heard of Rodney Allen King?"

"Uhh…did he play for the Patriots?" joked the ratback.

"Nah. He got beat to shit by the cops about twenty years ago. They would've got away with it, but someone caught the whole thing on video." I held up the phone and panned the scene. "Now pretty much everybody can shoot footage on their cell phone."

"Phones can break," said the ratback. I stayed just out of his reach as he lunged at me, but he was faster than I expected. He grabbed my wrist. At the same moment, something much more powerful latched onto my waist and ripped me out of his grasp.

Somehow I held onto the phone as I staggered and rolled to the ground, wondering what had just hit me. I turned my head and saw Moss getting up next to me. Boosh and Wee Wee stood nearby, holding their boards menacingly like cavemen with clubs. They advanced on the football players, who were no longer yucking it up.

"Hey, Doyle, let him go," said the Mohawk.

"'Cause of those guys?"

"No, 'cause of *that*," he said, pointing at my phone. "We don't need this."

Doyle considered a moment, then appeared to get an idea. He looked at Mac's legs in the garbage, as if for the first time. "Hey, look at this, you guys. Someone threw away a perfectly good Jew."

A couple of the football players laughed, but the Mohawk, who appeared to have marginally more brains than the others, muttered, "You're making this worse. Shut up and get him outta there."

Doyle raised his eyebrows but did as he was told. He pulled Mac out of the garbage and laid him on the ground. Then he and the rest of the football players walked quickly away from the scene.

The skateboarders tossed their boards to the ground and rode up to Mac. "Dude, you okay?" asked Boosh.

Mac nodded, getting up. He wiped smelly grime from his face.

Wee Wee held his nose, and said, "What was in that trashcan—a skunk?"

"I gotta get to my class," said Mac.

"No way," I said. "You gotta get to the showers. And change your shirt."

"I don't have another one," said Mac. I looked around at the skaters. They were in T-shirts, but Wee Wee was wearing a hooded sweatshirt over his. He nodded and unzipped it.

"Here, bro, wear this," he said, handing it to Mac.

"You sure?" Mac had a great deal of trouble accepting generosity.

"Yeah, just get it back to Moon when you're done with it. And maybe don't wear the hood."

"Well, thanks," said Mac.

"So, man, was that like random mischief, or did you tug on Superman's cape?" asked Boosh.

"The latter, I guess," said Mac. "I won a bet with Doyle."

"What kind of bet?" I asked.

"I bet him I could do more sit-ups. And I totally kicked his ass," Mac said with obvious satisfaction. He grinned through the filth on his face.

"Yeah?" said Moss. "How many'd you do?"

"I lost count after three thousand," said Mac. The skateboarders hooted.

"Tre grand!" said Boosh. "You a sittin' up mofo, bro!"

"How'd you stay awake?" asked Wee Wee.

"I think I dropped off, but I can do 'em in my sleep," said Mac.

"What about Doyle?" asked Moss.

"He owes me fifty bucks."

"Yeah, but how many'd *he* do?"

Mac snorted. "Not even a thousand. Then he threw up."

I had a terrible thought. "In the trashcan?"

Mac nodded weakly and there was a collective moan of disgust.

The tardy bell rang like a sonic punctuation mark ending the episode. Moss said, "Better jet, huh?"

213

"Yeah," I said, then, to Boosh and Wee Wee, "You guys go. Tell Mrs. Cross I had an accident and I'll be there in a few."

The three skateboarders rode off and left me alone with Mac. I looked at him a bit more critically. "Mac, you *knew* you could win that bet."

"Yeah, but Doyle didn't."

"Doesn't matter," I insisted. "You hustled him."

"'*You can't cheat an honest man.*' W.C. Fields."

"'*Well, did you learn anything from this?*' Mom."

"Oh, yes, several things." Mac was surprisingly chipper under the circumstances. "First of all, Doyle eats an enormous breakfast. Eggs, bacon, sausage, toast…"

I laughed, looking at my friend with the evidence plastered to his face. "I can see you're not exaggerating. You have a pancake in your ear."

Mac nodded. "Unfortunately, I can taste it." He laughed, too. "You're gonna love this one. When you were walking over Doyle musta been looking at your shirt. I could hear him talking to himself." Mac continued in a pretty good imitation of Doyle's big, dumb confused voice. "'*Kony 2012. I think I went to that concert. I can't remember if I liked it or not.*'"

Chapter Thirty-Eight
Jasmine

I CAN'T EXPLAIN IT myself; but abandoning a lifelong habit of obedience to unreasonable authority, I found myself at Jasmine's apartment against Mom's express orders. Though we'd worked on the phone, we hadn't seen each other since Mom's ban had gone into effect. Jasmine was taking her high school equivalency test the next day, and we both wanted one more face-to-face practice session.

We'd been working steadily for two hours, covering all the subject areas, but especially math. I'm pleased to say that it was no longer a weakness, but instead an area of strength.

"You know, I'll be surprised if you miss a single problem."

"Shut up!"

"I mean it. You know this stuff backwards and forwards."

"Stop," she said, pushing me. "You're gonna jinx me."

"Good students don't jinx. And you're a good student."

Jasmine looked at me for a long serious moment. "Thanks to you. You believed in me."

"What's not to believe in?" I said with my best Yiddish accent.

Jasmine giggled and wrapped her arms around me. We kissed for the first time in months. It was like slipping into a pair of comfortable, but very exciting shoes.

"Uh, I probably shouldn't tell you this," I started.

"Uh-oh."

"Kissing you feels sort of…incestuous."

"Oh, is that all? I don't remind you of your mother, I hope."

"God, no. Just sort of like the really hot older sister I never had."

"Well, get used to it, mister. I see a lot of sisters in your life, older and younger."

"As a matter of fact," I started, wondering if it was a good idea to be sharing this, "there kind of *is* a girl at school."

"Oh?"

"You're not mad?"

"Well, I don't know yet," teased Jasmine. "I'll have to hear more."

So I told Jasmine about Sarah. She asked a lot of questions, most of which I didn't know the answers to. At one point she commented with mild disgust that men never seem to find out about the things that matter.

"If I asked all that stuff, she'd think I was gay."

"Yeah, you're right. But you'd be her new best friend."

"I don't want to be her best friend."

"Don't worry, she likes you," said Jasmine with the certainty of one who knows. "Did you tell her about me?"

"Sort of, but no details. She was surprised by my 'unfinished business.'"

"Oh, *now* you'll be irresistible. I hope she deserves you."

"I hope so, too."

Jasmine punched me playfully. "What have I created here?"

"I couldn't have done it without you, that's for sure." I had a sudden thought. "You and I, we're like the Wizard of Oz for each other. You might say I gave you brains, and you gave me a heart."

"I like that, Moon," said Jasmine. "And I think this Scarecrow is not done with school."

"Oh?"

"I want to go to college."

"Yeah," I said, warming to the idea. "You should. What do you want to study?"

She shrugged. "Don't know."

"Well…what do you want to be?"

"Don't know. Maybe just a waitress. But I want to go to college."

"Well, then you will. And I'll have to stay one step ahead of you."

"I'm counting on it. Sarah or no Sarah, you're still my tutor."

I realized that I'd kind of assumed that, like a parent might take for granted they'd play an ongoing role in their child's life.

"Not that you need one, but I accept."

"Now that that's settled," said Jasmine, changing the subject, "how's your mom? I was surprised you came over tonight."

"Well, she doesn't exactly know. She hasn't changed her position on anything."

"Are you talking?"

"I'd have to say no."

Jasmine looked at me soberly. "If she were anyone else, you could take a loss and write it off." I raised my eyebrows at her unusual choice of words. "I've been watching investment shows lately."

"Did you come into some money?"

"As a matter of fact, I did. Freddy tipped me a fifty."

"*Really?*"

"He was drunk and thought it was a five," she laughed. "I'll give it back to him tomorrow."

"Maybe he won't take it."

Jasmine rolled her eyes at me. "You have a very positive view of human nature. And you're going to need it to deal with your mother.

Someone's going to have to show a lot of maturity to get your relationship back on track."

I sat a moment. "Surely you don't mean *me*."

"Surely I *do*. Everyone else took one step back. That makes you the reluctant volunteer."

Chapter Thirty-Nine
Howlelujah

IT WAS LATE AFTERNOON in early October when Mom and I pulled to the curb in front of the Covenant Presbyterian church on Sepulveda. The summer heat had persisted, with practically every day breaking a high of eighty, and many of them soaring into the nineties. But the days were getting shorter, and you could finally feel autumn taking hold; the temperatures would have to abate soon.

It was the first time I'd ridden in Mom's convertible. Though she'd had it for a couple of months, we naturally hadn't been on good terms, and Moss and I were maintaining as much distance from her as we could. That included taking the bus and bumming rides from anyone but Mom. So transporting via the dude magnet was in itself a step towards détente— a reluctant acceptance of Mom's new normal. Now that I'd had the topless experience, I had to admit it was pretty cool.

"Nice ride," I observed, as Mom freed herself from the hair protection she donned for open-air trips.

"Glad you like it," she stated neutrally. "Are you sure you want to do this?"

"Yeah, it was my idea." The more I'd thought about Jasmine's advice, the wiser it had seemed. In a few hours we'd see if I still considered joining the diplomatic corps such a smart move.

Mom raised her eyebrows slightly. "What is the attraction of a Presbyterian church in Westchester?"

"Didn't I explain?" I said, knowing that I'd kept it from her. "This is not a run-of-the-mill service. It's called 'Canines at Covenant.'"

As if responding to the cue, several people strolled past, leashed dogs at their side.

"You've got to be kidding," said Mom. "They're bringing their dogs to church?"

"Oh, yeah. Dog and God are like *that*." I crossed my fingers to show how tight they were. "Same three letters and all that." I looked at her, not sure how she was taking this.

"One thing I'd like to know. Is 'dog' *God* spelled backwards? Or is 'God' *dog* spelled backwards?"

I grinned in relief. We always got along better when Mom was laughing, but it had been a long time since I'd heard her say anything remotely humorous. "Depends on who you ask, I guess. C'mon, let's go see the show."

About a dozen dogs and their people were stationed in a chapel set up with dog beds, water bowls, and folding chairs on a carpet that was, hopefully, stain-resistant. Along the wall, a couple of stiff-backed elderly worshippers sat on traditional hard wooden pews and cast doubtful glances at the latest additions to Covenant's flock— who in turn ignored the disapproving glances and happily sniffed each other's butts. Mom gave me an inquiring look about where I wanted to sit, and I made for the dogs.

We picked up a card with the particulars of the afternoon's service, noting a big bowl of dog biscuits next to it on the table. Nice touch, I thought. I put one in my pocket, figuring it would come in handy later.

I considered it might have been a mistake when I felt a set of paws plant on my lower thigh. I looked down to see a small beagle staring up at me hopefully, its long tongue drooping from a drooling mouth.

"Ella, be good," her owner, a middle-aged woman in sweater and jeans, said sharply. "Sit." Ella gave a rueful look and squatted to defecate. "For heaven's sake, that's *not* what I said!" Her owner gave a sharp tug on the leash to pull Ella out of her crouch, then dragged her reluctant dog towards an outdoor area that had been designated for the excretory needs of four-legged worshippers.

Mom smirked at me. "You had trouble with the difference between "s" and "sh" when you were little, too."

"And you jerked my leash sharply until I got it right."

"I *never!*" said Mom, laughing, as we took folding seats and surveyed the congregation.

It seemed to be as good a cross-section of the dog world as you'd be likely to find at any church in LA. On our left, a pit bull lolled on its back, allowing a golden doodle to prod its belly with a moist nose, as the owners looked on good-naturedly. *The lion lies down with the lamb*, I thought. Next to them, a black Lab and a long-haired dachshund tangled leashes and headed in opposite directions, bounding happily through water bowls and dragging their confused people after them. A Chihuahua was dressed in a shark costume, making it appear that the monster had actually consumed the dog. Its owner was taking it door-to-door, collecting treats in a "doggy bag."

There was a chorus of barking behind us. We turned in our chair to see a squat corgi frantically rushing from side to side, doing its best to corral two elderly women who were trying to make their way to the pews. The women halted in consternation, as the corgi's owner reined her in. "She's a herder," the owner explained. "She doesn't like people to leave."

"The pastor will approve of that," commented one of the ladies, as they edged past the nervous dog. Once they were on their way to the pews, the corgi calmed. Apparently she didn't fret about the ones who got away.

Ella and her owner returned to the chapel and took seats near us. Or at least her owner did; Ella took one look at me and plunged her nose into my crotch.

"Ella!" her owner cried. "My God, I don't know what's gotten into her!"

"Oh, it's not *her*, it's Moon. All the bitches do it," said Mom, giggling.

"Mom!"

"Is that a biscuit in your pocket, or are you just happy to see her?" Mom was laughing hysterically, slapping her thighs, and Ella showed no sign of calming down. Amid her licking and sniffing I managed to dig the biscuit out of my pocket and hand it to her. She took it greedily, then plopped down and set to eating her treat.

I turned to Ella's owner and stuck out my hand. "Hi. I'm Moon Landing, and this is my mother, Mae West."

"I don't know which part of that sounds more incredible," she said doubtfully. "I'm Dorothy Simmons. And you've met Ella."

"Yes, we're well-acquainted," I said. Hearing my voice, Ella tilted her head up at me with a look that could only be described as suggestive. She grinned at me and licked her chops.

"Get a room, you two," said Mom, sending herself into gales of laughter. People were starting to turn and look, as we were actually becoming more of a spectacle than the dogs.

"Do you come here regularly?" I asked, hoping to break Mom's silly fit.

"On, no," said Dorothy. "I don't care for church, myself, but I thought it was time to see to Ella's spiritual needs."

"*Her spiritual needs?*" said Mom, aghast. "Really?!"

"You don't think dogs should have a relationship with God?" asked Dorothy.

"Please," said Mom. "They should have obedience training."

Dorothy looked at me apologetically. "I'm sorry. I'm not good at disciplining."

I patted Mom's hand. "Neither am I. This one needs a muzzle, but I can't bring myself to put it on her."

Mom snorted and elbowed me, her eyes dancing playfully. We were getting along a lot better than I'd thought we would.

The pastor took a position at the front of the group and nodded to a pianist seated at a battered upright, who began to play a hymn. Around us the owners, cued by the "gathering music," redoubled their efforts to bring their dogs under control, and we could hear choruses of "Sit! Stay!"

The pastor looked on benevolently for a few moments, then his booming voice filled the room, as if God Himself were issuing a commandment. "SIT! STAY!" There was a yelp from a cowardly Jack Russell terrier, but the last of the dogs took their places on the cushions, and their owners took a seat on their folding chairs.

"PRAY!" the minister thundered. The elderly worshippers in the pews chuckled. "Seriously," he continued in a calm voice. "Lord, thank you for all the gifts that you have given to us, including our four-footed friends here with us today."

The service was wonderfully brief, lasting barely half an hour. Apparently my attention span was similar to that of an average dog, because it suited me just fine. My favorite part was the offertory, when they distributed doggie treats along with the collection plates.

Amazingly, the Bible reading was from my old nemesis, the Book of Job! The pastor used a modern translation, selecting the passage where God brags about all the things he can do that Job can't. The hipper language made God sound sarcastic and even more obnoxious than in the King James, like some irate gangsta who's been dissed by a homie. The pastor's conclusion was that since God is all-powerful, Job was wrong to question the Almighty about any unfair treatment he'd received. God knows best and all misfortune is for a good reason. Naturally I didn't agree, but the dogs took the sermon lying down so I thought I'd better not make a fuss.

After the service Mom and I took a drive up the coast to enjoy the warm twilight, stopping to eat fish and chips and beer-battered shrimp at Neptune's Net. I tried to ignore the way she was ogling the bikers and concentrate on the sun setting over the surf. It had been a good day and I didn't want to screw it up.

Our accord was fragile, a pond that had just thawed but that could easily skin over with fresh ice were the temperature to drop a few degrees. I hated to risk that, but I had to take a chance. Mom was going to find out sooner or later, and this way there was a chance she'd react positively.

"So you might have noticed Moss has been getting some snail mail," I started cautiously.

Mom nodded and chewed a shrimp. "What's that about?"

"Free Flow Tour. He's competing in the finals in a couple of weeks."

"This is a skateboarding thing?"

I nodded. "A *big* thing. The top amateur skaters from all over the country are going. And the winner gets to skate with the pros starting the next day."

"I don't understand. How could this just *happen*? Did he compete in something else?"

I explained to Mom about the Windward West competition. She stopped eating and wiped her fingers carefully. She frowned, sipping her beer.

"Your father and I had an agreement that you weren't to see him," she said. I could hear the ominous, stubborn note slipping into her voice.

"This happened months ago, before you reached that agreement," I said. "Which you ought to revisit, since it's so crazy. You can't keep us from seeing our father for the rest of our lives."

"Not for the rest of your lives, no." I waited, but she didn't say anything else.

"The finals are Wednesday the seventeenth, and we're going with Dad," I said.

"That is against our agreement."

"Then Mr. Smith will be our chaperone. But we're going. That's it." I added, "It would be nice if you'd go, too."

"I hate skateboarding."

"It's not about skateboarding, it's about your son."

"I have to work."

"I think you can take a day off for this."

"Well, we'll see."

Everyone knows what that means.

After that, I guess neither of us knew what to say next. Finally, Mom announced, "I'm going on a cruise in December."

"A cruise? What does that have to do with this?"

"Nothing. I'm changing the subject."

"Okay," I said, trying to control my annoyance. "Tell me about your cruise."

"It's just for a few days. Cabo, Puerto Vallarta, and Ixtapa."

"Mexico?"

Mom nodded. "Never been."

I just couldn't make sense of what she was telling me. "This seems very weird. Where did this idea come from?"

"The opportunity presented itself."

"Are you going with some guy?" I asked, impressed that she had found a cub who would actually shell out for more than a couple of drinks.

"No, it's not like that," Mom assured me. "I'm going with Betty."

"With *Betty*?" This was not at *all* reassuring. "Then it must be some kinda 'Moms Gone Wild' thing."

"That's rather offensive, Moon," Mom said sharply, glaring at me, but I stood my ground.

"Tell me this is not a cougar cruise."

She held my eyes for long moments and finally conceded. "Well…it *is* a cougar cruise."

The bikers gave Mom an admiring look when she got into her red convertible, and she gave them a coquettish smile in return. Then we drove home in silence, the cool night air reflecting the chill that had crept back between Mom and me.

Chapter Forty
To the Flow

I DIDN'T ACTUALLY INVITE Mr. Smith to accompany us to San Francisco for the Free Flow Finals. Maybe I was underestimating him, but it just didn't seem right to ask a man like Mr. Smith to spend several days hanging out with Boosh, Wee Wee, and Moss. So I let it go, and hoped there would be no repercussions.

The competition was going to take place on Wednesday afternoon. Dad picked us all up in his SUV the minute we got out of classes on Tuesday, and we hit the road. We sailed out of LA before the traffic got bad, and I-5 was straight and fast.

You'd think that with four teenagers on a road trip it would have been a raucous ride, but just the opposite. I sat between Boosh and Wee Wee in the back, helping them with their geometry, while Moss held down shotgun and worked on a paper for English class. Dad just focused on the road and enjoyed the drive.

We finished our assignments by the time it got dark and retreated into our private iPod worlds. Dad pulled off for a bathroom stop and some burgers, but we jumped back in the car to eat on the road. Before we left the lot, Dad turned in the seat to look at us in back.

"What're you guys listening to?" he asked.

"Music," said Boosh.

"What kind of music?"

Boosh looked at Wee Wee. "What would you call it?"

"Post punk? Adult alternative?"

"I don't know," said Boosh doubtfully. "But it's not classical."

"I didn't imagine you'd be chillin' to Beethoven," said Dad. "Name a band."

"Lil Waync?" said Wee Wee.

"That sounds like rap," said Dad.

"Yes, come to think of it, that *is* what it's called," said Boosh. "Parents don't usually like it."

"Try me," said Dad. Moss plugged Boosh's iPod into Dad's sound system, and Lil Wayne's "My Homies Still" burst out of the speakers.

"Turn that shit *way* up," said Dad, as he pulled back onto the highway. We grinned at each other, and Moss cranked it. A relentless string of expletives, derogatory epithets, and *gangst* uncoiled for the next few minutes. Dad chewed a burger and pounded the steering wheel, nodding his head to the rapper's flow, while the rest of us snickered. The song ended, and Dad pulled the iPod cord.

"He's good with the rhyming words, isn't he," he said. "What else you got?" he asked Moss.

"This old band before your time."

"Who's that? Sinatra? Bennie Goodman?"

"Not *that* old. You know Led Zeppelin?"

Dad looked at Moss in surprise. "Plug it in." In moments the explosive guitar riffs from "Dancing Days" heralded Robert Plant's plaintive voice. Dad grinned and said, "This was *our* rap. Parents hated it."

Dad began to sing along, and I was shocked. "You sound good, Dad."

"Yeah," said Moss. He turned the music low, and Dad sang the chorus semi-a cappella.

"You coulda been a rock star, Mr. Landing," said Wee Wee.

"Coulda, woulda, shoulda," said Dad, laughing. "No regrets."

We drove through the night eating, listening to music, and joking. But I couldn't stop thinking about who my parents had been before they became the people they were now. I'd lived with them my whole life, and they still surprised me.

We slept late and stumbled outside to discover San Francisco. The city on the bay, noted for its blustery weather, was instead toasty and headed for the eighties without a cloud in the sky. With hours to go before the competition, Dad took us on a driving tour of the city. He told us about the Summer of Love while we ate a big breakfast in the Haight, then we went to the Golden Gate. We walked across the bridge, enjoying the breeze and the sight of dolphins in the bay far below. Looking back at San Francisco's gleaming skyline, it felt like life had a lot to offer us.

We arrived at the Civic Center in the early afternoon, walking past the majestic gilded dome of City Hall. Flanked by long rows of porta potties, towering white tents billowed from the ground like ghosts, as workers hustled to set up displays for the sponsoring vendors—Stride, Mongoose, Dog Funk, and Toyota. Paul Mitchell and the National Guard had a presence as well, and I wondered what particular connection they had to the world of extreme sports.

After a bit of wandering, we found the competitor check-in booth for Alli Sports. Moss made contact and the rest of us enjoyed the scenery: lots of athletes in their teens and twenties toting knapsacks and boards, and cute girls accompanying them. There was one guy everybody seemed to be paying attention to. I nudged Boosh.

"You know that guy?"

He shook his head. "BMX, I think. He's a pro."

"How do you know?"

"The ink," he said simply, and I realized he was right. Almost every visible bit of skin on this guy was covered with tattoos, and his frisky girlfriend had a gallery of her own. Several other guys had plenty of body art, but the younger riders checking in were blank canvas. "Pros don't need parental consent," he added.

Moss went behind the counter and posed while the official photographer, a real babe, shot several digital photos. "Turn to the right," she ordered, and he gave her a profile. "I thought I was skating, not going to jail," said Moss with a wry smile.

"Your mistake," she replied without missing a beat. "Bend over and spread 'em for the cavity search, honey."

The riders hooted, and I think Moss actually blushed.

Meanwhile, the BMX rider had taken a seat at a long table nearby and was bent over paperwork. He frowned at the forms like he was taking a final he hadn't studied for.

"How many exemptions I want?" he asked his girlfriend.

"What's an exemption?"

"Yeah, right," he said with annoyance, and noticed me eavesdropping. "Are you the IRS?"

"Uh, no…"

"An accountant?"

"Do you want to owe money, or get money back?" Dad asked him, coming to my rescue.

"What kinda question is *that*?" The BMX rider was getting more confused and more annoyed by the moment.

"The kind of question you have to ask yourself when you're filling out those forms. If you put down one exemption, they're going to take out a lot of money. But you can file at the end of the year and get a refund. On the other hand, if you take a lot of exemptions, they won't withhold much—but you may end up owing at the end of the year. Your choice."

The rider stared at Dad in sudden comprehension. "Thank you for explaining that. Sorry I was rude."

"No worries," said Dad. "Paperwork makes us all ornery."

There was still at least an hour to go before Moss could even get on the street course to practice, so we walked east to check out the BMX dirt layout. It was pretty impressive. Enormous mounds of compacted earth loomed from the pavement, as if dug up by giant gophers. They looked even more incongruous in the elegant urban locale, set off by bronze statues of gold prospectors and flanked by ornate museums. As we took in the vista, a rider shot out of a launching area and plummeted down a ramp that catapulted his little bike high in the air in a backward 360 over the first mound. He touched down and plunged to the bottom and then up the next hill, as another rider took off to follow him.

I'd never seen BMX dirt riding in person, and it was both amazing and hypnotic. They soared so high and stayed airborne so long that it seemed like they were performing on a different planet that had a fraction of the gravity we were used to. To my eye they were all flawless, but my jaw dropped on tricks in which the riders came totally out of the saddle and did their own acrobatic stunts, like gymnasts performing on a pommel horse, before hopping back on at the last second.

"Remind you of the Cossack Death Drag?" I asked Dad.

"Ha! Not hardly," he said. "Though at least these bikes don't spook at a snake and drag you through a cactus patch."

We wandered back the way we'd come, where another set of BMX riders were finishing their practice runs on the skate street course. Our "friends and family" passes got us through the chain-link barrier, and we mounted a staircase in the east end to an observation area.

The BMX riders seemed like they were moving in slow motion on their pint-sized bikes after the super-sized drama we'd just watched on the dirt course. Even for skaters, these obstacles didn't seem like much compared to the kind of thing I'd seen Moss handle on city streets. I said as much to Boosh and Wee Wee, but they didn't agree.

"Oh, I think the Iron Chef can cook on this course," said Boosh.

Moss was walking from side to side along the viewing platform, studying the course from all angles. Wordlessly he descended the steps and walked completely around the layout.

"This has got historical value, bro," said Wee Wee. "See that 9-stair? That's a tastier replica of the Hubba Hideout ledge, where the San Francisco homies used to go to score crack. They just demoed the real thing, RIP."

Boosh pointed out a feature in the center of the course. "That slanted brick wall with the stone seats—that's a nod to the China Banks, probably the most famous skating spot in the city. This is a cool course!"

"What's even better, *we* get to skate it," said Wee Wee, brandishing his board.

"But you guys didn't qualify," I said lamely.

"Nah, but everybody's invited to take some runs during the warm-ups," said Boosh, waving his board. "Check out that little guy." He pointed at a kid who appeared to be about eight years old, gripping the barrier rails and looking forward to the bike riders exiting. "He's just waiting his turn to thrash."

I was a little flummoxed by the impropriety of this. "Won't that bother the competitors?"

"Dude, don't stress," said Wee Wee. "*They* aren't." He waved at several skaters who were joking around, trading stories, and paying no attention to the course whatsoever.

That changed a few minutes later, when the BMX riders exited. Moss, Boosh, and Wee Wee hit the course along with about three dozen more skaters, who had loads of pent-up energy. Dad and I watched them career down the runs with abandon.

"Looks like someone raised the speed limit," said Dad.

It absolutely felt that way. The skaters were much more aggressive than the bikers, and missed a lot more tricks than they made. I walked east to watch them grinding a handrail along a stairless incline. Though they seldom landed their tricks cleanly, I was impressed at the way the skaters bailed out in mid-air, separating from their flying boards like cowboys coming free of a bucking bronc to land on their feet, unharmed.

The level of the skaters was sure a lot higher than it had been at Woodward. And even though Moss seemed totally unconcerned, I couldn't help gauging his chances. Only the top skater got an invitation to compete with the pros the next day. I watched as Moss noodled around the course, totally relaxed and unhurried, oblivious to the manic energy that surrounded him.

Dad nudged me. "Who's that guy there, with the tight Levi's?"

"That's Austin Zito."

"Looks pretty good."

"Yeah, he won at Skatelab out in Simi. He's right up there."

Dad turned to look at me. "Do you know these guys?"

"Well, not personally, of course," I said. "But some of them have been here two, three years in a row. There's footage of all of them on the Internet."

"And I imagine you studied it," said Dad.

"Maybe a little."

Dad laughed. "Hope you didn't tell Moss anything."

"I know better than that."

"I'm sure you do. You're gonna make a good father," he said, putting his hand on my shoulder. "Helluva teacher, too. I enjoyed listening to you tutor Tweedle Dum and Tweedle Dee."

"You mean Tweedle *Wee*?"

Dad laughed. "Yeah, that's what I mean."

"Really, they're pretty sharp," I objected. "Especially Boosh. He catches on fast."

"I don't doubt it. But not everybody woulda looked under the hair to find his brain."

Chapter Forty-One
In the Flow

ABOUT TWO HOURS LATER, twenty-six sweaty skaters clustered around a tall blond who was explaining the rules. The twenty-seventh skater didn't speak English; he was standing in the viewing area with a man he called "*Tío*." Uncle.

After the blond finished her speech, a skinny competitor with a red beanie hiked himself over the rail and explained to the uncle, "It's a modified jam. Seven minute heats, skaters take turns on the run. They'll let him know when to go. He's in the fourth heat, after Josh Love. Tell him they're only going to score the top trick on the run. Nothing else matters—just the top trick on the run."

The uncle nodded his thanks, and turned to translate to his nephew. Meanwhile, the first heat was getting started. Boosh and Wee Wee joined us in the viewing area, but Moss stayed on the course, off to the side.

"Which heat is Moss in?" I asked.

"Fifth, got a while to chill," said Boosh. "Some good skaters out there, bro."

"Seemed like they were falling a lot," I said.

"Land or slam, man," said Boosh.

"And they can land some pretty sick tricks," said Wee Wee. "This is gonna be cool."

I guess I'm not a very good fan, because I felt better every time I saw one of Moss's competition go down, and I cringed every time a skater landed something special. By the time Moss's heat came up there were three skaters who appeared to be locked for the final round of five. Jonathan Reese, who skated in the first heat, still had the top score of 84.00, followed by Austin Zito and Brent Bell. Several other skaters were tightly clustered in the mid-seventies, and I figured anyone else who could break eighty would make the finals.

Moss was skating in the last heat. I wondered what his strategy would be, and I didn't have long to find out. His first run, he landed a clean kickflip backside Smith on the flat bar—a solid, if unspectacular score. Finishing the run, he went for a much more difficult trick on the next section of the course—and hit it. Get a good trick under your belt, then go for a great one. It seemed like a cautious and prudent strategy. No wonder Moss immediately abandoned it.

His next run he brusquely hiked himself atop the counter we were all leaning on that overlooked the course. Planting his board smack on the ledge, he jumped on and pushed off, riding sideways on the bar, dodging water bottles and cups of trail mix, then bent to grab his board and plunge onto the course. He flew up to the 9-stair Hubba and launched a lofty 360 flip, clearing the last stair by a generous margin and sticking the landing. The small crowd, just family and friends, roared its appreciation.

Moss did finesse tricks as well, laying them down on every part of the course—something the judges admired, though I don't know if it counted in the scoring. Maybe it did, because when his score was announced it placed him solidly in the final five.

Moss skated over to grab a water and catch his breath before the final round. He was flushed and sunburned and grinning happily.

"Good riding," said Dad.

"You gonna release the Kraken?" asked Boosh.

Moss laughed and shook his head. "I dunno."

"What's the Kraken?" I asked.

"Monster sick trick. It's geometrically impossible. But with your assistance, Wee and I figured out how to make it work," said Boosh. I was about to ask a follow-up math question, when Moss's entire body suddenly went rigid.

"Holy shit," he murmured, more to himself than to any of us. We all turned to follow his gaze, and emitted similar expressions of shock. Maybe we'd been in the sun too long and were seeing a mirage—because picking her high-heeled way towards us, through skaters and their families, was none other than our mother. And she wasn't smiling.

We grew silent as she approached. Even some of the people around us hushed, sensing a cosmic disturbance.

"Hello," said Mom neutrally. "I flew up, in case you hadn't noticed."

"Glad you came," said Dad evenly.

"No sarcasm, please."

Dad raised his hands in surrender.

"You missed the first rounds, but Moss made the finals," I said.

"Oh, I've been here," she corrected. "Sitting at the other end." She waved toward the sparsely-populated grandstand at the east end of the course. "Thought I'd get out of the sun for a while."

"Good idea," offered Wee Wee.

"Though it appears you tan very well," said Boosh.

Mom considered him as a snake eyes its prey. "And you are…?"

"Boosh."

"Boosh...*what?*"

"Boosh please-don't-use-your-teacher-voice-on-me-Mrs.-Landing-I'm-very-fragile," he said, cringing comically. We all burst into laughter, and even Mom smiled, having achieved her intended intimidation.

"Once a third grader, always a third grader," she commented, then looked at Dad. "Are you going to move down to the other end?"

Dad looked momentarily surprised at the suggestion, then pursed his lips. "I believe this viewing area's big enough for the both of us, Janice."

"Don't bet on it," she snapped back.

"Well, let's give it a try," said Dad levelly.

They called time for the finals. Mom gave Moss a peck on the cheek which he reluctantly accepted, then he hopped back over the barrier and onto the course. Boosh, Wee, and I took places between Mom and Dad, hoping we wouldn't get crushed like buffer states between the great powers.

The final five skaters would each take extended solo runs to showcase the best they had, then participate in a final jam. The rotation was announced and Moss was to skate fourth.

Extended solo runs gave each skater a much better opportunity to develop a rhythm, and the first three competitors showed an interesting contrast of styles, but all were very good. Austin Zito had a few bobbles and outright falls on his solo run, and then Moss was up.

At its best, street skating is fluid and lyrical, and the tricks are integrated into the sheer act of moving from one place to another. However, perhaps due to the scoring systems, competition skaters tend to emphasize one trick after another with no particular rhythm or scheme. That's why the runs that Moss laid down on his solo portion were very different from everyone else's.

The course sloped downhill from where we were sitting at the western end, and that's where everyone started their first run that afternoon. Everyone except Moss. Instead, for his first line, he worked his way uphill, and we could see the theme was a progression of ollies, board jumps to the top of obstacles—first a small one onto a ledge, a larger one to the top of the China Banks—then a big 180 kickflip to the top of a picnic table set above a rise on the final plateau.

Pivoting on the wall he reversed course, kickflipped onto the Hubba ramp with a full head of steam and threw down a switch heelflip 50-50. He surmounted the China Banks again and did a nose grind along the entire edge of the coping, like a surfer shooting the curl of a wave.

The whole time Jimi Hendrix's classic "All Along the Watchtower" blasted from the sound system, and the rhythms of Moss's skating were accentuated by Hendrix's soaring guitar line. It was almost an unfair advantage.

Heading back up the course, Moss rode hard up the China Banks and pulled off a trick you might see on the half pipe, but almost never on a street course. As his board began to shoot over the coping at the top, he grabbed it with his left hand and planted his right hand on the edge of the coping. He balanced momentarily on the extended arm—legs, feet, and board coiled high above him—then pivoted and plunged back down the bank. The small crowd roared its approval, and Moss headed for the opposite bank. To show this was no fluke, he executed the mirror image of the trick, now planting left hand and doing the board grab with his right.

To wind up his solo run, Moss turned back the way he had come. He hit the handrail with a frontside feeble and finished with a flourish as the last strains of Hendrix faded away.

The crowd yelled, and I turned to Boosh and Wee Wee who were grinning and shaking their heads.

"Was that the Kraken?" I asked.

"Not *even*," said Wee Wee.

The last skater took his solo run as we savored Moss's success. Interim scores were not announced, but everyone watching that day knew that Moss was way out ahead of the competition and headed to skate with the pros the next day.

There was a short break before the final jam, and Moss skated over to say hi.

"Very tasteful, maestro," said Boosh.

We all chimed in and Moss smiled, wiping sweat off his face.

It was a great moment for him.

It was a great moment for *all* of us.

"Cougarlicious?"

The voice was soft, unsure, and inquisitive. Reflexively, Mom turned to see who it was: the tattooed BMX rider we'd met at the competitor check-in. He was staring at Mom like she was some kind of royalty.

"Wow, you look *just* like your picture online," he gushed. Mom stared at him, tongue-tied. Moss and I caught each other's eye.

The rider's beautiful girlfriend entered the scene with a brusque, "*Excuse* me," glaring at Mom.

The BMX guy gave Mom an awkward smile and put his arm around his girlfriend. "Let's grab a Dew, babe," he said, leading her away.

I thought the scene might somehow blow over—and it could have, if Mom hadn't glanced at Dad just as he was raising his eyebrows slightly.

"*What*?!" she demanded, like a street thug spoiling for a fight.

"Nothing," said Dad with a shrug, backing off. But now Mom was on the defensive, when she was most volatile.

"My personal life is none of your business," she flashed, thrusting her head past me to get at him.

"Fine. Let's just calm down and enjoy the rest of this. It's Moss's day. Let's not ruin it."

"*Ruin it*? I'm not ruining it!" she yelled. She turned to see Moss just as he rolled his eyes. She spun back on Dad. "You have no right to even be here. You are in breach of our agreement!"

Dad was breathing deep, trying his best to avoid throwing fuel on the fire. "Yeah, we're gonna have to revisit that agreement."

"You bet we are! In court! That's where we'll revisit that agreement!"

"Whoa, Mrs. Landing, chill," said Boosh. "It's all good."

"It is *not* all good," exclaimed Mom. "Do you have any idea what you're saying, you idiot?"

"Don't call him an idiot," said Moss.

Boosh waved him off. "I got this one, bro." He turned on Mom, regarded her calmly, then stated very clearly, "It may *not* all be good—but *you're* making it worse. You've got two half grown sons who could use a full grown mother."

Mom's jaw dropped and she was once again speechless. Her eyes flitted around our group and you could almost see the pieces coming together, like tumblers in a lock aligning, and the door to the vault swinging open. Moss skated away from us as the finalists assembled for the jam.

"I'm...sorry," she murmured, in a voice too soft for him to hear.

I don't know if her words would have made a difference, but they might have.

Skaters started their final runs, laying down a barrage of tricks all over the course. But Moss hung back, for a minute, for two minutes. People in the stands began to murmur.

Dad gave me a worried look. "Moss rules?"

I shook my head. "I hope not."

Just then Moss pushed off and headed away from us. He skated past obstacles, picked up speed and headed downhill, aiming at the handrail. He was going very fast.

"It's the Kraken," said Boosh.

"But he's coming in *way* too hot," said Wee Wee.

Other skaters turned to look, and some even stopped. Moss crouched, then popped the tail of the board into a massive ollie. He and the board immediately rose to a height of four feet or so, then he hooked a wheel under the rail. The board caught and abruptly stopped its upward flight.

But not Moss. He tucked in head and knees and soared into the air, rotating and executing forward flips like an Olympic tumbler. But he was higher than any gymnast had ever been—maybe ten feet in the air at the peak of his jump.

At the time, no one was counting. On film later, it would show that he completed three forward flips before he came down at the end of the handrail. He was a foot or so to the left of the metal obstacle, and it looked like he would clear it fine, his arms tucked neatly to his sides.

Then, at the last moment, he held his right hand out slightly from his body. It smashed into the metal handrail with a sickening whack that was heard all over the course, and Moss crumpled to the ground.

Two paramedics who had been stationed outside the course sprang into action and rushed to Moss's side. The competition was halted and the other skaters formed a mass around him. Mom and Dad rushed down the stairs to get to his side. All over the course people were struggling to make sense of what they had just witnessed.

I looked at Boosh. "He Krakened up, man," he said simply.

"No shit. How much of that was on purpose?"

Boosh and Wee Wee looked at each other.

"It's not the way we planned it," said Boosh.

"But I'd say it was *all* on purpose," said Wee Wee. "I think he reached out and busted his hand intentionally."

"Why?" I thought so, too, but I couldn't understand it.

Wee Wee pointed at the mob around Moss. Mom and Dad were now at the center of it, along with the paramedics. "Seems like he got someone's attention. *Finally.*"

Chapter Forty-Two
Reheated Macaroni

THE COMPETITION RESUMED after the paramedics tended to Moss. There was no persuading him to go to the hospital before the jam finished, so we all stayed to watch the outcome. It didn't take long.

When there's a gruesome crash in NASCAR, they wave the yellow caution flag and the other drivers all slow down. That convention is unknown to skating. Instead, the other four skaters totally went for it in the last seven minutes. Austin Zito particularly turned up the heat, overcoming his bobbles on the solo run to walk away with first place. If Moss couldn't win, I was glad Austin did. We all liked his style.

The news at the hospital wasn't particularly bad. Moss's feet and ankles weathered the landing okay, and his only injury was to his right hand. He fractured the fifth metacarpal and the cast they put him in would stay on for four weeks. Mom said that writing lefty might actually be a good thing and would help develop another hemisphere of his brain.

"Hopefully the one where France is located, bro. The mademoiselles got mad love for thrashers," said Boosh.

"You know all the lingo you need. Stick to '*oui, oui,*' and you won't go wrong," said Wee Wee.

Still, Mom was not her abnormal self. She avoided any conflict with Dad, and they were united in their concern for Moss's well-being. Whether it was Boosh's words or Moss's accident, it appeared that something *had* gotten her attention.

Mac, Aron, and I were out eating pizza, and I was filling them in on these events.

"So is Moss bummed he didn't win?" asked Mac.

"He's making out okay," I said. "The YouTube clip of the Kraken has been downloaded about a million times."

"Make it a million and one," said Aron, studying his iPhone. "This is awesome."

"We don't even answer the phone anymore, just let it go to message. Sponsors are calling constantly and he's getting all kinds of offers to skate in movies. We're totally inundated with free gear—boards, shirts, pants, hats, shoes—"

"You can always send some of that my way," said Aron.

"You don't skate," said Mac.

"No, but I can sell it on eBay."

We gave him a look, then Mac asked, "So you can see your dad again?"

"Yeah," I nodded. "In fact, he had his own plan in the works."

I told them about Mr. Smith and how he had played golf with us a couple of months earlier. That led to him finding a buyer for the Fanatics property, who was willing to pay, as Dad put it, an "obscene" amount of money in order to tear down the bar and put up a high rise. Since Dad owned the property, he made a killing on the deal.

"So your dad's out of the restaurant business?" asked Mac.

"Not really," I said. "Mr. Smith pulled off another miracle. One of the anchor restaurants at the Grove went bust and they want Dad to bring Fanatics over there. Mr. Smith got Dad a great lease and they're even giving him a remodeling budget."

Mac and Aron stared at me for a moment.

"This is freaky," said Aron.

"What?"

"You recall the way the Book of Job ended?" asked Mac.

"What about it?"

"You know—when God gives Job everything Satan took away, and then some," Mac said.

"Uh, I don't really think…" I fell silent, considering the parallels.

"What of the scrumptious Jasmine?" asked Aron.

"She aced her test. She said it was ridiculously easy and she was way over-prepared. She enrolled in Santa Monica College."

"And that's the end of it?" insisted Aron.

I shrugged. "We're going to the beach tomorrow."

"To the beach? She'll be wearing a bikini," said Aron, his tongue practically hanging out.

"Presumably. It's not a nude beach," I said.

"But she doesn't need any more tutoring," objected Mac.

I shrugged again. "We're friends."

"Man, I hope I can be as cool as you when I grow up," said Mac.

Aron sighed. "I just hope you grow up."

Chapter Forty-Three
Ashes to Ashes, Sand to Sand

AFTER COOLING OFF for a few days, the thermometer had shot up again into the high eighties. Jasmine and I were enjoying one of the truly great days at the beach: crystal clear skies, sunny and hot, with a sweet breeze blowing. We walked along the surf line, picking our way through the parents and kids playing in the water.

I don't know when I've felt so good. I was overwhelmed with relief, and for once I could enjoy the moment without worrying what was going to happen next.

We meandered up the beach from Venice to Santa Monica dodging Frisbees and squealing infants, and I filled Jasmine in on all of the news. She listened carefully, nodding, and when I got done she said, "You left someone out."

"Who?"

"Your mother."

"I told you what she did…"

"Yeah, but how is it now? Did you work things out?"

I was quiet, thinking of how to explain it. "I'm still kind of in shock. It's like Mac said. For forty years, all anyone worried about was the Soviet Union. They were our big, bad enemy. People thought the Cold War would last forever, and then one day, completely out of the blue, it was over. The mighty Soviet Union crumbled under its own weight and the world changed overnight."

"You're saying your mom's changed?"

I nodded. "I think she has. She's not back to her old self, but the reign of terror has lifted." I hesitated, then confided, "She even cancelled her cougar cruise."

"*Cougar cruise?*" Jasmine said with horror. "What is that?"

"Use your imagination."

"What does she want to be when she grows up? The female Hugh Hefner?"

"You say that like it's a bad thing."

Jasmine laughed. "I'm glad you still have a sense of humor about this."

"I try to stay in the moment." I steered Jasmine into the surf up to our knees. Reaching inside my pocket, I brought out a small bag of multicolored sand.

Jasmine's eyes lit up. "The Wheel of Time!"

"I think we should release it." I poured some of the sand into Jasmine's hand, and the rest into my own. "You ever see LeBron James throw the powder at the beginning of a game?"

"Oh yeah," she said.

Together we flung our sand high into the air, spreading our arms wide like NBA superstars. The sun glinted off the colored grains, as they rained down to patter into the onrushing swell. Jasmine and I smiled at each other, then turned to make the long, pleasant walk back to Venice.

Chapter Forty-Four

The Book of Moon

IN THE BEGINNING, I WAS NOTHING.

In the end, I'm everything.

Sounds great, doesn't it? I'd *like* to say it—but I can't. It isn't remotely true. Not even in my most spiritual moments.

I'm still nothing. But I feel a lot better about it. I'm not an anti-theist, not even an atheist. I'm open to the possibility, despite plenty of evidence to the contrary. In my heart of hearts, I don't know if I'll ever believe in God. And I'm not too worried about it.

I'd like to believe in people, though. I think that's more important, and it's not easy, either. Still, sometimes they surprise you and do wonderful things.

Sarah and I hadn't given up on Kony 2012, and in the waning days of October we made a push to enlist recruits to our cause. Boosh, Wee Wee, Moss, and the rest of the skaters were the first to join us. They helped us recruit the stoners. Mac somehow roped in the football team, and the rest of the athletes followed suit. After that, it was a domino effect, and the entire school enlisted in our cause. Literally every kid in school wore their red Kony 2012 T-shirts every

Tuesday, when the teachers wore their red union shirts.

Afloat in that red tide, I felt encouraged that so many people were at least willing to put on a shirt once a week. It's not much, but if everybody does just a little bit, that might be better than a few people trying to do it all. As we hit the homestretch of 2012, Kony may still not be infamous enough to shame the governments in the world into taking action—but we're going to keep it up until they do.

Meanwhile, Sarah and I have decided that our attraction has grown beyond the confines of the Club Meeting period and spend as much time together as possible. The more I hear about her parents, the lawyers, the less I'd ever want to be one. One aspect of their work I find unappealing is the focus on asking questions they already know the answers to. Responses that surprise and entertain are much more intriguing to me.

The search for my Tahiti remains ongoing, and maybe that's the way it's supposed to be. Not knowing what my future holds is sometimes troubling, but if the Book of Moon were already written in its entirety, that would be far worse. The chapters continue as long as you live—and maybe after that, though I don't think so. While browsing the stacks at the library last week, an elderly man and I both reached for the same volume on career counseling. When I gave him a look of surprise, he flipped me a white-dentured grin and said, "I'm trying to figure out what I want to be when I grow up." Following up with a question about what he'd done so far led to insight no reference material could offer.

Mom and I have resumed our monthly trips to church. We're still not looking to join so much as window shopping—and spending time together. Though we plan to visit a much wider variety of churches and temples, reflecting the wonderful diversity of our city—

our country—our world—it's always easy to fall back on the places near home.

That's why we now found ourselves in the congregation at the Holy Spirit Catholic Church on Pico. After multiple experiences with the faith, I was actually getting a little more adept at the "stand up, sit down, *fight, fight, fight!*" rhythm of the service.

And then came the sermon.

It was about my old pal Job. Did they put out a recall on the rest of the Bible, or *what*?!

I listened carefully, hoping the priest would find some way to make sense of Job's trial at the hand of Satan. But like every other sermon on this topic, he put the blame squarely on Job, claiming the book was a lesson on the folly of doubting God's judgment. When tragedy befalls us, it is surely part of a higher plan for our life, and we must take comfort in knowing that God has the details worked out, even if we can't see how the pieces of the puzzle will come together. Blah, blah, blah.

This sanctimonious interpretation sorely tested my newfound religious equanimity. I squirmed uncomfortably, and Mom actually put a hand on my leg to try to hold me still. I caught the eye of an old black woman who was scowling at me, and I made an effort to endure the sermon's foregone conclusion.

"I need waffles," I muttered, as we slowly meandered out of the church.

"Text your brother," said Mom, and I pulled out my cell phone.

Moss took a pass on our religious excursions, but most of the time he could be counted on to join us for breakfast. "Chow bound," I sent.

Vendors selling Mexican corn-on-the-cob and snow cones were set up outside the church, and generous parents bought the treats for their dressed-up kids. It's the least they deserve for sitting through that BS, I thought sourly.

Mom and I walked a few blocks east to Roscoe's Chicken and Waffles, where there was a substantial wait for a table. She went to the bathroom, and I put our name on the list. I heaved a sigh and settled on one of the banquettes.

Just down the street six months earlier, I had heard the story of Job for the first time. It had deeply disturbed me, like a gloomy diagnosis that demanded a second opinion, which I'd never really gotten. Still, whether God's arbitrary actions made any more sense or not, at least my life had righted its course, and that was some consolation. I no longer felt I had a passenger seat on the Jobean train wreck.

Setting cosmic thoughts aside, I turned to the weighty issue of whether to order an omelet or a waffle. As I considered the merits of each, I felt a tap on my shoulder. I looked up to see a black man in his early twenties frowning at me.

"Gramma want to see you," he said, hitching his head in her direction.

"Me?" I was pretty sure there was no one I knew in this neck of the woods.

"Yeah, you the one. C'mon."

Doubtfully, I followed him around the corner to a waiting area, and immediately recognized the old lady who had frowned at me in church.

She was perched on a bench, leaning on a walker. Surrounding her was a family that must have extended over four generations, all dressed immaculately in stylish suits and dresses.

Her face was puckered into a sour expression, like she'd bit into a lemon. I figured that was because of me—my fidgeting during the sermon must have offended her. She beckoned me nearer and I approached apprehensively, not knowing what to expect but hoping it wouldn't be too bad. She pried one trembling hand from her walker and laid it gently on mine, patting me softly.

"It troubles me. Always has. Troubles *you*, too."

"What?"

Her eyes locked on mine. "You know what. *Job*."

She paused, waiting until I was ready for what she had to confide, then concluded: "No two ways about it. The Lord did him wrong."

I felt tears start to well in my eyes and I blinked them back. Her voice dropped an octave and became softer.

"But you can't take it to heart, child. You can't take it to heart. *Even God makes mistakes.*"

"And...we have to forgive Him," I said without thinking.

She nodded slowly and smiled. "We have to forgive Him—for a lot."

I had a sudden thought and said, "If we can forgive God..."

"Yes. That's exactly it." She pointed a bony finger at me, and intoned slowly, "If we can forgive God...*we can forgive each other.*"

There was a soft chorus of "amen" from her family. I thanked them and withdrew awkwardly to find Moss watching. He held his board and regarded me curiously.

"*Qué pasó*, bro?"

Before I could answer, Mom rejoined us from the bathroom. Without thinking it through, I wrapped her in a hug and said softly, "I forgive you, Mom."

"I never apologized..."

"I forgive you anyway."

I held her tight as her body started to shake, and I realized she was crying. I felt another arm encircle my shoulder as Moss embraced us both.

"I *am* sorry," she sobbed. "I *am* sorry."

Holding my mother and brother close, the answer came to me.

I'd order an omelet and talk Moss into getting a waffle.

Fortunately, he agreed.

THE END

It's *so* important in the publishing world,
that they've coined a catchy name for it.

It's called "*social proof.*"

Without it, you're dead in the water.

SO IF YOU'VE ENJOYED *THE BOOK OF MOON*,
PLEASE CONSIDER REVIEWING IT AT AMAZON.
I'd appreciate it <u>immensely</u>.

I know this book is not for everyone.

But if it was for *you*—
—just a brief note expressing your thoughts—
—would help potential readers decide whether it might be for *them.*

Then come visit me at my webpage:

www.georgecrowder.com

Sign up for the mailing list—
—which I'll only use to notify you of new releases—
—and download a free short story!

Acknowledgements

BIG, BIG THANKS to my beta readers—you know who you are—whose enthusiasm for early drafts of this book made me think it might be worth sharing with the world at large. If it weren't for you, I never would have had the nerve.

The baddest of the betas is my wife, Liz, who held my hand throughout the first draft. Only someone who has lived with a neurotic writer can appreciate the patience and love required to get him to the next day and the next chapter. Thanks for putting up with me, hon. I owe you another trip to Italy—and I'm gonna make sure you collect.

A shout-out and a standing offer of a cocktail to my numerous writing partners over the years—Marc, Terry, Joey, Richard, and especially, Mark Saha. Whatever writerly skills I possess are largely due to my work with you guys. I know Joey would be the first to agree with this.

Then there's my dad. If it weren't for his positive reaction nearly forty years ago when I broke the news that I'd rather be a writer and a bartender than get my MBA, I'd probably be a CEO, outsourcing jobs and stashing profits offshore. Thanks for having the faith, Dad. As I recall, you were pleased that at least I wasn't going to wind up a lawyer.

A non-alcoholic toast to my maternal Granny, who for years replied to any inquiries regarding her grandson's profession by remarking, in her best *Downton Abbey* manner, "Oh, yes…George is at the bar," hoping they'd think I *was* a lawyer.

Here's to my mom, who, if there's any justice, basks in an afterlife principally surrounded by her beloved poodles. I am indebted to Mom for much of what passes for my sense of humor. She did in fact drag me to many places of worship—and I repaid the investment in my spiritual growth by forbidding her a pagan Christmas tree, once upon a time. For reals, no good deed goes unpunished.

I am oh-so-fortunate to have found my wonderful cover designer Dane Low, who came up with something for this book I never could have dreamed. Thanks for making sure this thing didn't look like a thriller or a romance. Though it might've sold better…

Fist bump to Ozzie Ausband of Blue Tile Obsession, who kept my skating sequences at least semi-legit. To my surprise, riders are not actually superheroes, able to ollie over six-foot cinder block walls in a single bound. At least not *yet*.

Cheers to my proofreader, Helen Baggott, who found far more mistakes than I'd have imagined. Who'd have thought it would take a woman from England to teach me how to spell "Spider-Man"?!

Mil gracias to longtime amigo Luis Contreras, a supremely gifted artist who's been beautifying my life for more than twenty-five years. His logo perfectly captures the gentle loving spirit of the granddog for whom Chelsea Press is named.

Last, kudos to my supremely talented and tactful editor, Tim Parolini, whose contributions improved the book immensely. Such was his insight and diplomacy that he persuaded me to make almost every alteration, which Liz could hardly believe. Any subpar content has, I'm sure, been retained against Tim's objections.

It's been a delight—and having done this once, I can't wait to do it again.

About the Author

No surprise, George Crowder has done time with the Buddhists, the Baptists, the Catholics, and the Jehovah's Witnesses. Well...maybe *some* of that's a surprise...

He has worked variously as a bartender, waiter, restaurant manager, window washer, grocery clerk, delivery driver, telemarketer, bead stringer, and screenwriter. Failing upward, he turned to education, and spent twenty-two years teaching third, fourth, and fifth grade, and as an elementary math specialist.

Pastimes include woodworking, tennis, hiking, playing guitar, speaking Italian, eating Italian, drinking Italian, and fraternizing with three adorable grandchildren.

He is the best-selling author of, uh, nothing... *yet*...

Follow George on Facebook and at www.georgecrowder.com.